Love Letters

IN THE SAND

SHARON STONE

This trade paperback original is published by Alyson Publications,
P.O. Box 4371, Los Angeles, California 90078-4371.
Distribution in the United Kingdom by Turnaround Publisher Services Ltd.,
Unit 3, Olympia Trading Estate, Coburg Road, Wood Green,
London N22 6TZ England.

First edition: August 2004

04 05 06 07 08 a 10 9 8 7 6 5 4 3 2 1

ISBN 1-55583-852-9

Library of Congress Cataloging-in-Publication Data
Stone, Sharon, 1955–
Love letters in the sand : a novel / by Sharon Stone.—1st ed.
ISBN 1-55583-852-9 (pbk.)
1. Women novelists—Fiction. 2. Women musicians—Fiction. 3. Lesbians—Fiction. I. Title.
PS3619.T683L68 2004
813'.6—dc22 2004046354

Credits
Cover photography by Ulf Sjosdtedt/Getty Images.
Cover design by Matt Sams.
Author photo by Lawrence Salerno.

Chapter One

L.C. Hackett sat on a barstool in the Bel-Air home of her best friend, Mandy Gilbert. She hooked the heels of her well-worn boots over the lowest rung on the stool, rested her elbows on her knees, and tapped her Heineken bottle against the bar in time with the music coming from the stereo in the adjacent room. Three Grammys lined up on a mirrored shelf above the row of liquor bottles caught her eye. Another person might have been impressed, but L.C. had two of her own at home collecting dust on a curio shelf.

She looked at her reflection in the mirrored wall behind the bar and frowned. What the hell had she been thinking when she got her hair cut this way? Fingertips combed through black feathery hairs, none of which was longer than an inch now. She felt bald and her ears were cold all the time. Turning her head side to side, she appraised her new do. Oh, well, most of her life she'd wished she'd been born a boy; at least now she looked like one. Fuck it—too late now.

She looked around the spacious home, built in the familiar style of Hollywood's heyday with a grand staircase in the center that split the house into two wings, each with two living areas and various other rooms. One could stand at any point near the front wall and have a clear shot through the entire first floor. In the west living room, Tracy Chapman and Sheryl Crow discussed which brand of pick each preferred for the acoustic guitar. Joan Osborne and Natalie Merchant sat across from L.C. in the den comparing notes on the coziest venues in Manhattan. Every room boasted several of the best female artists in the music industry.

L.C. smiled, her head bobbing in approval. "This is one of the advantages of being a success in the record business," she said to Carol Ann, one of her backup singers she had known since the lean days, who was standing beside her. "You get to hang out with the most talented people in the world."

Mandy had walked by just in time to hear L.C.'s remark. "You got that right," she said in a cocky voice, as though the statement had been meant only for her. The petite redhead plopped down on the stool next to L.C., kicking up her short, skinny denim-clad legs and tapping L.C. playfully on the thigh with a size-4 boot.

Mandy and L.C. had been best friends for nearly 12 years and were practically inseparable. They both had gotten into the record business at about the same time. Mandy hit the charts 11 years ago—the year after L.C. rocketed to fame—with a hard-driving rock album that won her two Grammys: Best New Artist and Record of the Year. She had made sort of a comeback two years ago, winning another Record of the Year award. Mandy hated the term *comeback* because in her mind she had never gone away—she had put out an album almost every other year. Just because they hadn't sold as well as her first didn't mean she had disappeared. She constantly teased L.C. about when she was going to make *her* comeback and top the charts again because the same thing had happened in her career. The response was always the same: "When I get inspired."

"Nice group tonight." L.C. took off her black leather jacket and pushed up the loose sleeves of her white silk shirt midway on her muscular forearms.

"Yeah," Mandy replied, pleased with the turnout for her get-together. She paused, crinkling her nose slightly. "Sorry about Veronica," she said.

L.C.'s smile evaporated. "Yeah, well, it was bound to happen sooner or later."

"I didn't invite her—she just showed up with Elizabeth, I swear."

"Don't sweat it," L.C. said, patting her friend on the knee but managing only a feeble smile to show she meant it.

Carol Ann glared at the thick-waisted, surgically enhanced 20-something—with coal-black hair cut like a '20s flapper—who was giggling obnoxiously in the next room. Carol Ann never could understand why L.C. had gotten involved with someone almost half her age in the first place. On second thought, she knew exactly what the attraction had been. "Just what do silicone implants feel like, anyway?" she asked L.C.

"Carol Ann!" Mandy scolded.

"They're not silicone, they're saline," L.C. said, just to set the record straight.

"What's that?" Carol Ann asked.

L.C. shrugged. "Salt and water, I guess."

Carol Ann pondered a moment. "Weren't you ever afraid with all that pulling and squeezing you'd end up with two big ol' blobs of taffy?"

Mandy and L.C. just looked at each other, not sure whether their friend was trying to be funny, or whether she was just that dense, or whether she had simply consumed one too many beers. It was hard to tell with Carol Ann sometimes. "What the hell is she trying to be with that hair, anyway?" the stocky blond said.

"It's her new image," Mandy explained. "Her manager wanted to give her a dramatic look before her first album is released."

L.C. snorted in disgust and shook her head as she stared at

her recent ex. An angry smirk appeared, and Mandy wondered whether L.C. was even aware she was reacting; she seemed so focused on the girl and oblivious to her surroundings.

Even though L.C. had repeatedly denied it, it was obvious to her two friends that she was still stinging from what the bitch had done to her. Everyone in the industry knew about how Veronica had pulled a real Eve Harrington on L.C., pretending to be her devoted friend and lover while all the time she was merely scheming to break into the music business. The girl didn't seem to mind climbing over the back of one of the industry's biggest names to get there either. It had been tabloid fodder for the last two months.

All of L.C.'s friends knew her record label had only signed Veronica as a favor, and they rallied around L.C. in support when the label refused to drop the upstart after the breakup. This naturally prompted L.C. to switch companies, and her new label immediately put her to work writing songs for another album, which everyone thought was the best medicine for her, all things considered.

"So where's Connie tonight?" L.C. said in a transparent effort to change the subject.

"She's coming," said Mandy. "She went to some book signing across town first. She wanted to get a book autographed."

"Books?" Carol Ann scrunched up her face as she took a swig of beer.

"Yeah, you know, sheets of paper with words on them sandwiched between two covers?" Mandy teased. Carol Ann didn't seem to appreciate her sense of humor, but it made L.C. laugh.

"Oh, God," said Carol Ann. She hooked her thumbs in her Levi's front pockets, throwing one hip out as if to brace herself when she saw Veronica heading their way. "Here she comes."

The three prepared themselves for a possible close encounter.

L.C. swiveled her barstool around, turning her back toward the devil child.

"Disaster averted," Carol Ann said after a second. "They're leaving."

"Good," L.C. groaned, then took a long swig from her beer bottle. She heard the front door open, and after what she figured had been plenty of time for Veronica to say her goodbyes and leave, she relaxed.

"I still can't believe they gave that screech owl a contract," Carol Ann said.

L.C. snickered. "Well, the one good thing about it is that I don't have to listen to her butchering *my* songs anymore."

The words were still hanging in the air when from behind her came a voice belting out the chorus of L.C.'s signature song, "Forever and Always Yours"—the one she had won her Grammys for 12 years ago in her breakout year. The first thing L.C. thought was that if this was Veronica, she'd had a vocal chord transplant because this was an exquisite, powerful voice.

L.C. swung her stool around and was blinded by the sight before her. Time and space disappeared, and she found herself mesmerized by a dazzling six-foot woman with golden hair curving down to her waist and long legs with even more curves up to her neck. This vision stood with her arms outstretched, leaning slightly back, belting out *her* song. And doing it well. L.C. stared, openmouthed, as a smile of disbelief crept across her face. Her brain was frozen, but she felt a tremendous flattery from this homage that made her heartstrings tingle.

This woman had some aura or energy that locked onto L.C. and drew her in like a magnet. It wasn't anything about what she was wearing: a simple white oxford shirt with long sleeves, thin black leather belt, black-and-white houndstooth slim-cut skirt ending midthigh, black opaque stockings, and three-inch heels.

Was it something in her face? L.C. studied the details: eyebrows wickedly arched over cat eyes of emerald green flecked with chestnut brown, a slender nose perched above the most luscious lips she'd ever seen, which were painted crimson, revealing a perfect string of white pearls as she sang.

Perhaps it was her body: shoulders just broad enough to be strong-looking but leaving no doubt she was all woman. Long arms reaching out with feminine fingers, perfectly manicured—natural, no polish. Her slender waist spread into wide hip bones that announced their presence from beneath her wool skirt. Then L.C.'s eyes took another ride down the curves of those long, lean legs. It finally registered that there wasn't just one particular thing about this woman that was so appealing—it was everything.

What seemed like hours had actually taken only seconds, and L.C. was suddenly shaken out of her dream state by the applause and laughter for the impromptu performance by the beautiful blond, who was now upon L.C.—who still had that open-mouthed smile. Somehow the singer had gotten to her feet during all this and was now standing in the middle of the room shaking hands with the stranger.

"Oh, beautiful lady," the blond said softly, then paused for a brief moment, in which L.C. was certain she detected a change in the woman's expression, "you have been touched by the hand of God, and you're one of the lucky ones whose path has allowed them to develop that potential to its fullest. I am so happy for you."

Now, L.C. Hackett had been writing songs for nearly 25 years, and she considered herself quite good with words and expressing herself, but suddenly every word in her vocabulary had been knocked clean out of her head, and she couldn't speak. She was aware of her mouth moving slightly, trying to form words, but nothing came out. And before she knew it, she felt her hand slip from between the woman's warm, soft hands as the beautiful stranger was ushered away to be introduced to the others who had gathered around. L.C. was left standing alone, grinning like a slow-witted bastard.

Mandy sauntered over and threw a compassionate arm around L.C.'s shoulders. "Way to go, Shakespeare."

L.C. shook her head at what had just happened.

"You know," Mandy continued, "they say you only get one chance to make a first impression. I'd say you just made a doozy."

Carol Ann tried not to laugh, but this was the first time she had ever seen L.C. Hackett freeze up at the sight of a beautiful babe. Margaret and Susan, who had witnessed the brain freeze, also gathered around, sharing a hearty laugh.

Finally L.C.'s gray cells thawed. "Jesus!" she said, throwing her hands in the air. "She probably thinks I'm a half idiot. Oh, man." She continued to shake her head in humiliation.

Mandy gave her a reassuring pat as she guided her back to the bar. "I'm sure that if she thinks of you at all, she'll think of you as a complete idiot." L.C. glared at Mandy. First, for her insincere effort in comforting a friend in need, and second, because she was able to be so goddamn clever with her words. Words! What the hell had just happened here?

Nona came bounding up and nearly knocked Mandy over. "Man, is she hot." She craned her neck, standing on tiptoe, trying to get another look at the dish standing a few feet behind L.C. Then she leaned in and whispered, "You don't think she's one of us, do you?"

"Yeah," Mandy said flatly. "Life is ju-u-ust that fair."

"Who is that, anyway?" Susan asked. "She was hauled off before she could even introduce herself to you."

Connie, who no one seemed to notice had arrived with the mystery blond, poked her smiling face through the bodies surrounding L.C. "It's Sydney Sanders."

"Who?" Margaret asked.

"Sydney Sanders! She just won the Pulitzer Prize for fiction," she said, bursting with excitement as she waved her book that had been autographed by the author an hour earlier.

Carol Ann did the eye roll. "Oh, yeah...she was on *Leno* last night—I remember the hair."

"I can't believe I froze up like that," L.C. said, still trying to shake it off. "But Jesus, what do you say when you're confronted with a walkin', talkin', life-size Barbie doll?"

"Barbie doll?" came a voice from over L.C.'s shoulder. The singer turned and found herself unexpectedly looking into the face of Sydney Sanders once more. "If I were a Barbie doll I'd have boobs out to here," she said, grabbing her oxford shirt and pulling out as far as it would go. Everyone laughed except L.C., who had turned fire-engine red and was busy saying a silent prayer: *Dear God, just take me now...please.*

Sydney looked down from atop her Bruno Maglis at the red-faced woman. "You know," she said, looking directly into L.C.'s blue eyes with a confident, almost teasing smile, "if you're going to live in L.A., you really should start using sunscreen—your face is red as a lobster." And as she passed by, she brushed a feminine finger against L.C.'s hot cheek.

This simple touch sent a warm sensation shooting through the flustered L.C., but this time the tingling was noticeably south of her heartstrings.

While the women around her gossiped and chattered, L.C. drifted off for a brief moment, recalling the touch of that finger, the sound of that voice, the strange expression when she had first spoken—wait a minute. What was that Sydney had called her? Beautiful lady? Had she imagined that? She'd been called many things in her life, but never beautiful. And what had she said about a God-given talent? She could recall the feeling of complete sincerity in the words, but not the words themselves. Fuck—what the hell was her problem with words tonight? And what was that little change in expression she had noticed—sadness, regret, envy? She couldn't define it, which only intrigued her more.

The group adjourned to the living room, while the commotion surrounding Sydney shifted into the adjoining den, and guests made themselves comfortable in plush, upholstered chairs and sofas positioned to invite conversation. Several pairs of eyes were still ogling Sydney, who was standing, talking to a group of women. "Man, I'd like to wrap those legs around my neck like a New York pretzel," Mandy said hungrily, causing an outbreak of laughter.

"You are so crude," L.C. said, even though the idea appealed to her too.

Mandy cocked her head and narrowed her eyes. "You mean you're not about to slide off that couch there, buddy?"

"Hey—stay out of my pants," L.C. warned.

"That's one thing you'll never have to worry about."

The others all knew the two had been best friends forever and were just kidding around—their banter didn't mean anything. Still, Carol Ann frowned. "I don't know what you guys are getting so torqued up about anyway. She's just another cheesy bottle blond."

L.C. gave her a look. "What's your problem? You don't even know her."

"Oh, I know her." Carol Ann narrowed her eyes. "She was the cheerleader who dated all the jocks, her daddy's filthy rich, and she plays tennis at the country club. Her family winters in Palm Beach, she got a Porsche for her 16th birthday, and I'll bet you a million dollars she was a model."

This time the joke was on Carol Ann because Sydney had

walked into the room just in time to hear her remarks. "Actually, I was a dancer." She took a seat on the end of the sofa across from L.C. and Carol Ann. Tension fell over the room; no one was sure how Sydney would react to the insults.

"Were you any good?" Carol Ann asked, as though she already knew the answer.

"I was very good," Sydney said confidently, stretching out her long legs before crossing them.

"Then how come I've never heard of you?"

"Because agents and producers were always promising to put me on Broadway or in the movies…if I'd let 'em fuck me." That struck a familiar chord with a few of those listening because it was the same crap in the record business. "Even my own agent—the guy who was supposed to watch out for me and protect me—got in on the act. They all said they wanted to help me, but all they really wanted was to help themselves."

"Is that why you started writing instead?" Margaret asked.

"Partly. When I was in grade school I was being groomed to be an Olympic gymnast—"

Carol Ann rolled her eyes. "Oh, please," she grumbled. L.C. jabbed her in the ribs with an elbow.

"But by the time I was 12, I was already 5 foot 8 and 122 pounds. I outgrew my arm strength, and all that extra height and weight really increases the centrifugal force when you're swinging around on the uneven bars. And let me tell you, you go flying across a hardwood gymnasium floor a couple of times and you figure out pretty quick that Mother Nature is telling you it's time to give it up. So, after abusing my joints and ligaments and tendons through six years of gymnastics and six years of cheerleading—"

Carol Ann jabbed L.C. back. "Told ya!" she snarled.

"I was a prime candidate for a serious injury. I tore the cartilage and strained the anterior cruciate ligament in my right knee one day. Well, the doctor I had wasn't worth a damn, and the therapy program I was on wasn't doing much of anything. So after six months of physical therapy, I still couldn't walk right, let alone dance. I finally got fed up and just started stretching and working on my own doing basic ballet positions and ballroom dance steps for balance and weight transference.

"Two months later I was walking and running short distances again. But I still couldn't bend my knee all the way like a dancer needs to and wasn't willing to risk another injury, so I gave that up too." She let out a pathetic laugh. "Not bad, huh...washed up in two careers before I even hit 30." She smiled, but it didn't mask the pain of unfulfilled dreams. L.C. wondered whether this was what she had detected in Sydney's cryptic greeting.

"Anyway, one day I got to thinking about all those poor people out there suffering and thinking they're going to be disabled for the rest of their lives all because of a couple of little but important things they aren't doing right. So I went back to that therapy clinic and showed them what I'd been able to accomplish. Well, they were shocked. I ended up working with them for several months developing a physical therapy program for patients with leg and hip injuries that don't respond to traditional treatments. Sometimes it's just a matter of fooling the brain."

Sydney could tell by their faces they didn't really understand. "OK, when an injured leg doesn't heal right away, you start favoring it and using it improperly. Well, the knee bone's connected to the thigh bone, etcetera, etcetera, and after a while the whole body gets out of balance and muscles start tightening up, working the wrong way to overcompensate, then everything gets out of whack. Before long, the brain begins to think this abnormal usage is normal.

"But people don't think of dancing as physical therapy, so

they relax more, which allows things to stretch the way they're supposed to and to stand erect for a better plumb line through the entire body, which gives proper balance and masks the weight shifts. Plus they don't think simple dance steps are going to hurt them like physical therapy exercises often do. So you see, sometimes the mind is the key to healing the body. Anyway, they've had tremendous success with the program over the years. In fact, they're still using it today." Sydney smiled modestly.

Someone from the next room came up and tapped Sydney on the shoulder. "Excuse me, I hate to interrupt, but is yours the little black purse with the shoulder strap?"

"Yes," Sydney replied, sitting up.

"I think your cell phone's ringing."

"Excuse me, ladies." She hopped up and headed back to the bar where she'd left her purse.

All eyes went to Carol Ann. They knew she was silently eating her words and no one really wanted to make her choke on them. After a moment, L.C. broke the silence. "Wow," she said, shaking her head pathetically, "what...a...*bitch*." Several giggles and spit-laughs escaped. "God—don't you just hate people like that?" she continued, "it's always me-me-me-me-me!" By this time the entire room was doubled over laughing.

Carol Ann held up her middle finger an inch away from L.C.'s face, but L.C. still laughed along with the others. Then L.C. noticed Mandy's eyes were locked onto the leggy blond who was standing at the bar with her back to the room, one hand over her ear to block out the noise. As she talked on the phone, her weight shifted back and forth, creating a sensual swaying motion in her legs and well-rounded hips. After 30 seconds of watching Mandy watching Sydney, L.C. felt a tinge of competition, and she didn't care for it a bit. "Will someone get her a coaster for her tongue?" she said, only half kidding.

Mandy snapped out of it and realized that remark was directed at her. "Cunt," she spouted back affectionately, turning back around to face L.C. She didn't see Sydney slip through the sliding doors out back to block the noise while she talked on the phone. But L.C. did.

"If anyone's a cunt, I'll bet Blondie is," Carol Ann groused. "I mean, look at her—she's got prom queen written all over her."

"Will you stop," L.C. said. "Geez—I feel like I'm caught in this evil web of negativity you're casting out. *Help me! Help me!*" she said in a shrill, quavering voice like the human-headed fly in the original B-movie. Her dead-on imitation caused another wave of laughter. Then L.C. stood up. "I can't stand this negative atmosphere anymore. I'm going outside for some fresh air."

Someone reminded her that this was L.A., but she went outside anyway.

Chapter Two

The entire back wall of the den leading to the pool was sliding glass doors, and L.C. pushed the end panel open and went out. Sydney was lying on one of the chaise lounges, no longer talking on her phone, but L.C. still closed the doors behind her.

"You just enjoying the night?" L.C. said, looking up at the clear sky full of stars.

"No, some people are smoking, and I saw someone just light up a cigar. I'm *really* allergic to cigars—my face breaks out in itchy red welts. So I'm just waiting it out."

L.C. pulled up another chaise, then threw her leg over, mounting it like a horse. "Oh, by the way, sorry about that Barbie-doll comment," she said, looking a little uneasy.

Sydney just laughed. "If that's the worst thing ever said about me, I should be so lucky."

L.C. figured girls like her took their fair share of slams during their lifetime, and the comment probably hadn't bothered her too much. She took a swig from her beer, then noticed Sydney didn't have a drink in her hand. "You want a beer or something?"

"Um, just some Evian if she has it," Sydney said, smiling appreciatively.

"I think you're out of luck there," L.C. replied. "Water, huh? You a member of a club with a 12-step program or something?"

"Oh, no. I'll have a glass of champagne at a wedding or on New Year's, but I just have to be careful not to overdo it."

"How come?"

"Partly because alcohol puts me to sleep, and partly because for some reason champagne makes me really horny. Must be all those tiny bubbles tickling me inside," she said with a giggle.

L.C. wondered whether the tiny bubbles in a bottle of beer might have the same effect since there was no champagne in the house. "You sure you wouldn't like a beer instead?"

"No, thanks," Sydney said. "I really don't like to drink. I've always taken care of my body. You can't function at 100% as a gymnast or a dancer if you drink."

"OK, so let's recap: You don't smoke. You don't drink," L.C. said, counting on her fingers, "I bet you've never done drugs either," she said, holding up a third.

"Nope."

This was getting disgusting. "So what—did you spend most of your life in Catholic school like I did?"

Sydney looked a little shocked. "You were raised Catholic?"

L.C. laughed. "Oh, yeah. They *love* to see me, come reunion time."

Sydney felt somewhat awkward talking about this, even though the whole world was aware of L.C. Hackett's sexual preference—she had never made any bones about it. But Sydney had never discussed this sort of thing before, and it made her uncomfortable. For a moment they both pretended the awkward silence didn't exist, then L.C. spoke.

"So I hear you won the Pulitzer for your book?"

"Yeah. I was shocked, actually."

"How come?"

"Because it's not exactly a flattering portrait of men, and the majority of people on the Pulitzer committee are men, so…"

"Don't be offended or anything, but I haven't read your book."

"I'm not offended," Sydney told her. "I've never bought any of your albums either."

Touché. "So what's it about?" L.C. asked, caring a little less at this point.

"Oh, God." Sydney's hands dropped to her side. "I'll give you the Cliff Notes version: It takes place at the turn of the next century when male nature has gone unchecked by society for a hundred years. It's basically a wake-up call to women to rebel against the abuse. I hope you don't mind if I don't go into all the details, because this is all I've talked about for the last five months." Her brow suddenly knotted, the gears in her brain straining. "This is October, isn't it?"

"Yeah, for another 10 days, anyway."

Sydney shook her head, as if to clear it. "I've been on the road since early summer doing talk shows and book signings and lectures—I've completely lost track of time. And between the limited conversation topics and the lack of sleep from going Amtrak, with the train stopping at every little Podunk town all night long, and living in noisy hotels with people coming in drunk at 2 A.M., elevators pinging, ice machines grinding, people leaving at the crack of dawn to catch the red-eye, housekeeping with their vacuums at 7 A.M.—I am so sleep deprived, I want to scream."

"Why are you taking the train? You afraid of flying?" L.C. asked, almost hoping the woman would say yes and reveal a flaw.

"No, I simply refuse to patronize an industry that shows so little regard for its customers," Sydney said. "I can't count how many thousands of dollars I've lost having to cancel a trip at the last minute—airlines don't give refunds, you know. I don't know of a single business that takes your money before you use its product and then keeps it even if you don't use it. What kind of communist way to run a business is that?" L.C. laughed out loud.

"Oh, they say you can use the ticket toward another flight within a year, but sometimes you don't go anywhere during that time frame, and I've ended up losing money for several first-class tickets. And who designed those seats anyway—Quasimodo? The human spine doesn't go like this." She cupped her hand to make a crescent shape. "Where's the lumbar support in that? And even the first-class seats aren't much better. But the last straw was the rude flight attendants. I tell you, if I'm paying 10 times what the people in coach are paying for the same flight, I at least expect courtesy." She shook her head defiantly. "I won't do it."

L.C. let out a sigh. "You are the most principled person in the world, aren't you? Damn!"

They both laughed, then a thought popped into L.C.'s head and out of her mouth before she knew it. "You're welcome to stay at my home, if you like. I've got a house in Malibu, and the ocean waves really rock you to sleep at night." She noticed immediately Sydney didn't react the way she'd wanted, and L.C. felt a twinge of embarrassment.

"Oh, that's so sweet of you," Sydney said, "but have you really thought about what you're doing, here? I mean, you know how when relatives visit, and by the third day you want to boot them all out? And that's people you know and love. I'm a total stranger. What if I snore and leave dirty dishes all over the place?"

"Not a problem," L.C. said flatly, eyes averted to her beer bottle.

"What if I squeeze the toothpaste from the middle instead of rolling up the end? It might be a little too much too soon, don't you think?"

L.C. kept her eyes lowered and shrugged her shoulders, as if to say it was no big deal. But Sydney felt an unmistakable embarrassment radiating from the singer. She felt bad too, knowing the woman's feelings were hurt. "Hey," Sydney said, "I'll tell you what. Tomorrow I have a book signing in the morning, then lunch, and a lecture at UCLA at 2—how about if after I finish, I pack an overnight bag and come out for one night and we can have a slumber party?" she said with a grin.

L.C. had never done the slumber-party thing as a girl and thought it a bit late to start, but she appreciated Sydney's enthusiasm for recapturing her youth.

"We can do each other's hair," Sydney said in a Valley Girl voice as she twirled the ends of her hair around an index finger. "And we can make prank phone calls and have pizzas delivered to the Back Street Boys!"

L.C. had to laugh at this. "Sure, I'm up for it."

"Great. Um, look, I'm not familiar with L.A., so you're going to have to fax me a detailed map of how to get to your place, OK?"

"Will do. Where are you staying?"

"At the Beverly Hills Hotel."

"I'll fax you tomorrow," she promised.

"Oh, shoot!" Sydney said, leaping to her feet. "I forgot to call my agent about something—that phone call I just got. Will you excuse me a minute?"

Before L.C. could respond, Sydney had rushed back into the house, frantically punching numbers on her phone. Then the singer heard the glass door slide open again, and the living room gang poured out poolside. They all wore the same expression. L.C. leaned back, arms crossed, and prepared herself for the inevitable onslaught.

"So, will you be hitting the sheets tonight at your place or hers?" Carol Ann teased, knowing L.C.'s reputation.

"It's tomorrow night—my place," L.C. boasted.

"Bullshit," Mandy replied. "She's straight. Connie told me. Sydney mentioned to her that she's married...or was married, I forget."

"So?" L.C. said, like it was nothing to worry about.

"You're not seriously thinking 'conversion,' are you?" Mandy said. "Not even you could pull that off."

"Oh, please. L.C. could charm the panties off a nun," Carol Ann said in all seriousness, causing groans of disgust.

"Gross!" L.C. said, and put her hands over her contorted face. "Now I'm flashing back to sixth grade and picturing Sister Mary Kathryn naked under her habit. Oh, man!"

"Sydney wouldn't go for you anyway," Mandy said. "She's too straitlaced."

"Yeah? Well, I'll be sure and tell her you said that when she comes over to spend the night tomorrow."

"In your dreams," Mandy sneered.

"In your wet dreams," Carol Ann added.

L.C.'s cocksure expression never faltered. "Seriously."

"You lie!" Carol Ann said loudly, her sixth beer apparently affecting her hearing levels.

"Nuh-uh. After her lecture she's coming over, and we're having a slumber party. Al-l-l night long." L.C.'s blue eyes twinkled with a glint of mischief.

"Liar, liar, pants on fire!" Carol Ann shouted.

"I mean it," L.C. said with a big smile.

"Your nose is longer than a telephone wire!"

Margaret wasn't going for this bullshit either. "You two were just talking, and you know it." She looked at her friends. "She's zoomin' us."

"I don't know," said Mandy, who was beginning to wonder. "When did L.C. Hackett ever see a tasty morsel like that and not try to sample it?"

L.C. shot her friend a look. "You're reducing the woman to a plate of hors d'oeuvres?"

"Nah, she's too big to be an hors d'oeuvre," Carol Ann said. "She's a prime cut of USDA choice."

"Jesus, what a cliché," L.C. said. "Can't you do any better than that?" She got serious for a moment. "No really, I'm just doing her a favor."

They all cracked up. "I'm sure you think you are," Mandy teased.

"I didn't mean it that way."

"Yeah, right," Carol Ann said.

L.C. had had enough. "Whatever. Anyway, you shouldn't talk that way about her. She's really nice."

Carol Ann was having a hard time with her friend's denials. "Look at how you defend her…you come to her rescue like Sir Galahad." Then she noticed L.C. looked away. A Cheshire grin spread from cheek to cheek on Carol Ann's face. "Oh, my God. This isn't just a lay—you're smitten!"

L.C. rolled her head from one shoulder to the other. "I am not. She's just nice."

Carol Ann knew she was on to something good here and intended to work it. "You are the smitten kitten!"

L.C. acted nonchalant just to get this schnauzer off her ankle. "So I have good taste in women, so sue me."

"Pf-f-fht! Get in line," Mandy laughed.

"Ain't that the fuckin' truth," L.C. said, her thoughts shifting to the three pending lawsuits against her—one by her former manager, who felt that since he had discovered her 15 years ago he was entitled to 10% of everything she had made since; another by her former record company citing breach of contract when she left over the Veronica incident; and one by a woman in Minneapolis who claimed the singer's voice had sent her into an epileptic fit causing her to fall down a flight of stairs, thus wrenching her back and rendering her unable to work for the last 14 months. "Fucking vultures," L.C. groused. She was going to clarify that she meant the people suing her, but then she thought of the $450 per hour her attorney was charging and decided it pretty well fit both, so she let it go.

Margaret suddenly sat up. "Straighten up, here she comes."

Sydney walked over. "All taken care of," she said to L.C. "Oh, I jotted down the number for the Beverly Hills, and my room number." She handed her a piece of paper. "So I'll be hearing from you tomorrow, I guess."

"Absolutely." L.C. slipped the paper into her pants pocket, giving the others a sly "eat your heart out" smirk.

Lisa had followed Sydney out and said, "Hey, the party's moving to a bar—the Little Dutch Boy—come on!"

Everyone agreed it sounded like a plan and headed for the door. "Wanna join us?" L.C. said to Sydney.

"Oh, thanks, but I'm half asleep right now, and I've got a long day tomorrow." Her brow wrinkled. "I'm sorry, what was the name of that club she mentioned?"

"The Little Dutch Boy," said Margaret.

"I don't recall seeing that mentioned in the magazine in my hotel room that lists all the hot spots in town."

"It's a dyke bar," Carol Ann blurted out, delighting at the opportunity to shock the woman.

Sydney got flustered but tried to keep it hidden. "Oh...well, then shouldn't it be called the Little Dutch *Girl*?"

Carol Ann rolled her eyes and let someone else take this one. Margaret politely explained the connection between the famous story of the little Dutch boy, the dike, dykes, lesbians.

Carol Ann couldn't resist just one more. "Yeah, what did he do, put his finger in a dike?"

An audible gasp popped out of Sydney. She quickly covered her mouth and stopped in her tracks at the sliding doors, turning bright red. Mandy tried not to let her guest see she was laughing when she passed by; Margaret and Susan followed suit. L.C. was the last to go by the flustered blond. "You should try a little of that sunscreen yourself," she said, then brushed a finger across Sydney's cheek.

A cacophony went off inside Sydney's head. What the hell was that? If L.C. had been a guy, she would have interpreted it as flirting. But this was a whole new game, and she wasn't familiar with the rules. *Was* L.C. flirting with her? Do women flirt with women the same way men flirt with women? Had L.C. misinterpreted that same gesture when she had done it earlier? Or was she the one misinterpreting? Good God, what had she done? Sydney blinked hard to clear her head, but it didn't help—her mind was racing at 90 miles an hour.

Well, so much for getting a good night's sleep—she was wide awake now.

Chapter Three

At 2:45 the following day, Sydney was winding up her lecture at the coliseum-style classroom in the communications department at UCLA. All the standard questions had been asked: How long did it take you to write the book? Are you a feminist? What did it feel like to win the Pulitzer Prize? And all the standard answers had been given: A year. Yes. Surprise and shock. At last, someone asked a question she felt had substance, one that would exercise her mind beyond these rote responses. "What inspired you to write the book?"

"I'm glad you asked that," she said, just before the doors behind the back row slammed shut, echoing loudly. All heads turned toward the rear. To everyone's surprise, in walked L.C. and Mandy. The presence of two famous rock stars generated a big buzz among the students, who watched intently as the women made their way to a cluster of empty seats in the back row.

The two looked like a couple of Hell's Angels to Sydney, with their lightweight black leather jackets—sleeves pushed up—black jeans and boots. Then she noticed that L.C. had worn the same outfit last night. The only difference was today her white silk shirt was unbuttoned down to the tip of her sternum, which Sydney guessed was an effort to shock any young, fragile mind that was in range of getting a good shot down her blouse as she leaned forward, resting elbows on knees, staring directly at

Sydney with a big grin plastered across her face. Mandy was kicked back in a seat with one foot up on the back of the chair in front of her. She sported the same cocky grin. It was obvious these two felt right at home stealing the spotlight.

Maybe it was the arena-style seating, but suddenly Sydney felt like a Christian being fed to the lions. Surely they wouldn't say anything to embarrass her. Then she thought of last night's "finger in the dike" remark and how these women got such a kick out of shocking her. She cringed, then smiled a pathetic, helpless smile. "Ladies and gentlemen, I think it's safe to say I'm about to be heckled by two of the most gifted artists the world has ever seen." She extended an arm of introduction, "K.C. from the Sunshine Band and Melissa Gilbert from *Little House on the Prairie.* Let's hear it for 'em!"

A burst of laughter filled the auditorium and everyone applauded. No one laughed harder than the two women in the back row. When the commotion died down, Sydney said wistfully, "Don't you two have a world tour or something to go to?" Another burst of laughter.

"Nope," was all L.C. said. The grin got bigger.

Sydney's eyes rolled back in her head and she let out a sigh, then braced herself. "All right, what was the last question—I'm sorry, I've forgotten."

The student repeated her question. "Oh, yeah," Sydney said. "Well, if you all don't know, I was a newspaper journalist for many years, and I found out very quickly newspaper journalism is all the negative things in life—it's all rape, robbery, and murder. Think about it, how much happy news do you ever read in the newspaper? So, after about 10 years of reading this garbage, day after day, month after month, year after year, I was reading a crime brief one day about a woman whose car had broken down on the Interstate and she accepted a ride from some guy who stopped and said he'd take her to a gas station for help."

A few students groaned; a few heads shook sorrowfully. "Yeah, you already know what's coming, don't you? The guy took her out, raped her, then stabbed her and dumped her body on the side of the road. After I read the two paragraphs—which, by the way, is all a rape gets anymore; it's so common it's not worth wasting the space for a real story. Anyway, I said out loud, 'This stupid woman! Doesn't she read the papers? She should have known.' Well, about two minutes later my stomach knotted up and I felt ill. It had just hit me, what I'd said. I'd blamed this poor woman for this horrible thing that had happened to her just because she trusted another human being. Now, how sad is the state of our society when even women fall prey to this attitude of blaming the victim?"

The lighthearted atmosphere in the room turned serious. Even L.C. and Mandy weren't smiling any longer. "There's a real problem in our society, folks, when men view women as mere receptacles for their lusts. Once he's through with her body, he disposes of it like so much other useless garbage. We've stopped blaming men for the most abominable behavior. And part of the reason is because we women don't stand up for ourselves. We don't talk about the abuse. We don't draw attention to the problems in the right way."

The room was dead silent, and L.C. and Mandy exchanged glances.

"I mean, where is our outrage?" Sydney continued. "When was the last time you heard of women joining forces to boycott a football game in protest of one of the star players being charged with rape or spousal abuse? Spousal abuse—hell, it's wife-beating! Even the terminology has been cleaned up and made politically correct so it's not so offensive. Well, it *is* offensive. Yet today men have this attitude that if an opportunity presents itself to commit a crime against a woman, that somehow makes it OK. If there's no one around to witness it, then it's not really a crime. Let's face it, females have become the victim sex.

"And you know what's almost as bad? Because we've made it less offensive and because we're so used to hearing about it that it doesn't outrage us anymore, in a way we're accepting it without even realizing. And we all just go about our own lives and do nothing to change things. I find it all *very* offensive. It doesn't work that way—it *shouldn't* work that way.

"Anyway, that one incident at the newspaper really shook me up, and a few months later I decided it was time for a wake-up call in America. A year later this was the result." She held up her book, and the room erupted in applause.

A male student raised his hand. "It sounds like you don't like men...are you gay?"

Once again the attention turned to the two women in the back row. "I like to borrow from the classics at times," Sydney said with mock dignity, "and I think the best answer to that question comes from a classic episode of *Seinfeld.* It's the subway episode where Elaine is explaining to an older woman that she's on her way to be the best man at a lesbian wedding. The woman gets disgusted and walks away, and Elaine calls out after her: 'I hate men, but I'm not a lesbian!' "

Somewhere in the auditorium a voice shouted out, "Not that there's anything wrong with that," which set the room off.

"I must say, though," Sydney continued, "that after decades of dating and being married, I have come to the conclusion that women will never be able to find the emotional satisfaction they require from a man."

"Why's that?" someone called out.

"Have any of you ever heard of *Brain Sex?*" Several in the audience laughed, but Sydney could tell no one knew what she was talking about. "It was this wonderful series on the Learning Channel, a study about how male and female brains process information. One test had men and women look at the photos of faces expressing different emotions and then asked them to identify those emotions. Afterward, they showed a scan of how much of the brain was being used to interpret those emotions. Well, the women scored higher than the men and used significantly less of their brains to do so. But the men scored horribly, and had to use much more of their brain to interpret the images.

"But in another test, subjects were given pictures of naked people of the opposite sex, and males responded significantly stronger than females. Long story short, male and female brains are wired differently—males are visually stimulated creatures and females are emotionally stimulated. Which means the age-old communication problems between the sexes aren't just from males being socialized poorly, as we once thought. So it seems to me that if men are genetically incapable of making a woman happy, then the logical choice would be for women to engage in relationships with other women...unless they want to play Get Thee to a Nunnery, which would be terribly lonely, don't you think?"

From on high a familiar raspy voice called out, "On behalf of the membership committee, I'd be happy to welcome you aboard."

The room burst into laughter. Sydney looked up at Mandy's smiling face. "Are you guys still giving away a free toaster oven to new members?"

"If that's what it takes to get you on board," came the reply.

Sydney clasped her hands and acted like she was pondering. "Is it a GE?"

This exchange broke up the room to the point where Sydney deemed it impossible to get serious again. She checked her watch. "It's almost 3," she told the class. "This seems like a natural stopping place, so let me thank you for coming and for your questions—I enjoyed talking with all of you."

For the next 15 minutes, Sydney was tied up with shaking hands and autographing copies of her novel. When she finally made her way to the top of the arena, L.C. and Mandy walked out with her. L.C. gave her the once-over, checking out the form-fitting black Armani skirt suit with white silk blouse. "Nice outfit," she said, with a touch of mocking.

"Yeah…it's like looking in a mirror, huh?" Sydney shot back. Mandy snickered at the clever comeback, then rubbed her head, which throbbed from a hellacious hangover. "So what are you two up to today?" Sydney asked as the three strolled toward the exit.

"Not much," L.C. said. "I freeloaded at her place last night and figured I might as well give you a ride instead of faxing you a map and all that bullshit."

"Oh, how sweet," Sydney said, still scrutinizing L.C. The way she dressed and spoke reminded her of a free-spirited hippie—the *Easy Rider* type. Then she stopped. "Oh, God," she said, looking at the women in black leather. "If you've got a motorcycle out there, I am going to scream."

Mandy laughed. "She just sold her motorcycle," she said reassuringly as L.C. opened the door for Sydney. Then Mandy laughed again right in L.C.'s face as she passed through the door. "She spent a *year* searching all over Europe for that damn thing, then when she finally finds it, she gets rid of it." The tiny woman shook her head hopelessly at her friend, thinking back on the countless times L.C. had done this—how she'd always get so excited pursuing a special toy, then shortly after she got it, she'd lose interest.

L.C. shrugged it off. "It was too much work. That thing needed constant attention—I was always in the garage tinkering with it to keep it running right. I don't have that kind of time."

Sydney's eyes scoured the parking lot for the car she thought fit L.C.'s personality, but was pleasantly surprised when she found them heading for a slick, banana-yellow Jaguar. It was one of the classic XKE roadsters from the '60s—a two-seater with a long nose and rounded back, V-12 engine, and spoke wheels like circles of Fourth of July sparklers all on fire from the California sun.

L.C. opened the passenger door for Sydney, who was going to make a comment about chivalry not being dead, but she thought about L.C. touching her cheek last night and decided not to provoke anything. When Sydney sat down, her skirt rode up high on her thighs and L.C. caught Mandy getting an eyeful. A wordless conversation passed between the two friends. L.C. cocked an eyebrow: *You're trespassing on my claim—knock it off!* Mandy shrugged: *A girl can dream, can't she?* Sydney waved goodbye to Mandy, who had hopped into her BMW, and the two cars drove off in opposite directions.

After dropping by Sydney's hotel for her overnight bag, the two stopped at a grocery store to pick up ingredients for the gourmet dinner Sydney had volunteered to cook so they could relax at home instead of going out. At the entrance, Sydney stopped and turned to L.C. "Gee...you guys are sure liberal out here," she said. L.C. asked what she meant. "Bristol Farms is selling skinny lesbians." L.C. followed her line of sight and looked at the poster of specials in the window: LOW-FAT HOMO. GAL. $2.69. L.C.'s belly started jiggling, then she giggled so hard she had to stop for a moment and collect herself.

An hour later they turned onto Sea Shell Drive in Malibu and pulled up to the gated home shrouded by an acre of professionally landscaped greenery of palm trees, shrubs, and row after row of multicolored flowers. Sydney noticed the name "M. Mitchell" above the mail slot, which L.C. explained was the name of the author of her favorite book, *Gone With the Wind*, adding that the ruse was unfortunately necessary to keep rabid fans from knowing who really lived there.

She punched in a code and the gate opened. Once they had driven past the tropical camouflage, Sydney could see the beautiful sprawling home and hear the ocean coming from the other side of the house. A black Land Rover and a sea-green Mercedes sedan were parked in the driveway. "You got company?" Sydney asked.

"Nope, just some of my toys."

Sydney followed L.C. to the door, which was actually the back door because it was an oceanfront home, and waited while she fumbled with her keys. L.C. pushed the door open then stood aside, but Sydney didn't move. She stood on the porch, arms crossed, with what L.C. thought looked like a sneer.

"I'm not going in there," Sydney said.

L.C. was confused and on the verge of being insulted. "Why not?"

"Because this is the kind of house I've dreamed of my whole life, and if I go in there, I'm going to fall in love with it and I won't want to leave, and then I'll end up eating my heart out over something I can't have." She shrugged defiantly. "I'm not going in there."

L.C. stepped around behind the blond and playfully nudged her with a shoulder toward the door. With a smile, Sydney grumbled, "Oh, man!" and grudgingly shuffled inside.

The inside of the home was exactly what she expected from a millionaire rock star—huge and well furnished. To the left of the entrance hall was a large kitchen with every possible amenity, including a Jenn-Air grill, a built-in deep fryer, and a walk-in subzero refrigerator-freezer. The emerald-green granite counters complimented the mottled-peach tile backsplash behind the stove, which was recessed into an archway and crowned by a solid copper Vent-a-Hood up to the 12-foot ceiling. The flooring was of large natural sandstone tiles. All the earth tones gave the room a feeling of warmth, but something didn't seem quite right to Sydney.

There were no smells. No garlic or oregano wafting from their spice jars, no burned-on remnants of steaks on the grill or boiled-over spaghetti sauce on the stove coils; the chrome drip plates beneath the coils were spotless and gleaming; no fresh fruits or vegetables ripening in a bowl. This beautiful kitchen looked brand new and untouched. She'd bet a bundle that huge refrigerator was full of take-out cartons.

Once she stepped into the main living area, the first thing Sydney saw was a shiny black grand piano in the far corner. "Oo-o-oo!" she cooed, walking toward the black jewel with her arms outstretched, hypnotized by the object that drew her closer and closer, completely oblivious to the spectacular view of the ocean framed by a 30-foot glass wall that opened to the beachfront deck and heated pool. "Steinway," she said, sounding impressed. Then she positioned herself in the curve of the piano's body and leaned back, arms stretching out sensually over the instrument, head tilted coyly against a shoulder. "Me likey," she said in a throaty but intentionally silly voice.

L.C. put her hands in her pockets and enjoyed the show for a moment. "I'm betting that with those long fingers of yours, and by the way you're feeling up my piano, that you play."

"Indeed I do," Sydney said, taking a seat on the bench.

L.C. walked over. "Go ahead."

Sydney threw back her head with a laugh. "I stopped playing in front of other people a long time ago." She gently ran her fingertips up the pearly white keys. "When I was a girl, my mother used to drag me out like a trained monkey to play whenever anyone came over." She looked somberly at L.C. "Why do parents do that? It's like they're living out their own failed dreams through their children…even if the children hate it."

L.C. noticed the ice in those hazel eyes and knew she'd hit a sore spot. Afraid of making things worse, she said nothing.

"We had this beautiful antique piano she'd gotten me to learn to play on, and she put all the family pictures in these ornate silver frames on top of it. I could always tell when I'd displeased her because when I'd come downstairs in the morning, her picture of me would be facedown." She forced a smile. "In case you haven't figured it out, my mother is a big red button, even though she's dead, and I strongly advise you not to push that one unless you're willing to suffer the consequences—and I do mean suffer."

"Should I get out my motorcycle helmet just in case?" L.C. said, trying to lighten the mood.

"Wouldn't do you any good—I do my damage with words. I'm very good with words, but when I get angry, I become fuckin' eloquent." She ran her fingers the other way down the black keys. "Lost a really good friend that way a long time ago. But I've worked on it over the years and I'm keeping it under control very well in my old age." She hit a chord on the piano, then took a deep sigh. "Well, I guess we should bring the groceries in before things start melting."

Chapter Four

The two had a ball making a complete mess of L.C.'s spotless kitchen while Sydney worked her magic, concocting a scrumptious coq au vin. L.C. admitted to being helpless in a kitchen—which was why she had a personal chef who prepared all her meals in advance and froze them—so her participation was limited to chopping the onions and mushrooms and stirring the sauce.

After dinner, L.C. watched while Sydney put together a spectacular baked Alaska in minutes. Sydney pointed out that if they had made the ice cream and pound cake from scratch instead of buying them, not only would it taste better but it would be healthier too. She showed L.C. the nutritional chart on the carton of Häagen-Dazs macadamia nut ice cream. Each half-cup serving provided almost 75% of the recommended daily allowance of fat. While Sydney piped the meringue over the ice cream and cake, she began a friendly lecture on cholesterol and how just one egg contains 213 milligrams, declaring it no surprise that a cholesterol crisis existed in America. L.C. poked fun at her perfection, to which Sydney replied that her first gymnastics coach had her eating wheat germ when she was only 6 years old, so what did L.C. expect?

After five minutes, Sydney pulled the tray out of the oven, and the dessert boasted a perfect golden-brown meringue.

"Viola!" she cried, purposely mispronouncing the word to show she was, indeed, not perfect.

They ate dessert in the living room, listening to the ocean waves outside while L.C. spent her daily half hour on the phone with Trudy, her personal assistant, running over the day's phone messages and instructing the girl on replies to issue tomorrow. The singer apologized for the interruption but said it couldn't be helped, which Sydney understood.

After taking the dirty dishes back to the kitchen, L.C. stopped at the living room entrance and flipped a switch on the wall. The recessed lighting dimmed and the ceiling was filled with tiny white lights twinkling like stars. Thus began the singer's standard prelude to sex: Set the mood with romantic lighting, wait for the opportunity to get close enough for physical contact, then move in for the kill.

"That is so cool," Sydney said, her head tilted back as she marveled at the lights.

"I had the whole house done like that," L.C. said. "I get to sleep out under the stars every night of the year, rain or shine." But when she looked over, she noticed Sydney's eyes were no longer transfixed on the stars. "You've been looking at that piano all night," L.C. said in an inviting way.

Her guest smiled shyly, then walked over and sat at the instrument again. "All right," Sydney said, "I'll play something for you." She ran her fingers up the entire keyboard like a concert pianist warming up, which got L.C.'s attention. "We'll have a little pop quiz: Name That Composer!"

"Man, a song from you doesn't come cheap, does it?" L.C. said, joining Sydney on the bench and thinking the opportunity to get close had just fallen into her lap.

Sydney began playing Chopin's famous *Prelude*. L.C. recognized the melody immediately but didn't know who the composer was. When the last note was struck, L.C. said, "I'll take a guess and say Mozart."

"It's Chopin."

L.C. raised her hands as if to say, "Of course." Then she wondered aloud, "Isn't he the one who fell in love with that French writer who wrote under a man's name and wore men's clothing—oh, who was that...George Sand?"

"Yes ma'am."

"She must have been a real scandal in her day."

"She was, from what I've read."

"More power to 'er," L.C. said, raising a fist of solidarity. "But didn't their love affair end tragically—someone intercepting their love letters so they each thought the other didn't care?"

"You're thinking of the PBS series," Sydney said. "Unfortunately, they took a bit of dramatic license. Their version had Sand's daughter intercepting the love letters because she was secretly in love with Chopin and wanted the affair to end so she could have him. She didn't even tell her mother when he wrote that he was dying, and he died thinking Sand didn't love him anymore, all because of the daughter's interference.

"But in my studies," Sydney went on, "we had to read biographies on the great composers, and I read an excellent one by an ancestor of the Polish royal family who were patrons to Chopin. It didn't happen quite that way. He and Sand split up long before he died—she got into a relationship with someone else. The sad thing was that they had this white-hot passion for each other that never burned itself out. For years after they split, each was still deeply in love with the other but too proud to admit it. Foolish pride," she said sadly.

"His whole life was sadness and tragedy, actually," she said. "He was ill for so much of his life with tuberculosis, which eventually killed him. And if you listen closely, you can hear that melancholy in his music." She played the song again softly.

"Listen to how delicate and sweet the melody is, all the way through, until just near the end." She looked into L.C.'s eyes when she hit a certain note. "Right there, the change in that one chord, that one note changing from a natural to a sharp—that's all it takes to reach into your heart and make you feel his pain. It's like he goes along hiding his true feelings behind this simple melody, then at the end it becomes too much and his facade cracks—just that one little note—it's like a single tear rolling down his face. And then he regains his composure and covers up again at the very end." She finished the composition with reverence. "Sometimes it's the simplest things that make the greatest impression and endure."

L.C. gazed at the beautiful face next to her, no longer with a look of lust, but with respect for this woman who shared such a deep understanding of the thing that was her own life. "You didn't just learn to play the piano—you studied music, didn't you?" L.C. said with a note of admiration.

"I did indeed," Sydney grinned. "My first piano teacher told my mother I had the makings of a concert pianist. Mother wanted to send me off to a conservatory in London, but I was immersed in gymnastics—that's what I loved. So I devoted most of my time and effort to that instead."

"Which is why your picture spent so much time facedown on the piano, huh?" L.C. understood now.

"You know, it's funny...I used to be able to compose when I was a child. I used to hear the most beautiful melodies, and it was such a thrill to put those sounds down on paper with little black dots. It was almost like a foreign language—each note was a letter, each chord a word." Her face lit up with the innocent joy of a child discovering something wondrous.

"Sometimes I'd put words to the melodies," she said. "Oh, the lyrics weren't great or anything. I mean, what kind of life experience can you have to draw on when you're 8 or 10 years old?" She laughed. "Little did I know what was right around the corner." L.C. was intrigued as to what she meant but sensed Sydney didn't want to go into it at that point.

"I originally wanted to play the piano because it made me happy, but after so many years of being forced to practice and perform, I lost the ability to create my own songs. I just couldn't hear the music anymore."

She sighed, then clasped her hands on her lap. "Well, enough about me. Let's talk about you for a while."

The two moved out to the deck and got comfortable on a pair of all-weather chaises, which they positioned side by side. "So, what would you like to know?" L.C. said.

"What's it like having all those famous people as your personal friends? That party at Mandy's just blew my little Midwestern mind."

"Yeah, I was the same way when I first started in the business, but it's no big deal anymore—I'm so used to hanging out with them. It's just like anything else. After so long, you just get used to it."

Sydney dared to get a little personal. "So...are you and Mandy just good friends, or were you ever..." She left the question hanging, unable to say the words.

"Just friends," L.C. said with assurance.

"She's so cute and petite. And what a voice coming out of that tiny package. What is she—like, five-one?"

"On tiptoe," L.C. said, then gave Sydney a good once-over. "You must be around five-nine without shoes?"

"Exactly." Sydney pictured Mandy and L.C. standing next to each other. "I guess she would be a little short for you, huh?" She sized up L.C. at about 5-foot-6.

L.C. took in a breath of sea air. "Ah, you'd be surprised how quickly a height difference disappears once you're horizontal."

Oh, my! Sydney hadn't meant it *that* way. Immediately she considered changing the subject, but now that the subject had been broached, she was tempted to delve further. "Well, since we're getting sort of personal here, there is something I've been curious about," she said, biting her lip. "But if you don't want to answer, just say so and I'll respect your right to privacy."

"Fire away," L.C. said, raising a hand in the air.

Sydney's face took on a naughty expression. "Have you ever had sex with a guy?"

L.C. laughed at the tame question. "Nope."

"Oh, my God!" Sydney said. "Never in your whole life?" L.C. shook her head. "So you have no idea what it feels like to have a penis inside you? Wow!"

That mischievous expression returned to L.C.'s face. "Oh, I have an idea," she said.

Oh, dear! Well, what did Sydney expect? After all, she had opened that can of worms—now they were crawling out. Then came the natural response to her question.

"Have you ever had sex with a woman?" L.C. asked.

"No-o-o!" Sydney said. For a moment she was too embarrassed to speak, but she felt at ease with L.C. and quickly opened up. "You know, I honestly can't imagine what it would be like with a woman. I look at these women men drool over, like Pamela Anderson, and it does nothing for me. In fact, I think she looks slutty with that makeup and her clothes. Oh, sure, I can appreciate the lines of the female body—it's pleasing to the eye in an artistic way—but I don't get...aroused. No, I don't think I could ever give up the penis. I don't care too much for what it's attached to anymore, but I do like the penis. So that might be a problem."

L.C. leaned forward and got very close. "You know," she said in a confidential manner, "I have a little box under my bed with an assortment of ways to solve that very problem."

Sydney's eyelids fluttered like a window shade that had been pulled too tight then snapped. She didn't even want to think about what sort of pornographic Whitman's Sampler lay under that woman's bed. Worms, worms everywhere!

L.C. leaned back again. What a babe in the woods.

Sydney mustered up her courage once more. "Speaking of hiding stuff under beds, can I ask you another question?"

"Honey, I don't think you can take it," she said, sounding concerned.

"Do you read *Playboy* like guys do? I mean, you like women the same way guys do, so do you look at stuff like that too...or porno movies?"

"I've been known to purchase a *Playboy* now and then, but I don't subscribe."

Sydney shook her head. "I don't understand why men have such a need for naked women as entertainment," she said. "It's an epidemic. You've got strip joints and whack joints in every city in America. It's so dehumanizing. My first husband had a box of *Playboys* that I asked him to get rid of when we got married, and he said he would. Years later I found them in the back of his closet. When I asked him why he'd lied to me and asked him again to get rid of them, he refused. Even though he knew how much it upset and offended me—his wife—he still wouldn't do that for me. Why does a married man need that sort of thing?"

"In most cases I'd say because the wife let herself go and the man didn't find her sexually attractive anymore. But with you, that doesn't seem to be the case." L.C. took a quick glance at those great legs stretched out beside her.

"I tell you, that testosterone must be like electricity buzzing in their testicles to put them in constant need of an orgasm," Sydney said. "And they don't even care if it's a human outlet." Her expression grew serious. "You know that's how syphilis came into existence, don't you?" She could tell by L.C.'s puzzled face that she didn't. "Really—it's because some guy fucked a sheep."

L.C. smiled in disbelief.

"I'm serious. That's why we have the scourge of syphilis in the world today. Now how fuckin' horny does a guy have to get to screw a sheep? Geez, can't you just see it...a shepherd's tending his flock in the meadow, when one sheep catches his eye and he says, 'Ooh! Why don't you just ba-a-ack on up here, little feller?'" Sydney moved her hands and pelvis as though fucking an imaginary sheep, which had L.C. double over laughing. "You know, I've had some hormonal surges in my day, but I have *never* been tempted to go outside my own species. Lord! It took me decades of dating men and two marriages before I finally figured out the problem with men is that they're on a never-ending quest for the ultimate orgasm."

L.C. asked what she meant by that.

"Think about it. They're willing to risk their marriage and family and financial security all for the chance at a bigger and better orgasm. After being with the same woman for so long, they eventually lose interest. Then they see a young girl with longer legs or bigger boobs or a firmer ass and they just have to have it. And it's all because they think this new chickie will get them off in a bigger and better way. For them, sex has to constantly be hotter, steamier—there's no emotional involvement for guys. It's purely a physical thing with men, you know. You never hear about guys leaving their devoted wives for another woman with a more advanced degree." L.C. admitted that was true.

"I don't think men are even capable of feeling love the way women do because love requires respect, and I don't know too many men who genuinely look at women as equals, which is what it takes in order to have respect. I really believe they simply confuse lust with love in the beginning of a relationship, and once that hormonal high wears off, so does the relationship. Males just haven't evolved beyond that primal urge to copulate with as many females as possible. How sad and pathetic."

"I never had the need to give it much thought," L.C. said, gazing off, unconcerned.

Sydney drifted off too, but after a moment she turned to L.C. "Please tell me it's not like that with two women," she said, almost pleading. "I mean, I know that with same-sex couples, one's usually more feminine and one's more..." She hesitated, trying to find the right word. "Well, more..."

"Butch! Just say it, will ya? It's not going to offend me—God knows I've heard worse." L.C. was getting a little fed up with this woman's naïveté.

Sydney grew uneasy. "I'm sorry, I can't use that word."

"Why the hell not?"

"Well, because in my world when you call a woman 'butch' it's an insult. That word has been given such negative connotations, I just can't use it." L.C. felt bad once she understood that Sydney wasn't being naive; she was simply trying not to hurt her feelings with her choice of words.

"Anyway, let's just say one woman is usually more masculine," Sydney said. "But I'd like to hope that with those women you'd have the best of both worlds—masculinity tempered by feminine sensibility." She looked deeply into L.C.'s eyes. "Is that how it is?" she asked, hoping for reassurance.

L.C. thought a long time. "Now that I think about it, most couples I know didn't break up because one was fooling around. Mandy and her girlfriend just split up about a year ago and they'd been together, geez, almost 15 years, but it was over money issues. Most of them split up mainly because of pressures from family or friends or work, or just day-to-day life. It's not easy for gay couples, even today. They have a lot more crap to deal with than you can imagine."

Sydney looked out at the moon shining on the ocean and smiled. "This is nice, having someone to talk to again after all these years."

L.C. was a little confused by her words. "I'm sorry, I thought you were married until recently?"

"I was...and I've never been so lonely in all my life."

How sad, L.C. thought, *to be married and still feel alone.*

"He never talked to me," Sydney explained. "After my second husband and I had been married about six years, it dawned on me that I knew hardly anything about his life before we met. He never talked about his childhood, his friends, his family. He never talked about *anything.* I was always the one initiating conversation—or trying to. You'd think that after that long together, conversations would flow effortlessly. Well, you may as well grab a piece of string, tie it to a molar, and slam the door because trying to get this man to talk with me was like pulling fuckin' teeth."

L.C. admired Sydney's sense of humor about something that obviously was very painful.

"And now that I think about it, all men are like that," she said. "I mean, look at you and me—we've known each other a mere 24 hours, and neither of us has shut up the whole time." They both laughed. "And we can talk about anything too. It's almost like we've known each other forever."

Sydney took L.C.'s hand on the armrest next to hers and held it as she gazed out over the water again. The dark-haired woman looked at their joined hands—her own, with the thick wrist and fingers, nails bitten down all jagged; Sydney's, with its long, delicate fingers and manicured nails. L.C. smiled; this was a nice feeling. She had to admit that she'd been pretty lonely since

Veronica moved out, and it was good to have another warm body in the house again.

The conversation continued flowing, and the two women talked until 10 minutes after 4, when the need for sleep became too strong to ignore any longer.

At high noon, L.C. emerged from her bedroom in her well-worn Detroit Red Wings jersey, hair disheveled, eyes mere slits. On her way to the kitchen to make coffee she passed through the living room and stopped cold. There was Sydney on the floor doing leg lifts in what was either a pink bikini or sexy underwear—L.C. was one of those who eased into consciousness in the morning and couldn't tell at this time.

"Morning," Sydney said with a perky smile, but L.C. didn't respond and kept staring at Sydney with a peculiar expression. "What?" she asked, sitting up.

L.C. took in a deep breath, ran a hand quickly over the top of her head several times, fluffing up the tiny black hairs. "You may find this hard to believe, but it isn't every morning I wake up to find a beautiful half-naked blond lying in the middle of my floor with her legs in the air. Trust me on that one," she said, then shuffled off to the kitchen.

The aroma of freshly brewed coffee soon filled the house, and L.C. went out to retrieve the morning paper. She settled in on the couch, letting her eyes adjust to the light reflecting in from the beach while she attempted to browse the arts and entertainment section. "Want some coffee?"

"No, thanks," Sydney said in the middle of a set of hamstring stretches, "I don't touch the stuff."

L.C. threw up her hands. "Of course not! That goes without saying. I forget I'm talking to Miss Perfect here."

Sydney wasn't sure whether that had been meant as a jab or a joke.

"Do you have *any* vices at all?" L.C. asked.

"I used to be sort of addicted to chocolate, but I stopped eating it for about a year, and now I only allow myself to indulge once a week or so."

L.C. rubbed her aching head while she laughed hopelessly. Then she looked up in anguish. "If you have the power to avoid it, *it's not a vice*!" she shouted. Good grief! This innocent couldn't even see her own perfection, which was getting more annoying by the minute. 32

Sydney finished her morning routine and joined L.C. on the couch, reaching for the sports section. "Checking the hockey scores," she explained.

L.C. was shocked. "*You* know hockey?"

"Yes, ma'am," Sydney said haughtily.

L.C. decided to test her. "So what's icing?"

"The stuff Kerry Fraser puts in his hair," came the swift reply.

L.C. laughed and nodded admiringly. If this woman knew enough about the game to refer to one of its referees whose perfectly coiffed hair was the source of jokes throughout hockeydom, that was good enough for her. "A woman after my own heart."

It was then Sydney noticed the large, red heart tattoo on L.C.'s right biceps peeking out from beneath the cut-off sleeve of her jersey as she read the paper. It made Sydney a little uncomfortable. She'd known only one woman in her whole life who'd gotten a tattoo, and it was a teeny little butterfly on her shoulder blade that didn't show when she was fully dressed. What on earth would possess a woman to get a tattoo that big on her arm where it would show all the time?

L.C. was in the middle of a story about the dwindling of scholarships for students in the arts when her eyes drifted over the top of the paper and onto Sydney's pink lace bra. The straps and border were exquisite lace flowers chained together at the tips of two petals—not a plain flat lace, but thick, with dimension, almost like each flower had been hand-crocheted. The cups were of lighter and darker stripes of smooth pink silk with just a hint of shine on the lighter stripes, pushing up firm breasts into a full, well-rounded cleavage. These were real too. L.C. could tell by the smooth line of skin from the collarbone to her nipples—not like the abrupt angle Veronica's implants caused, like lumps of clay that hadn't been molded to a smooth fit against her chest.

The bikini panties were totally lace flowers, letting Sydney's creamy skin and pubic hair show through. Hmm, so Carol Ann had been right about her being a bottle blond. L.C. fidgeted, adjusting her position on the couch. Damn—didn't this chick know this was killing her? "You must have been to Victoria's Secret?" she said casually.

Sydney feigned insult. "I don't wear-pol-y-est-er lin-ger-ie!" she scolded, playfully smacking L.C. on the arm with each syllable.

"Excuse me," L.C. said. "So where'd you get those? They ain't Playtex."

"There's a little shop on the Boulevard des Capucines in Paris that has the most scrumptious lacy tidbits," she purred.

"They look pretty flimsy. Aren't you afraid you'll tear them or spill something on them by wearing them all the time?"

"Hey, if I'm paying $3,000 for lingerie, by God, I'm going to wear 'em."

The paper dropped from L.C.'s hands. "You paid $3,000 for underwear?! How much did those things cost?" she said, nodding toward the pink lingerie.

"Mm, I think this set was $400."

"Holy shit!" L.C. couldn't take her eyes off the silken lacies. "Are they all like that?"

"No. Some are black, some are red, some are peach. Some are really sexy, some are cut from a distinct era with sort of a retro look, and some are just pretty to look at."

L.C. helped herself to another serving of the delicious pink confections. Judging by the way she was tingling between her legs, she figured they were worth every penny. "So what's on your agenda today?" she said, changing the subject before she started drooling.

"I have a book signing at 3," Sydney said, "so I'll need a ride back to my hotel pretty soon. I hope you don't mind all this driving back and forth into town."

L.C. didn't mind, but she also saw an opportunity here. "You know, why don't you just pack up the rest of your things when you're back at the hotel and check out and just spend tonight out here too? It seems silly to pay those outrageous rates for just a few hours of sleeping."

"I'll need a ride to the train station tomorrow, you know," she said with a slight frown.

"I don't mind. Really. It's no big deal. You live in L.A., you drive a lot. It's fine. I think I can put up with your perfection one more night," she joked.

Sydney thought a minute about whether she really wanted to do this again. L.C. was a little surly in the morning, but then, she knew a lot of caffeine-addicted people who were like that before their first cup. Plus, she'd been on the road alone for months, and it was nice having some human companionship again. "Well, all right," she smiled. "Thanks for the offer."

L.C. said it was no problem, that she had to go into town to talk with her producer today, then suggested the two have dinner at the hotel since she had to come by for her there anyway. Sydney said it was a good idea, and they agreed to meet at her room at 7.

L.C. showed up wearing a man's suit, which for some reason surprised Sydney. She hadn't really thought about it before, but L.C. probably didn't even own a dress. And she did look good in that dark, well-tailored suit that brought out the contrast of her black hair and flawless fair skin.

Sydney wore a chic smoke-black gown sprinkled with tiny black studs that picked up the light in a subtle fashion. The dress clung to her curving waist and hips, draping over her legs with a slinky flow as she walked, one shapely leg revealed through an off-center slit with every other step.

The suited woman had the bellman load Sydney's suitcases into her car, then the two went downstairs to the restaurant. Sydney was a little apprehensive about being seen in public with L.C., but hardly anyone looked at them the whole evening. Apparently it wasn't a big deal in L.A. to see a gay woman dressed like a man. Plus, everyone recognized the singer, and for some reason, thought Sydney, artists and celebrities have always been afforded more tolerance for their eccentricities and going against the norm.

After dinner L.C. helped Sydney on with her long black velvet coat. Sydney flipped out all that blond hair and noticed L.C. admiring her golden locks until they were both distracted by a group of 30 or so college football players hovering around the front doors while waiting to check in. The boisterous bodies practically blocked the entrance. "You want to see something funny?" Sydney giggled. "Watch this."

L.C. stood back and eyed the woman as she walked toward the door—nothing special, just walking. Soon, one after another of the young men noticed the tall blond, the long hair and coat flowing as she stepped, and one by one they stepped aside. It was like Moses parting the Red Sea. When Sydney reached the door, a handsome muscular blue-eyed blond held the door open for her, and she breezed on by.

L.C. looked at the pathetic sea of open-mouthed, bug-eyed boys awash in Sydney's wake. She shoved her hands in her pockets and followed, but she didn't have the same kind of luck making her way to the door. One boy almost backed into her.

"Sorry, fella," he said, turning around.

"No problem," came the feminine voice.

"Whoa!" he said, realizing his mistake. "Sorry, lady."

She heard a few snickers, then someone said, "Hey, that's L.C. Hackett!" One player wondered out loud whether the two women were "together." Then she heard the blond jock who had opened the door for Sydney snicker, "Elsie? Isn't that the name of a cow?" Hoots and hollers erupted.

L.C. joined Sydney, who was waiting a few feet from the door. "What did he say?" the blond said angrily.

"Nothing." L.C. kept her hands pocketed, eyes on the ground as they walked silently to her car.

Sydney couldn't help notice L.C.'s mood had deflated. She had barely spoken the first half-hour of the drive home, giving one-word answers or a shrug whenever Sydney tried to engage her in conversation.

Once home, L.C. poured herself a drink, and the two made themselves comfortable on the chaises, still in the same cozy position from the night before. Sydney figured she'd let L.C. start the conversation when she was ready. She didn't have to wait long.

"So what's it like living the blond life?" L.C. said rather sarcastically.

Ah, so that was how things were going to go the rest of the evening. "It has its advantages and disadvantages," Sydney said matter-of-factly.

"I'll bet you dated all the cool jocks in school, huh?"

Sydney wasn't about to apologize for her life. "I had my share of them, yes."

"I'll bet you could've had any one of those guys at the hotel go home with you tonight, right?"

Sydney had to laugh. "I don't think so. Once they got a good look at the lines around my eyes, they'd cool off. But if I were 20 years younger, that boy who opened the door for me might have been in big trouble." She gave L.C. a wink.

"I guess blond attracts blond, huh?"

"I don't know about other women, but for me, blue-eyed blonds have always been my Achilles heel. I can't resist 'em. Probably because the first boy I was really head over heels about was a blue-eyed blond. Must have imprinted on that."

"What?"

"Imprinting. In the animal kingdom, babies get attached to the first creature they see after they're born—they think it's their mommy who'll feed them and protect them."

"I get it."

"Unfortunately, my gorgeous blond turned out to be a real bastard. In fact, now that I think about it, most of the guys I dated ended up being bastards. You think they're all going to be Mr. Perfect when you meet them, then you quickly discover they're just another nose-picker and ball-scratcher. I remember one night at a party when I was 16, I'd had too much to drink and passed out—"

L.C. almost came out of her chair. "What?! You? Drinking? Oh, my God—she's human after all!" L.C. rejoiced.

"Yeah, yeah. Hey, I was just like all teenagers in high school, testing the ropes once in a while. Anyway, I woke up in the middle of the night with my best friend's boyfriend trying to undress me!"

"Horny fucking bastards," L.C. said.

"He'd taken my friend home, then came back and decided he was going to have his way with me while I was unconscious."

"That's disgusting. What did you do?"

"I knocked him off the bed and screamed and kicked him until he got the hell out of there. And you know what, the next day when I told my girlfriend, she got mad at me. *Me*!"

L.C. took a drink and leaned back again. "I know women like that. They think their man is perfect and he would never lie or do anything wrong, when the truth is they *all* do shit like that all the time."

Sydney detected a touch of anger in L.C.'s voice. "Ain't that the truth," she said. "You know, I could have gotten some horrible disease from him, or gotten pregnant. He could have ruined my life, but he didn't care—just as long as he got his rocks off—that was all he cared about." Her head fell back against the chaise. "Men can be such fuckers. You have no idea."

"Oh, don't I?" L.C. said, her pained face looking down into her drink. "Men are cruel to me because they don't like my body...they're cruel to you because they do."

Sydney thought back to when she had been in school and how cruelly boys teased the girls who weren't as pretty as the others and figured L.C. must have had her feelings hurt countless times throughout her life. "So I guess we're in the same boat, huh?" Sydney said with a sympathetic smile.

L.C.'s eyes met Sydney's. "And where is this boat taking us?"

This took Sydney by surprise. She didn't know whether L.C. meant "us" as a couple or whether it was just a polite response. Plus, she hadn't even expected a response. She tapped her fingertips on the armrests trying to get her brain to reengage.

"It's...hard to tell...when you have only one oar to guide you."

An uneasy silence prevailed. Sydney could tell L.C. was searching for something to say back. And she could understand why it was taking so long—even she didn't know what the hell that meant. Suddenly Sydney's face went hot. Oh, God—what if L.C. said something romantic and turned this into some sort of verbal foreplay?

"You know what I think?" L.C. said softly.

Sydney was almost afraid to ask. "What?"

"I think someone should throw out an anchor on this metaphor." Her eyes rolled and she took a healthy drink.

Sydney cracked up and turned red. "OK," she said, hanging her head. "Even a Pulitzer Prize winner can't hit a home run every time."

"I don't know how you do it," L.C. said, "locked up for months alone. Just you, your computer, and your imagination."

The mood lightened and the two relaxed again, words coming without hesitation. "You make fun of me for being so disciplined, but otherwise I couldn't be a writer. There's no one to set a deadline or ring a bell to start my day."

"I suppose you're right," L.C. admitted, then her mind wandered. "You mentioned the other night something about how you'd mellowed in your 'old age,' and tonight you said if you were 20 years younger—just how old are you?"

"Forty-one soon."

"No way!"

Sydney grinned.

"I guess all that healthy living paid off."

"No, I'm just a genetically superior human being."

"So how much work have you had done?" L.C. chuckled.

Sydney sat up defiantly. "I beg your ever-lovin' pardon? I refuse! It's such a double standard—women going through hell and killing themselves to look more attractive to a man. How insane is that?" She threw her hands up in the air. "I'll tell you what, I'll have plastic surgery the day Al Pacino has those jowls lifted off the floor and Clint Eastwood has those gullies filled in with collagen and Jack Nicholson has that bowling ball sucked out from under his shirt."

"Amen to that." L.C. drank to the idea.

Sydney looked at the singer's smooth face. "So when's your birthday?"

"The 17th of next month."

"November 17th. Uh-oh. You're a Scorpio—why doesn't that surprise me?"

"Now, why do you say that?" L.C. said with a hint of defense in her voice.

Good Lord, there were so many reasons. First, even though Sydney had never put much stock in astrology, every Scorpio she'd ever known had been nothing but a horndog, so there had to be something to that aspect. Then there was the way that L.C. had burned two little holes in her nylons that night at Mandy's…the way she had sat perched atop the classroom at UCLA like a hungry predator…that box under her bed. It was obvious this woman was chock-full of hormones, constantly craving satisfaction. "Let's just say you have this aggressive sexuality about you," Sydney said, trying to be kind. Then she changed the subject. "So how old will you be?"

"Thirty-eight."

"No way!" Suddenly Sydney realized something and laughed. "Look at us, will you? Even we're buying into this baloney about what a woman should look like at a certain age, like at 40 she's supposed to be a dried-up old hag who's totally undesirable. I wish men would view women as individuals instead of stereotypes, like we're useless if they can't get an erection from looking at us. It's a new day—women are more active than our mothers and we take better care of ourselves. Sixty today is what 40 used to be."

"I think you're right. Look at Tina Turner," L.C. said. "The woman's still got it."

"I remember how active and full of energy my grandmother was when I was little," Sydney said, "and she was almost 80 when I was born. I used to sit on her lap, touching the deep laugh lines around her eyes and the corners of her mouth and thinking it was so neat to have skin do that. But her cheeks and forehead were so smooth even at that age. She just had the most beautiful face, full of character and life experience.

"I guess I grew up with a wonderful idea of aging because all my relatives were so much older than me. And I still don't want to look like a freshly minted coin at my age, with no details, no evidence of my life experience showing on my face. Those lines add so much character, don't you think?" While looking at L.C., she realized she was looking at the same distinct, round cheekbones as her grandmother's.

"No, I refuse to cop out to someone else's standard of beauty," Sydney continued. "Which is why I won't get sucked or lifted. That's why I wear my hair this way. I know the 'in' thing is that *Friends* look, pinned up with sprigs sticking out everywhere. Those girls look like freakin' Woody Woodpecker!" L.C. almost choked on her drink. "Whose idea of style is that anyway? They take all this beautiful long feminine hair, flatten it, pull it back and pin it up. Sometime you can barely tell the girls from the boys. But if some Hollywood hairstylist says it's fashionable, then they believe it, despite what they see for themselves in the mirror. Well, I refuse to let anyone turn me into a woodpecker…or a boy."

She noticed L.C.'s smile quickly disappeared. "Oh!" Sydney

gasped, putting her hand to her heart. "I didn't mean anything by that. It's just that guys prefer girls with long hair."

"Yeah...you proved that earlier tonight, didn't you?"

Now, that one stung. Sydney was surprised L.C. was so upset. "Is that why you've been in such a weird mood since dinner? I was just having some fun showing how guys go goofy over a blond. I wasn't trying to say I'm more attractive than you, honestly."

"Yeah, I know," L.C. said. "It's not your fault you turned into Cinderella and I turned into the pumpkin." A distinct bitterness came through in her voice.

"Well, it's obvious your feelings are hurt, but I think it's more what that guy said than anything I did." L.C. finally looked up, somewhat surprised and embarrassed because she thought Sydney had been out of earshot. "Yeah, I heard him," Sydney continued. "That was an awful thing to say, but I don't understand why you're so defensive. Just because it goes against the white male standard of beauty doesn't mean it's wrong for a woman to emphasize her masculine side. It works for you—it looks good on you. But on me it wouldn't. And all I can do is say what's right for me—there's no inherent criticism in that either." Still no response. "Why are you so bothered? You've been open about your sexuality for years—I thought you were secure with your appearance and who you are?"

"You know, I thought I was too. But for some reason tonight I felt so... I don't know, it just seemed that...oh, hell, forget it." She got up and leaned on the rail of the balcony, turning her back on Sydney.

Sydney didn't understand this at all. Her mind went over and over all the two had said to each other. Then suddenly all the tension in her disappeared. "Oh, my God... You're Cyrano," Sydney said softly.

L.C. didn't know what the hell was she talking about.

"You're Cyrano," she repeated. "He was a man with this beautiful soul and the most magical way with words and expressing his feelings, but he was stuck in a body he felt was ugly and repulsive because he had a big nose."

OK, OK, she knew the story.

"Only your whole body is your nose...and you think the fair Roxane here is going to look at you and see you as ugly and shun you for the handsome Christian." L.C. was too embarrassed to look her in the face anymore and turned away again. Sydney knew she had thrust home with that one. She walked over and stood beside the singer. "You want to know what I see when I look at you?"

Although she kept her eyes forward, L.C. felt Sydney staring at her. She squirmed beneath her skin, not used to this kind of scrutiny.

"I see beautiful, endless sky-blue eyes and a smile filled with the light from a sweet and gentle soul. And from somewhere within comes the most sublime sound, a voice that gets into people's souls and touches them and makes them *feel.* In your heart and mind you create the most beautiful sounds, translating emotions into words and music. You have a magical ability to take people wherever you want, to feel what you want, and with just a handful of words and notes you make another human being laugh or cry. That is such a gift! And you had the courage and strength to pursue this love of yours by putting yourself on stage in front of thousands of people where it's just you and your voice. It takes a very special person to be able to do that, and do it well."

L.C. turned away, but not before Sydney detected the tiniest quiver in her bottom lip. "So what if your hair doesn't flow in the breeze? So what if you don't have big doe eyes or a smooshy little nose—a waistline that doesn't curve in like an hourglass, and legs that are big and muscular? So what?" L.C. still wouldn't look at her.

Sydney took L.C.'s hand, rubbing her fingers over it with care and appreciation, as though she were treasuring a creation by Michelangelo. "You're beautiful, L.C.," she said with words imbued with genuine affection as she gently kissed the back of the strong hand. "God was having a good day when he made you."

Sydney went inside, and L.C. heard the door to her bedroom close. She blotted her eyes with her shirtsleeve and was glad Sydney had left when she did. The moist outline of two lips on the back of her hand glistened from the moonlight and caught her eye. For a brief moment L.C. allowed herself to believe those words, then she took a deep breath, tucked those feelings away, deep inside where they belonged, and turned the key.

The next morning, Sydney was surprised to find L.C. had gotten up before her and was already gone. She had left a note apologizing for not being able to take her to the train station, and placed a $100 bill next to it for cab fare, which Sydney left on the table.

That evening, an arrangement of two dozen yellow roses arrived for an M. Mitchell with a card thanking her for being such a generous hostess. The gesture touched L.C. because the only time anyone sent her flowers was once in a blue moon for congratulations on some career accomplishment; she wasn't exactly the candy-and-flowers type when it came to birthdays or dating.

It wasn't until the following day that L.C. got the courage to call Sydney's agent and track her down at a hotel in Sacramento. It took half an hour for her to mention the roses and ask how Sydney had known yellow roses were her favorite because that was something very personal L.C. had purposely never mentioned in an interview, wanting to keep some things about her life private.

Sydney said she hadn't known, there was no way she could know, it was just what came to mind when she thought of L.C.

By the end of the conversation, the two had agreed that Sydney would stay with L.C. the following week after her book tour was completed. She was scheduled to come back to California to hammer out a deal with Paramount for the film rights to her book. L.C. didn't say it, but she was looking forward to having Sydney back under the same roof. She already missed the companionship. There was far too much quiet around that empty house.

Two days after arriving back in Malibu, Sydney attended her first meeting at Paramount. The writer had left the house that morning excited about passing through the famous black wrought-iron gates she had seen in countless movies, but she came home that evening angry and drained.

L.C. asked what the problem was, and Sydney explained it wasn't anything about the money—seven figures was a fair price—it was a control issue. She was adamant there was no way she was going to hand over her story to a bunch of postpubescent hormonal boys who would most likely turn this sensitive women's issue into some soft-porn flick, so she was fighting to be the head screenwriter and one of the producers on the project. Naturally, the studio didn't want anyone but its own boys making decisions on a project, so it had become a battle of wills. After all, it was Sydney's name on the book, and this movie could affect her career and future sales if it tanked.

Since the topic of money had been broached, Sydney told L.C. she wanted to pay her share of the living expenses, which she felt only fair, but L.C. wouldn't hear of it. Sydney pointed out that L.C. had already generously offered her the use of the Mercedes until she could get back to Texas to retrieve her things that were in storage since her divorce, including her car, and she didn't want L.C. to think she was taking advantage of her. L.C.

said she could help out buying groceries now and then, since Sydney seemed to enjoy puttering in the kitchen, but there was no point in trying to share the bills since her accountant took care of them and they never even came to the house.

A few days later L.C. invited Sydney to her producer's house to do a test recording of a song she'd been working on. Sydney thought it would be fun to see how a record got made, so she went along.

The pair arrived at Rick Jenkins's home in Beverly Hills almost three hours past the time L.C., herself, had chosen to start. L.C. dragged herself in wearing a sleeveless black T-shirt and a pair of Army surplus camouflage pants that looked like they'd seen action in both world wars. Those who had been summoned were a little pissed at this point, but because L.C. Hackett was still a name in the industry who had a good sales record thanks to her strong and loyal following, no one had said "fuck it." They had waited...and waited...and waited.

Rick told L.C. he had gone ahead and had the musicians lay down most of the instrumental tracks after the first hour had passed, so now he was ready for the vocals. This was his way of letting the songstress know he was aware of her lateness, but that was as much of a scolding as he was going to give. His label was ecstatic at having signed L.C. Hackett, and he wasn't about to piss off a big money-making artist of her caliber. While Rick was busy getting an extra chair for Sydney to sit with him in the mix room where all the recording equipment was located, Carol Ann migrated over to L.C., who stood by the door that led to the recording area. "What the hell are you up to?" she whispered, giving her friend the evil eye.

"I don't know what you're talking about," L.C. said.

"I'm talking about the blond Amazon. I thought she left weeks ago."

L.C. looked her backup singer in the eye. "She did. She's back."

Carol Ann got the message. The boss had pulled rank, and that was going to be the end of it. "I see disaster written all over this," she mumbled, lowering her head. "So explain to me why we're here today?" she asked, sounding perturbed at having to give up her afternoon for a lousy test recording.

"I want to see how this song sounds with all the elements. I'm not sure about some of the harmonies and the glockenspiel I keep hearing in my head when I sing the song, and there's no point in me wasting time trying to make the words fit the music if it's going to sound like crap."

Oh, so we all have to waste our time, Carol Ann thought, but didn't dare say it. Now she knew why they had met at Rick's instead of one of the label's studios—L.C. never would have shelled out the bucks for this. "So why couldn't we all just get together at your place and sing and play instead of taking the time and expense to put down tracks?"

L.C. looked down her nose at her friend. "Because when I'm singing, I mostly hear my own voice from inside my head—I can't concentrate on other voices and instruments properly like I can when I'm listening to a completed record."

Carol Ann gave her a "whatever" look, then turned her attention to Sydney, who was wearing a short, pleated, plaid wool skirt with a black sweater, black tights, and saddle oxfords. "Did you leave your pom-poms on the 50 yard line?" she quipped, staring at the shoes.

Sydney walked over, laughing. "Cheerleader flashback—what's a girl to do?" She bounced lightly on her toes, looking very peppy.

Carol Ann looked her over carefully. "Apparently, put on an old uniform and regress back to high school."

L.C. interceded by pushing Carol Ann into the adjoining recording area, then followed, taking a seat on the stool positioned at the microphone in the center of the large room while the three backup singers sequestered themselves in one of the smaller glass booths in the back. Sydney took a seat against the wall and watched L.C. through the glass window.

Sydney couldn't help marvel at Rick's mastery of the massive console, which was about eight feet long with hundreds of switches and buttons. Every time he adjusted one, a computer screen centered above the windows registered the change. The sounds came through two huge speakers on either side of the computer screen that looked like their front covers had been peeled off. Sydney imagined this room full of equipment must have cost a fortune. She wondered whether the record company had paid for it or whether this had come out of Rick's own pocket, but of course she didn't pry.

It wasn't long into the session before Sydney realized what a force L.C. Hackett was, the way she dictated every move during the session, correcting the backup singers, telling Rick to downplay one of the instruments, blowing a take whenever she felt something wasn't exactly right. And the expression on her face when she spoke—the air of superiority. What a healthy ego this woman had. But then, Sydney supposed a strong ego acted as a protective shell in the entertainment business. How else could an artist keep going after a bad review or a tabloid scandal?

Regardless of the ego or the temperamental attitude, it was all worth it once that voice rang out. What an incredible sound came from this woman. After listening to L.C. sing for a while, Sydney noticed a warm, tingly feeling coursing through her body—a sort of mellow, almost floating sensation. She searched her vocabulary until she found the perfect word to describe how this voice affected her: intoxicating. Mm-m-m, that was it. L.C.'s voice was absolutely intoxicating...like hot buttered rum on a cold winter night. She closed her eyes, sat back, and enjoyed the libations.

Four hours later L.C. finally got the vocals down the way she liked. While Rick mixed the tracks for the umpteenth time and prepared to play it back, Sydney went into the recording area to talk with L.C. She mentioned she felt a little in the way sitting in there with Rick because she had absolutely nothing to do. It was at this point Carol Ann suggested Sydney should make herself useful by whipping up one of her special treats in the kitchen—where she belonged.

Sydney wasn't sure whether the woman had intended her to hear the remark or not, but either way she didn't care for it. Her eyes narrowed, and a strange smile crossed her face as the three backup singers crossed the room and joined them. "You know," she said, smiling at Carol Ann, "I've been sitting in the booth listening, and it absolutely amazes me how you can sit on that stool, hour after hour, and sing with that stick up your butt."

L.C. stifled a laugh because she could tell by Carol Ann's expression she had started to take this as a compliment until Sydney hit her with the coup de grâce. She got the feeling she was about to sample a taste of that verbal eloquence Sydney had warned her about.

"Kiss my ass," Carol Ann snarled.

"No way," Sydney said, eyes as big as silver dollars. "God only knows where that thing's been."

L.C. knew she shouldn't have laughed, but it just popped out.

Carol Ann stormed out of the studio, cursing a blue streak as she passed through the mix room. "I hope you're through with me today 'cause I've had all I can take of that she-devil!" she shouted at Rick.

He stopped what he was doing. "I gather you don't care much for L.C.'s new girlfriend?"

She snorted as she paced angrily, hands on hips. "You mean that blond freak of nature? No, I don't."

"Well, you're done here, so go blow it off," he said, then resumed his work.

Sydney had decided Carol Ann wasn't worth getting upset over and concentrated on the music when the final playback started. She was surprised at how much richer L.C.'s luscious voice sounded with the aid of professional studio equipment. Every quality was magnified tenfold. Rick played the song through twice, then came out to discuss a few points with L.C., dismissing the other backup girls for the day as their part was complete. Sydney was surprised L.C. let him have that one.

She and the singer stood and listened to Rick making his suggestions, most of which L.C. agreed with. When Rick went into a spiel of technical terms, Sydney started walking off, but L.C. reached out and hooked her around the waist with her right arm, drew her in, and held Sydney securely against her torso without missing a beat in the conversation.

This had such a familiar feel to Sydney for some reason. She rested her forearm atop L.C.'s and felt the hot skin against hers. Then she noticed the muscular biceps with the red heart tattoo against her own shoulder and suddenly felt as though she'd eaten a plate of butterflies. This reminded her of how one of her old boyfriends, a college football player, used to hold her at times, making her go all girlie inside. How strange she should feel that way now.

Sydney tried walking away again, hoping L.C. would simply release her, but the singer held tight. The blond stretched out her arms and leaned forward in a semistruggle to free herself. When she realized how silly she must look, she started flailing her arms.

"Danger, Will Robinson! Warning! Warning!" The conversation between L.C. and Rick came to a halt, and Sydney turned and faced L.C., grinning like a child behaving badly.

"What are you doing?" L.C. said, sounding a little confused.

Hearing that soft, sensuous voice so close made Sydney draw in a breath. At that moment she realized her face was only inches away from L.C.'s. "Uh…I'm trying to leave," she said.

"Why?"

"Because you guys are talking about Sennheiser microphones and Lexicons—whoosh!" she said, rushing her hand over her head. "I can't contribute to the conversation, so I was just going to go sit in the control booth and leave you two musicians to talk business. I'm not hopping a plane or anything," she said to reassure L.C., but there was a hint of teasing in her voice. Without a word, the singer let Sydney slip away.

From the booth, Sydney scrutinized L.C. as she talked with her producer and wondered what was it about that simple gesture that had been so appealing. Part of it was L.C.'s cocky confidence, as though she were entitled to determine Sydney's comings and goings the way her old boyfriend used to whenever the two were in public. He would do that sort of thing whenever he wanted to signal other guys that this chick was his.

That was it. This was another guy move. Had it been intended simply as a gesture of affection, or had L.C. done it in some territorial display when Rick came around? Did the woman with the velvet voice feel that way about her? She ran the scene over in her mind until those butterflies stirred again. Perhaps the bigger question was, did she feel that way about L.C.?

On November 17 Sydney and L.C. were getting ready to go to a birthday bash at Mandy's, but before they left, Sydney presented L.C. with a brightly wrapped gift with a large red bow. L.C.

opened the box and pulled out a pair of Nick & Nora pajamas, a Cloud 9 pattern of puffy white clouds against a blue sky. Sydney mentioned she'd gotten them so it would be like sleeping in the clouds under her starry ceiling. Plus, she figured that old Red Wings jersey might give out any day.

But when L.C. held up the bottoms, they were gigantic. Sydney was horrified, swearing she'd ordered a medium, and she grabbed the plastic sack. There was a big M on the sticker. L.C. checked the tag in the pajama bottoms, which said XL. Someone in packing obviously had been asleep on the job.

L.C. took another gander at the enormous pants and burst out laughing. Then she peeled off her jeans and climbed in. With her thumb, she extended the waistband a good foot and a half beyond her stomach. "I'll bet we could both fit into these!" she laughed.

Suddenly their eyes met, and the two exchanged a knowing glance. Sydney hopped up, shimmied out of her miniskirt, and climbed in with L.C. It was a bit snug, but they both fit.

The women cracked up laughing. "I have *got* to have a picture of this," L.C. declared, then the two started hopping like contestants in a potato sack race over to the cabinet where her camera was kept. L.C. set the camera on automatic, and they bounced frantically back over to the middle of the room. With the exuberance of a couple of mischievous preteens, they put their cheeks together, smiled ear to ear and shouted "Cheese!" just in time for the flash.

The very next day, Sydney came home from her meeting at Paramount crying her eyes out. The studio had refused to give her any level of control over the movie—not even offering to let her write the screenplay. The boys issued one final offer for the film rights only, tacking on an additional $400,000 to compensate her for being shut out of the production.

That evening, Sydney and L.C. discussed the situation for a long time. Sydney explained that this was her baby she had conceived and labored over and given birth to, and to hand it over *carte blanche* to these bastards was unbearable. L.C. said she understood but added that the entertainment business was a lot more cutthroat than the publishing business. She pointed out that if these guys were being such bastards at the beginning and obviously didn't want her on the project, that if she insisted, they could really make her life hell and sabotage her but good. She'd seen it done before and heard even more secondhand horror stories that started out just like this.

"Look how miserable you are right now," L.C. said. "Imagine feeling 10 times worse than this every day for the next two years."

Sydney trusted L.C.'s advice. After all, she had lived in L.A. for years and had had her own experiences with the film industry, her music being used on several movie soundtracks. Plus, the entertainer simply knew a lot of people in the film industry. Sydney called her agent the next day and accepted the offer, deposited a check for $2.4 million, then wrote off any hope of seeing justice done to her story.

Now that Sydney had her money, she mentioned it was probably time to get a place of her own. A queasy sensation gripped L.C. at hearing the announcement, but she recovered after managing to convince Sydney she should wait until after the first of the year and not ruin her holidays with the stress of house hunting. But Sydney did go out and buy herself a Mercedes of her own so she wouldn't have to impose on L.C. anymore for transportation.

When Thanksgiving rolled around, Sydney expected L.C. to have big plans to either have her family over or to go home for the holidays, wherever that might be. She was surprised to hear

L.C. had no plans at all. Sydney explained that she didn't have any plans this year either, since all her closest relatives were now gone and she was newly divorced, with her home now a storage cubicle in Austin. So she ended up cooking a turkey dinner with all the trimmings just for the two of them. During dinner Sydney asked L.C. why she wasn't spending the holiday with her family. The reply was simply, "*I* am my family."

Chapter Seven

One of the most anticipated events at the Little Dutch Boy was the annual Christmas charity show on the first Saturday in December, when artists who frequented the club donated their time and talent to raise money for an L.A. women's shelter. It had started out as an intimate gathering of regulars, but over the years word had gotten out about all the famous names that came to play and the event had grown into a standing-room only, all-night concert.

L.C. asked Sydney if she'd like to play the piano at this year's event, but Sydney declined the invitation, citing her disdain for playing in public. But she wanted to contribute to the cause and volunteered to sing one song, provided L.C. was on stage with her in some capacity for moral support. The two decided L.C. would play the piano while Sydney sang "Since I Fell for You." She had chosen this particular song because it didn't require much range and she felt her untrained voice could handle it.

For the third year in a row, L.C. had been enlisted to play Santa at the show, basically acting as master of ceremonies, which meant she'd be dressed in a red-and-white Santa suit all night long. Her role was to introduce the performers, tell a few jokes, sing some Christmas songs, and close the show by drawing the names of the door prize winners.

On the night of the show L.C. was busy most of the evening

with her duties, which left Sydney basically on her own. She enjoyed the performances at first, but before long she began thinking about her upcoming number. About two hours before she and L.C. were to go on stage, it hit her that this would be the first time she had ever sung in public. And it wasn't exactly an intimate gathering of friends either—there were at least a thousand people packed inside the club. And this crowed was used to the good stuff—the pros. What if her voice cracked, or she hit a clinker, or she couldn't reach the high note? Oh, God—what had she gotten herself into?

A waitress passed by carrying a tray full of cups of eggnog, and Sydney flagged her down, taking two off the tray. Half an hour later when they were gone, she had another…then another…and another. By the time the show's director came to get her, she was full of courage and ready to belt out a tune.

L.C. had made a slight change in wardrobe for the number with Sydney, having brought her white tie and tails out of the mothballs. Sydney had chosen a slinky black strapless evening gown slit to mid thigh that she wore with long black gloves for a look that harked back to the Golden Age of Hollywood. The two women in black contrasted beautifully with the white, concert-length grand piano rented for the evening. They received applause and whistles when they took the stage. L.C. flipped up the tails of her black jacket and sat at the piano while Sydney took her place in the curve.

The number started out as rehearsed, and Sydney's deep, throaty voice didn't waver from nerves as feared. Halfway through the song, though, all that highly fortified eggnog kicked in and Sydney started feeling a little saucy. She hopped up onto the piano, stretched out on her side with those long legs peeking through the slit in her gown, and began cooing shamelessly to the short-haired woman tickling the ivories.

The crowd instantly sensed the electricity generated from the stage and responded with a big "Woo-o-o!" They watched the two women, eyes locked on each other, with the gorgeous blond writhing sensually as she sang. At one point Sydney twisted her torso so that she faced L.C., then arched her back slightly, pushing forth her generous breasts and cleavage, a gesture L.C. couldn't help respond to, as she was pretty lit from sampling eggnog all evening long too. Her smile stretched from ear to ear.

The number brought down the house, and rumors flitted around the club about L.C. and her newest "roommate."

It was going on 3 A.M. when Santa came back out for the finale, which was a medley of Christmas classics. After L.C. finished, she sat on a stool preparing for the door prize drawing from her big white sack when she heard a torrent of hoots and whistles. From stage right pranced Sydney, dressed as Mrs. Claus in a strapless red satin dress up to her butt, white fur trim, and red high heels. The white ball on her red cap bounced with each step, as did her breasts. She gave L.C. a mischievous smile. "Change of plans, Santa baby."

She leaned in toward the microphone at center stage, practically sticking her ass in L.C.'s face. "Hello, everyone," she said coyly. "I'm Franz Liszt's lesser-known sister, Christmas." The audience roared with laughter when they got the joke. "I'm playing Santa's little helper tonight for the door prize drawing since he's had such a *hard* night already." Again the audience burst in hoots and hollers.

She asked Santa to open the bag that was sitting on the stage beside the stool, then bent over, straight legged, revealing her red tights mere inches from L.C.'s smiling face as she reached in and drew a name. The rowdy audience ate up the act. "Santa, will you read the name of our first winner?" she said, then leaned forward to hand Santa the piece of paper, her breasts nearly falling out.

For the second drawing, Sydney cozied up on Santa's lap, wriggling her tush in a mock effort to position herself just right. Everyone but Sydney sensed L.C. becoming more and more torqued up from the teasing and flirting, but only L.C. knew that her panties were so wet they were sticking to her crotch. How could she not be affected? Those luscious red lips inches away from hers, this mountain of firm cleavage practically in her mouth. Oh, God, but she wanted a piece of this Christmas candy.

After five names had been read, Santa focused her eyes on the last piece of paper Sydney had drawn and read the name, after which Sydney announced, "I think that's all for tonight, Santa." But L.C. took the microphone from her and said, "No, actually, there's one more prize to give out," and before the words had time to register in Sydney's brain, L.C. pulled down her white beard, and like a drunken sailor on shore leave, bent the blond backward and laid one on her, bringing the audience to its feet. Sydney quickly wrapped one arm around L.C.'s back and the other around the back of her neck and hung on for dear life.

The next thing Sydney knew, she felt L.C.'s tongue shoving its way into her mouth, exploring and playing with her own tongue in a raw, sexual motion. Sydney's hands clenched, fingers intermingled in short, black hairs and red velvet. She was breathing so hard and the front of her dress was stretched so tight she felt her nipples might pop out over the edge of the fabric at any moment.

A good 30 seconds later, Sydney found herself upright again. The first thing she became aware of was the rollicking noise from the crowd. This prompted her second thought, which was that she had just been kissed by another woman for the first time—in front of a thousand strangers. The third thing that registered was the sight of her bright red lipstick smeared around L.C.'s mouth, making her look more like a clown than a Santa.

L.C. took the microphone and said something to the crowd in closing, which didn't register, then Sydney felt the woman in the Santa suit put an arm through hers and escort her off stage. But once behind the curtains, L.C. dropped her arm quickly and walked directly to the dressing room without saying a word, which Sydney didn't understand at all after the way the woman had just kissed her.

While sitting at the vanity in the dressing room wiping the lipstick off her face, L.C. heard Sydney's voice from the doorway. "Well, that certainly took me by surprise," the blond said in a tone that sounded a little like a scolding.

L.C. looked over her shoulder and saw Sydney leaning against the door frame, arms folded. "One surprise deserves another," she replied, then removed her red Santa cap and white beard.

Sydney couldn't quite read the tone L.C. had used. "Are you pissed off because I horned in on your finale?"

She laughed pitifully. "It has nothing to do with that."

"Well, then, what is it?"

The singer turned completely around and faced Sydney. "Why do you keep teasing and flirting with me?" She saw this had taken Sydney by surprise because of her blank expression and half-open mouth. "You run around the house in French lace lingerie with legs and cleavage up to your neck, you come out here tonight in that barely-there evening gown and stretch out on the piano like it was a bed, seducing me with that love song, then you stick your gorgeous legs and ass in my face and sit in my lap with your tits in my face! I'm not a robot, you know," she said firmly.

Sydney still hadn't moved a muscle and didn't look as though she were able to respond, so L.C. continued. "I don't know if this is all just a game to you—that you don't take any of it seriously because you're not gay or because I'm not a guy. But I'm telling you, I'm flesh and blood, and this sort of thing does affect me, and I'm only going to take so much. So if you don't like the way I'm behaving, maybe you should think about the way *you're* behaving."

There. That put the ball in Sydney's court. She turned around and started taking off her makeup.

"Hey!" Sydney shouted angrily.

L.C. turned back around and saw the figure filling the doorway with her arms pressed against either side of the frame, hips cocked to one side, exuding a dangerous confidence that reminded her of Kathleen Turner in *Body Heat.* "I never said I didn't like it," the blond purred, then sauntered off.

Well, that was not the response L.C. had expected. But she wrote it off to the fact that Sydney had had a couple of drinks and was feeling a bit randy.

When she turned around to finish removing her makeup, something hit her. She looked at the face in the mirror and laughed. "You schmuck!" she said out loud. "You blow out this well-worded tirade, dumping it all on her so she has to make the next move, which would clearly tell you if she's interested or not, and with one sentence—a tiny handful of words—she dumps it all back on you! Now *you* have to go back out on that limb again and risk the rejection." She shook her tired head. "Man, she really knows how to play the game."

Mandy spent that night at L.C.'s, and at 1 o'clock the following afternoon they sat in the living room having their morning coffee while Sydney finished her exercises. "Does she do this every morning?" Mandy whispered.

"Like clockwork."

Mandy watched the curvaceous woman in the black lace

lingerie with a ponytail on top of her head that swished back and forth as she sat straddle on the floor doing side stretches. "Doesn't it drive you up a wall?"

"Fuck, yeah!"

The redhead got a chuckle out of her friend's torment. Having finished exercising, Sydney hopped up. "Have a good workout?" Mandy inquired, though not really interested.

"Yeah, it really gets the blood flowing in the morning. But then I do another hour's worth of exercise in the evening after dinner—a walk on the beach, bicycling, swimming, whatever. Makes you sleep like a baby." She bent over and brushed her long ponytail as she talked. "Plus my body's so used to it, now it starts craving that blood flow at the same time of day—it's really weird."

"Well, that must be how you stay so slim."

"Yeah, I exercise, eat right, and take care of myself." She threw her ponytail back and stood tall. "Well, I'm going to hop in the shower. I've got an early dinner with my agent in a few hours. Excuse me, ladies."

The two women on the couch watched Sydney's gorgeous ass until it was out of sight. Mandy gave her friend a look of envy. L.C. just smiled. "My woman…I think I'll keep her."

Mandy recognized the line from an old Geritol commercial. "So what are you doing about that?"

"About what?"

"About freakin' Judy Jetson there! What do you mean, 'about what'?"

"Nothing."

"Nothing? What about that kiss last night?"

L.C. shrugged. "A wild hair."

"You mean you haven't even made a move on her?"

"Nope. Every time I think the time is right, she starts playing some classical music on the piano or talking about something deep, and the mood gets really serious and I get caught up in it and lose track. I tell you, it's the damnedest thing I've ever experienced. Normally I would've dumped a chick if it had taken this long to fuck her, but for some reason I like having this one around—we have fun together. It's weird."

Mandy gave her a suspicious smile. "What—are you in love or something?"

L.C. leaned back and closed her eyes. "Oh, Lord, what's love got to do with anything?"

"Well, having been lucky enough to find love once in my life, I'd say it's worth looking for. I highly recommend domestic bliss."

"Honey, it's been so long, I've forgotten what it feels like. I wouldn't know love if it slapped me in the face."

Mandy tried to remember the names of all the girlfriends L.C. had gone through in the years they'd known each other. The longest relationship she could remember her friend being in was just shy of two years, so there were a lot of names on that list. Too many to recall. "So are you honestly going to sit there and tell me you've never been in love with any of the women in your life since I've known you?" Mandy asked.

L.C. didn't even have to think. "No."

"That's pretty sad, woman."

"Like I said, it's been so long I don't know what I'm missing anymore. I'm comfortably numb now," she said with a boastful smile. "It's safer that way. Besides, I—"

"*Lydia Charlene Hackett*!" came Sydney's voice bellowing from her bedroom.

Mandy's eyes grew big. "Uh-oh! All three names...boy, are *you* in trouble!"

L.C. went to see what was wrong, then quickly returned. "I

used up the last of her conditioner and forgot to get her another bottle like I promised," she said sheepishly.

Mandy laughed again. "You know, people were talking last night about what a great pair you two make."

"Really?"

"Yeah, someone was saying you two have each other's bodies."

"Excuse me?"

"It's just that she's got this real feminine body, but she's got a voice so husky it could pull a dog sled, and you're just the opposite. She's got a man's name and you've got a woman's name—*Lydia Charlene*," she taunted, knowing how L.C. hated her full name. "Maybe that old saying is right, opposites do attract. Anyway, judging by the fireworks you two set off, I'd say you've definitely got that chemistry thing going."

L.C. shook her head. "I don't know. Sometimes I think she's interested, sometimes I think she just wants to be friends, sometimes I think she's just playing games. She's a hard one to read."

"Did you ever think that maybe she just wants to get to know you first? That would be a first for you, now, wouldn't it, Little Miss Hit 'n' Run?" L.C. hated that name, which Mandy had pegged her with, and she glared at her this time. "Maybe it's good she didn't let you have your way with her right off the bat. Who knows, maybe love will finally find Andy Hardy."

"Very funny." L.C. finished her coffee, put her cup down, and closed her eyes. Her head was banging fiercely from all that eggnog.

Mandy finished her coffee too and stood to leave. "Well, I'm going to drag my ass home and take a nice long, hot bath. Call me and let me know what china pattern you guys register."

L.C. wasn't in the mood. "You're not dragging that skinny ass of yours home nearly fast enough," she shouted out after her friend.

Mandy still got the last word in by singing "Chapel of Love" by the Dixie Cups on her way out of the house.

Two hours later, L.C. was reading in her room, nursing a beer, being one who followed the "hair of the dog" philosophy when it came to hangovers. Sydney knocked at the door, then entered wearing only her underwear. She had done her makeup and had removed all the hot rollers except one, which dangled from a section in the back of her golden tresses. She looked strangely at L.C., who was reclined on a plush fainting couch, wearing cutoffs and a baggy tank top, a leg flung over the back and the bottle of beer cuddled against her side. "What's wrong?" L.C. said.

"My second husband used to lie on the couch like that and watch football."

"Yeah, but I bet he didn't leave lip gloss on the bottle," L.C. said, swilling her beer. Then she sat up. "Let me guess, you need some help."

"Yes, please," Sydney said pitifully. "This is what happens when I don't use conditioner on my hair," she added emphatically. L.C. got the message.

She sat on the couch between L.C.'s bare legs with her back to the woman and pulled the rest of her hair up out of the way, piling it on top of her head so no more would get tangled up in the mess. "So, is this a business dinner?" L.C. inquired, working the hair loose bit by bit.

"Nope. No business for a change. We're just going to enjoy a nice dinner and exchange Christmas presents."

As L.C. pulled the last strand of blond hair from around the curler, her eyes drifted to the long slender neck inches away, her smooth creamy skin with a peachy glow, the roundness of her shoulders, the outline of her shoulder blades. How many days had she looked at this body, lusted after this body? How many nights had she dreamed about touching and kissing Sydney? Today, at this moment, she could resist no longer, and she leaned forward and kissed the back of Sydney's neck, giving a gentle nibble with her teeth.

"Good God in heaven!" Sydney shouted, her head and shoulders scrunching up so quickly the women almost knocked heads. She dropped the armful of hair and rubbed that spot on her neck. "You have no idea how that affects me! Oh, my God, it just sends hot shivers up and down my spine," she growled.

"And you don't like that?"

"No, it feels wonderful, but—"

Here it was. The moment of truth. Sydney couldn't avoid this conversation any longer. She was so uneasy about the subject she couldn't even bring herself to turn around and face L.C. as she spoke.

"You know, I love you as person, L.C., I really do, you're so sweet and generous and gentle-natured, but I don't know if could ever love you…that way. I mean, I don't know if I could ever open up enough and relax enough to respond to you touching me…that way."

L.C. leaned forward again and whispered in her ear, "You mean *this* way?" Then she ran her hands around Sydney's front, cupped her breasts, and squeezed them gently. Sydney moaned, and fell back against L.C.'s chest, her head resting on a strong shoulder. With eyes closed, she took in a deep breath, pushing her breasts firmly into the strong hands. "I think we have our answer," L.C. said, sounding very pleased, then she reclined on the couch with Sydney in her arms.

Fingertips ran down the top border of the lace cups, pulling down just enough to uncover soft pink nipples, then flicked over their sensitive tips, teasing them to attention, making L.C. wish she could position herself to put her mouth around them.

Sydney turned her head and gazed at L.C., then leaned in and kissed her. God, what an incredible sensation! This wasn't like last night when L.C. had shoved her tongue into her mouth so brusquely—this was sensual, soft, and there was a sweetness about the way these thin lips caressed her own, sucking gently on Sydney's full bottom lip, then exchanging the caress on her top lip. Every kiss, every touch of these strong hands stoked the fire inside Sydney until her bones turned to melted butter.

And yet all the while her body was responding, her mind was in conflict with these glorious sensations, not allowing her to completely let go and enjoy. Her emotions simply didn't match up with the love scene playing out because she had felt this way only when a man touched her before. It was true that L.C.'s strong body, the taste of beer on her lips and tongue, her aggressive nature all reminded Sydney of being with a man, but she was a *woman*—not a man. Then Sydney asked herself a question: Was the important thing that someone was making her feel these sensations, or was it the sex of that particular someone? She didn't have the answer.

Sydney placed her hands over L.C.'s in a half-hearted effort to stop them as they squeezed and massaged her breasts, but it just felt too good—she didn't want this feeling to stop. L.C. whispered in her ear as she nuzzled her neck. "Your breasts must really be sensitive."

"You have no idea," she moaned. "Sometimes I think I could have an orgasm just from having my nipples played with. You don't know how wet this makes me."

L.C. took this as an invitation and slid her right hand down Sydney's bare stomach and under the lace border of her panties. She played with the soft tuft of hair, then slid her middle finger between Sydney's legs, which made them open up like a flower in bloom. The blond stretched her whole body, moaning passionately. "Good Lord, you are wet," L.C. said, as she gently massaged Sydney's clitoris all around the sides of the delicate pink rosebud. The more she stroked, the more Sydney's back muscles tensed, pushing her breasts out farther, seeking more stimulation.

Only minutes later, Sydney began gasping for air. The heat from her face radiated against L.C.'s cheek. Sweat from the back of Sydney's neck had darkened the fabric of her shirt. L.C. watched the beautiful face as the brow knotted, wet lips parting, drinking in air, chest heaving. The hands on top of her own gripped tighter around her wrists, and she knew this was a woman on the verge. L.C. hoped to put Sydney over that edge, but the woman couldn't seem to let go and let it happen. L.C. removed her left hand from Sydney's breast and took her firmly by the face and kissed her hard.

It was difficult for Sydney to breathe without her mouth open, and she tried to break free, but when she felt L.C.'s tongue slide into her mouth at the same moment the fingers from L.C.'s right hand slipped inside her, she was paralyzed with passion. In and out, hard and fast, the tongue moved in the same rhythm as the fingers inside her, filling her body with an intense rhythm until the sensation overwhelmed her. Sydney broke the kiss and let out a groan of exquisite agony as her back arched higher, hands clamping down so hard L.C. couldn't move her own any longer. L.C. felt a gentle intermittent throbbing around the fingers inside Sydney, and she smiled. Oh, yeah...this girl was gone.

When the pulsing stopped, the fingers slid out, briefly brushing over Sydney's clitoris, making her flinch. "Ooh, my body is supersensitive right now," she said while moving the hand up to her torso.

L.C. noticed a pained look on Sydney's face. "You OK?"

She rubbed her forehead. "Yeah...just waiting for my eyes to uncross."

L.C. knew the feeling. She smiled and kissed Sydney on the forehead as if to make it better. The two cuddled without speaking for a while, then Sydney laughed. "My thighs are actually shaking—I have no strength left."

L.C. suggested she lie down on the bed.

"I think I need to. I'm so spent I'm going to have to sleep this one off." She wobbled her way to L.C.'s bed. "Just 10 or 15 minutes and I'll be fine."

A couple of hours later Sydney awoke to find L.C. still reading on the couch across the room. She looked at the clock on the bedside table and sat up quickly. "Oh, good grief, is it really 5:30?"

"It is."

"God, I can't believe I was out that long!"

"Oh, your agent called about half an hour ago. I told her you were asleep—I said maybe you were coming down with a cold. She said to call her tomorrow to reschedule and to get better."

Sydney fell back against the bed. "Oh, no! I can't believe I blew her off after all the work she's done for me. Now I feel bad."

L.C. crawled onto the bed beside Sydney and wrapped her arms around naked shoulders and kissed the woman full on the lips. "You enjoyed that, didn't you?"

Suddenly Sydney turned shy. "How could you tell?"

"Mm, I think when your back went up like the St. Louis Arch, that sort of gave it away." Sydney buried her face in L.C.'s chest. "I know I took you by surprise," L.C. continued, "but I guess after last night I was so pent up I just couldn't stop myself."

Sydney stroked the strong arms around her. "Don't blame yourself for anything. I could have stopped you if I'd wanted to. I know how to say no. So don't feel like you have anything to apologize for." She tightened her arms around L.C., looking as though she wanted to say something more. L.C. waited quietly until Sydney found the courage.

"I...want to take care of you too," Sydney said, "but honestly I don't know if I can. I've never been with a woman before. And this is a lot for me to adjust to in one day. I mean, if you'd told me a month ago that I'd be letting a woman touch me this way—and *enjoying* it—I'd have bet everything I owned against it. So maybe in time, but for now..."

"I understand," L.C. told her. "I won't rush you."

Chapter Eight

New Year's Eve found Sydney and L.C. getting ready to go to a party a couple of miles up Pacific Coast Highway at Eric Clapton's beach house. The holidays always brought to L.A. industry folks who were escaping the harsh winters in New York and Europe, and the bash was expected to be a star-studded event. L.C. decided to wear an Armani tux with a casual cut and was ready before Sydney had even finished her makeup. "You seem awfully anxious to get to this party tonight," Sydney said, still in her robe when L.C. came in to see if she was ready. "Is someone going to be there you want to see?"

L.C. put her arms around Sydney's waist. "No, it's just that when I was in school, girls like me were hiding way back in the closet playing dress-up in Daddy's clothes. That's why I didn't go to my senior prom. I always felt cheated out of a lot of great life experiences because I didn't fit the mold. Well, tonight I'm going to the prom...with the prom queen." L.C. flashed Sydney a big grin.

Sydney smiled too because since their one and only sexual encounter the day after the Christmas show, she had been wondering how L.C. thought of her now—still as a girl friend or as a girlfriend. That question had finally been answered.

Upon arriving at the party, Sydney was nearly knocked over by the smell when they walked in. "Ah, the traditional rock 'n' roll holiday potpourri: pine, bayberry, and marijuana." Then she experienced a Salvador Dali moment. The house was carpeted wall to wall with celebrities. All the great musical artists she'd grown up with were there, live and in person—the groups she'd stood in line to get tickets to see, that she'd screamed herself hoarse over. Forget front-row seats—this time she was so close she could tell which cologne they were wearing, what they'd been drinking, and in one case what he'd eaten for the past three days.

As she and L.C. pushed through the crowd, she almost stepped on the foot of James Taylor. A few steps farther and she ran shoulder-to-shoulder into Robert Plant, who apologized for the mini collision. She heard a burst of laughter and saw Stevie Van Zandt laughing hysterically with Crosby and either Stills or Nash—she never could remember which was which, but she knew it wasn't Young, the one who looked like a psycho killer. In one corner Billy Joel, the Piano Man himself, was *actually playing the piano*, singing with a couple of people Sydney didn't recognize. He was chunkier and grayer, but he still sounded just as good almost 20 years later. Judging by the drums and guitars and amplifiers set up in the den, she figured she was in store for some world-class entertainment at this shindig.

She and L.C. separated while L.C. schmoozed with everyone, and it didn't take long for Sydney to feel out of place. She was hoping to see Mandy's familiar face so she'd know at least one other person there. Hell, even Carol Ann's puss would have been a welcome sight at this point. Instead she found herself hanging out by the far wall overlooking the deck in back and evaluating the architectural aspects of the beach house. She noticed this home was different, and she didn't like it as much as L.C.'s because the deck hung practically over the water and there was no beach in the backyard. The shoreline here was rocky and not good for swimming, unlike the 30 feet of sandy beach from L.C.'s house to the water, which was great for walking and sunning and playing volleyball. Ah, well, to each his own.

After saying hello to several spouses and girlfriends of the rich and famous, Sydney felt the need for security and started scanning the joint for L.C. She spotted her love wandering into the kitchen with Sting and followed like a lost puppy.

The singer introduced her girlfriend to the man making himself another drink, but to L.C.'s surprise Sydney said she'd met Sting before. "You don't remember?" she said to the musician. "Cairo...1980...you guys were there on world tour and shooting the cover for your next album."

A light flickered in his eyes. "I remember the shoot and the concert, but where did I meet you?"

"We were all staying at the Mena House hotel, remember? You three were sitting at the table next to mine at dinner." He still couldn't place her. "I was the one who insisted you try the mango ice cream."

"Now *that* I do remember," he said fondly, turning to L.C. "The most extraordinary ice cream I've ever tasted." Sydney's ego took a dive. Great. He could remember mango ice cream but not her. The three small-talked for a few minutes longer, all the while Sydney noticing how much he had changed since his prime. Yet he was still a devastatingly attractive man with a strong charisma that women, no doubt, couldn't help being drawn to.

Suddenly L.C. was dragged off into another room by Bonnie Raitt, and Sydney ended up sitting on a couch talking to some old balding grandpa type. At one point she thought she recognized the accent and figured this was the lead singer from Dire Straits; she couldn't recall his name, however. But it wasn't until well into the conversation that she discovered she'd been talking to Peter Frampton.

Once the music and singing began, Sydney relaxed and

enjoyed the familiar voices. Before long she felt like she was holding court at her own personal Woodstock. Although some of the bodies had expanded and some had withered, they all still had their chops and sounded great.

With the nonstop entertainment, hours passed quickly and before anyone realized it, the New Year was upon them. L.C. brought Sydney a glass of champagne, and everyone counted down the clock and shouted "Happy New Year" at the stroke of midnight. The two women drank a toast, and L.C. nuzzled up to her sweetie. "Can you handle another public kiss?"

"Let's find out," Sydney replied playfully.

L.C. gave her a quick kiss on the lips—no tongue this time. Sydney liked the sweet kiss, so there was no recoil. For some reason it didn't bother her at all to be kissed by another woman around these people. Hell, half of them had probably slept with a goat at one point in their lives—they wouldn't care if two women shared a New Year's kiss.

By 2 o'clock L.C. was pretty well snockered and feeling her oats, and she decided it was time to let down her short black hair and take her turn at the microphone.

After her first number, she tossed aside her tuxedo jacket because she had worked up a sweat. Sydney hadn't known that underneath the jacket L.C. was wearing a sleeveless white shirt—somehow sleeveless wasn't the most flattering look with formal wear. Someone commented on L.C.'s tattoo, and the singer defended herself, saying something about not being an angel. At that point, Sweet Baby James sang out the first bar of "I'm No Angel" by the Allman Brothers, and L.C. took the cue while the band geared up and Billy Joel played along on the piano.

Before long, the woman was into the song mind, body, and soul. She was absolutely mesmerizing, belting out the sassy lyrics. When she got to the line about showing her tattoo, she struck a bodybuilder pose, kneeling sideways while flexing the biceps with the heart tattoo. The move brought down the house, but when L.C. struck the pose, the white silk shirt that was unbuttoned down to the middle of her chest ballooned out and Sydney caught a glimpse of a small, bare breast beneath. This was the first time she had seen any of the intimate areas of L.C.'s body. How strange that it should be in a room full of people. She felt a little embarrassed but a little aroused too.

What a performer, Sydney thought, watching the woman put on a command performance for the rock 'n' roll royalty gathered that night. She realized L.C. had come along about 15 to 20 years after most of these people, and it seemed to her that this was an acknowledgment of L.C. as one of the second generation of rockers, as though she had been accepted into their ranks.

Sydney then noticed that when the singer turned a certain way, little sweat beads on her chest caught the light and glistened like glitter. Sydney's eyes followed one tiny drop that rolled down L.C.'s breastbone and out of sight under her shirt, and once again she pictured that bare breast in her mind. Then she noticed how the sweat made L.C.'s short hair separate into hundreds of equal strands, like row after row of petals on a black dahlia. It was all so exhilarating—the music, the energy, L.C.'s voice getting inside her. She was absolutely buzzing inside. There was no doubt about it, when L.C. was in her element, she exuded a tremendous sex appeal.

It was nearly 4 A.M. when the couple arrived home, and L.C. went directly to the sliding glass doors and opened them wide, even though the air was crisp and chilly. She removed her jacket then collapsed into a chair, fanning her open shirt to create a breeze on her damp front. "Man, I'm still burning up. Jesus, I look like I've been in a wet T-shirt contest," she said, looking down at her chest, "and I lost."

She reached for the white linen handkerchief peeking out from the breast pocket of her tuxedo jacket and was about to wipe the perspiration from her neck when Sydney suddenly shouted, "*Stop*!"

L.C. sat bolt upright and threw the handkerchief across the room. "Jesus! Was there a bug on it?"

"No," Sydney said quietly, with no expression whatsoever.

L.C. was more than a little miffed that her mellow had been completely disturbed, her heart now pounding in her chest and head. "Then why did you yell at me to stop?"

Sydney didn't speak. She walked over and stood between L.C.'s legs, knelt down, and planted her full lips on the woman's chest just below the collarbone. L.C.'s head fell back slowly and she let out a groan of pleasure. When the blond pulled back, she looked into L.C.'s blue eyes for a moment, then whispered, "I just wanted to taste you."

An intense tingling shot through L.C.—there was no misreading this message tonight. The woman on her knees leaned forward until their lips met in a slow, soft kiss. Sydney took in a deep breath and relished the smell of hot, clean skin and hair, wet with perspiration. She wrapped her arms around this hot body and pressed their chests together. What an incredible feeling, being so close to this beautiful face, this beautiful voice, this beautiful body.

Sydney's soft lips caressed a rounded cheek, an earlobe, a spot behind the ear just below the hairline, down her strong neck, along a collarbone, down her chest, all the while fingers unbuttoning tiny white buttons. With one hand, she pushed back the white silk and gently cupped a small breast, fingertips tracing the outer edge of the firm flesh protruding from the shirt.

Her lips parted and she brushed them back and forth across a brownish-pink nipple, barely touching, teasing, until it became erect. Back and forth, gently caressing…back and forth, wet tongue licking, tasting…back and forth, gently sucking, tongue flicking over the sensitive tip. Waves of passion rushed through L.C.'s body and she groaned loudly, hungrily.

Sydney stood and took her by the hand, but when they got to the middle of the living room, she stopped. "Your place or mine?" she said with a smile.

"You lead and I'll follow," came the response.

Sydney chose her own bedroom and led L.C. to the bed. As they lay wrapped in each other's arms, kissing and undressing each other, L.C. asked, "Why tonight?"

Sydney smiled shyly. "This may sound silly, but your voice has an unbelievable effect on me."

L.C.'s ego surged. "Really? What kind of effect?"

"Well, did you ever see a movie called *Love Potion No. 9*?"

"Is that the one where Sandra Bullock plays the geeky lab tech?"

"Yeah. Remember how that love potion made a person's voice supposedly stimulate tiny little hairs inside the ear canal, making anyone who heard it climb the walls in a sexual way? Well…your voice is my love potion. It gets inside me and I melt."

L.C. grinned. "Ah, so whenever I want to seduce you, all I have to do is sing, huh?" L.C. gave the woman another dose of love potion, and the two giggled and kissed as they explored each other's bodies.

After a while, Sydney whispered in L.C.'s ear, "Tell me how you need to be touched." And she did.

Hours later, the lovers lay naked, hot and sweaty on wet sheets. "Now I really need to take a shower," L.C. said, wiping the sweat from her chest with her hand.

Sydney said she could use one too, and the two hopped up and headed to the bathroom. Since Sydney had just washed her hair a few hours ago, she didn't want to do it again so she wrapped it up in a towel turban and came into the bathroom like Carmen Miranda doing a samba, singing what she thought sounded like Brazilian lyrics as she joined L.C. in the shower.

"What was that?" L.C. asked, admiring the smooth moves.

"Carmen Miranda!"

"No, the dance."

"Oh. That's the samba."

"You really were a dancer, weren't you."

"This stuff is easy. I could teach you the basics of any ballroom dance in five minutes."

"Are you serious?"

"Absolutely. Tomorrow we'll have our first lesson."

"You're on!"

The two took turns washing each other's sweaty bodies, then Sydney took the shampoo and stood behind L.C. while she washed her hair, which didn't take long, considering how short it was. She watched the foamy white lather wind its way through shoulder blades and down the curves of L.C.'s hips. *What a Botticelli babe,* she thought, admiring the woman's classic beauty: broad, rounded shoulders; small, firm breasts; thick waist; strong hips and thighs, all packaged in creamy porcelain skin. The tattoo on her arm seemed almost like graffiti defiling this lovely work of art. Body by Botticelli; tattoo by Cletus. She got closer to the back of L.C.'s neck and inhaled deeply. She loved the way her skin and hair smelled. What a treat for the senses this woman was.

Once back in bed for the night, they lay with legs intertwined, Sydney snuggled up next to L.C. with her head resting on her lover's chest. "You know, ever since I met you, it's been like a whole new world to me," Sydney said, "all these firsts that bring these incredible new feelings." L.C. kissed her on the forehead. "Right now I'm trying to figure out this feeling I have, this wonderful feeling, but sometimes it's hard using conventional terms to describe an unconventional situation."

"Well, you let me know when it comes to you," L.C. said, then closed her eyes.

A moment later Sydney said, "I think it's from the freedom of not having to worry about birth control for the first time in my life. You know, I can just let go and enjoy not having to worry about getting pregnant—not to mention the mess." Her head shook back and forth. Then she turned onto her side, facing L.C., her head propped up on her hand. "Did you know that I'd been having sex *nine years* before I found a guy who knew how to give a woman an orgasm?"

"You're kidding!"

"Nope. Nine friggin' years," she said, snuggling up to L.C.'s warm body again. "And that double standard they dish out when it comes to sex—that girls aren't even supposed to enjoy it because if you do you're a slut, and then you end up feeling guilty about feeling good. That is so unfair. God, remember what it was like when we were in school?" she said, thinking back. "I'm so sick of all the garbage of a patriarchal world," Sydney said. "It makes my head spin."

L.C. stroked the border of fine, soft hair around Sydney's face. "You're preaching to the choir, sister," she said quietly.

"This is so-o-o much nicer. And you like to cuddle and talk afterward," she said, giving L.C. a big hug. "What a switch." Sydney kissed L.C. on the chest then closed her eyes. "You know, there's something else about you that's very sexy. I think it's this confidence you have, like you've got it all together. I find that strength of personality very appealing too."

"Well, I'm not always like that. Sometimes I get so tired of having to handle everything, but it's just me—there's no group to share the responsibilities with, so if I don't do it, it doesn't get done and I have no career. Don't get me wrong, it's been a great life, but the downside is that I have no time to enjoy it. I'm always in a studio recording, or writing songs, or running around the world on tour."

"Well, seeing the world isn't so bad, is it?"

"Of course not, but I never get to enjoy the places I go to—we're in one day and out the next, and all the time in between is tied up with rehearsal and the show. Plus there's so much legal crap. God, sometimes I just feel...weary. That's the exact word I'm looking for. Weary."

Sydney began singing the opening verse of "Try a Little Tenderness," only she used the word "wooly" instead of weary, and mangled a few other words of the lyrics. L.C. laughed when she thought she recognized the deviation. "*Bull Durham*?" she asked. Sydney nodded. "Good scene," L.C. said, and the two snuggled up and softly sang to each other before falling sleep.

In the months that followed, the women settled into their relationship. Some days they were like two puppies, frisky and frolicking, playing on the beach or around the house. Sydney had kept her word about teaching L.C. basic dance steps, particularly the cha-cha, rumba and mambo, and frequently when L.C. came home, Sydney would sweep her up in her arms and dance her lady around the room to Latin rhythms.

At least once a week they tried to get out of the house and go to a museum or art gallery, or to a hockey game, or take a day trip in the car. Wherever they went, they chronicled their adventures in pictures and soon had three albums full of photos.

While in Aspen skiing, L.C. had come down with a horrible

cold and spent an entire week in bed while Sydney nursed her back to health. L.C. got a bit peeved that Sydney never got sick—not even a headache—but her girlfriend simply reminded L.C. that she was involved with a genetically superior human being.

Sydney also tried to schedule a gourmet night once a week and treat the two of them to a delicious multicourse dinner. The meals didn't always go as planned, however. Once Sydney made a chocolate mousse cake. The recipe began at the bottom of one page and continued on the next, but Sydney accidentally skipped the last ingredient on the first page—the egg whites. Her cake ended up looking like a chocolate plate. But they ate it anyway, and it tasted pretty good.

Then one night in April, L.C. decided to do something special for Sydney for a change. That was the night she brought out the Box.

L.C. placed the gray plastic box in the middle of the bed and Sydney climbed on, hands grasping her yellow chiffon nightie, feeling a mix of dread and anticipation. "Are you ready?" L.C. asked.

"I suppose so," Sydney said.

L.C. opened the box, and Sydney screamed and jumped back to the edge of the bed as though it were full of spiders and snakes. It contained four dildos of different sizes, shapes, and materials—some hard plastic, some soft and pliable. Sydney's mouth hung open, eyes big and round. "Where did you get these?"

"They do have stores that sell things like this, you know."

"No, I don't know!" she said honestly.

L.C. chuckled. What an innocent babe. "Are you going to sit there and tell me that you've never known one lesbian your entire life?"

Sydney bit her lip, debating whether or not to dish, but there was no way L.C. was going to let her keep this a secret any longer, and the singer soon wheedled it out of her. "Well," Sydney said confidentially, "when I was a dancer, this pretty, older woman hit on me after a show." She leaned in closer. "A former Miss America," she whispered loudly, looking as though she'd let the cat out of the closet.

"You're kidding," L.C. said. Sydney told her the name, but it didn't ring a bell.

L.C. turned her attention back to the box and began the demonstration. She took out a soft plastic penis about six inches long with a little crank on the stump that when turned made the penis scrunch up then spring out full-length over and over. "Oh, my God!" Sydney shouted, laughing hard. "It's a Jack-in-the-box!"

"How right you are."

Sydney giggled hysterically. "Honey, there is *no way* you are putting that inside me." L.C. demonstrated the others, but none in the assortment met Sydney's approval. "You don't really use these on people, do you?"

"What do you think I do with them—put 'em out on the curio shelf when company comes over? Of course I use them... and I'm damn good with them too," she said, wickedly wiggling her eyebrows.

Since Sydney had vetoed all the choices, L.C. was forced to the last resort. "Then maybe this will appeal to you," she said as she lifted the false bottom on the case and pulled out a strap-on with a huge black penis. Sydney was too shocked at the 12-inch cock to say anything. "It's called the Black Mamba, but I have my own nickname for it." L.C. quickly stripped down, climbed into the apparatus, positioning it properly, then stood proud, arms akimbo. "I call it...Mandingo!" she said, head raised high.

The sight set Sydney off in a fit of giggles as she rolled around on the bed. Like a macho stud, L.C. took a couple of exaggerated steps toward her. "Get away from me with that!" Sydney shouted through her laughter. The closer L.C. got, the farther Sydney backed away until she had to roll off the bed and back against a wall. The blond made a cross with two index fingers. "You go away from here now—I mean it!"

L.C. ignored the warning and chased her girlfriend through the house as the woman giggled and screamed, all the while Mandingo bouncing like a diving board, which only made Sydney laugh harder.

Finally Sydney ran out of steam and the strong woman caught up to her, grabbing her around the waist from behind. She stuck Mandingo between Sydney's thighs, and when Sydney looked down and saw the huge head poking out from between her legs, she let out a shrill scream of laughter. "You cannot be serious!" she roared.

L.C. practically carried her into the bedroom, then playfully pushed her onto the bed, scooted off her panties, and pounced upon her. After wrestling a few moments, L.C. finally maneuvered herself between Sydney's long legs and slowly slid the monster member inside her. Sydney thought it a little cliché that L.C. had dubbed the huge black penis Mandingo, but then she was quickly developing a tremendous fondness for clichés.

The women's bodies moved automatically in rhythmic undulations. Sydney enjoyed making love this way because they could kiss and feel their bodies pressed together instead of having to take turns pleasuring each other. She also liked having L.C. inside her body and the intimacy that sort of closeness created. "I love you," she whispered.

L.C. stopped moving and looked at the pretty face beneath her. "You have no idea how happy that makes me when you say that." She kissed Sydney passionately, thrusting her powerful hips again.

Sydney had expected to hear the words in return and was disappointed when she didn't. In the four months they had been lovers, not once had L.C. said them. But the physical sensations of the moment quickly rendered her unable to speak or think, and her mind and body drifted away on waves of intense passion.

Chapter Nine

Sydney was awakened the following morning by L.C. sitting down on the bed next to her. "Baby," L.C. said, gently shaking her by the shoulder, "do you have any tampons in your bathroom?" L.C. knew she had awakened her out of a sound sleep, but the expression on Sydney's face was beyond that. "What?" L.C. asked.

Sydney concentrated on the face of the person sitting next to her, the one she had just had the most incredible sexual experience with hours earlier. "I just never dated anyone who asked to borrow my tampons before," she said, rubbing her head. "It's another one of those new life experiences for me, you know."

While they ate breakfast out on the deck, L.C. groused incessantly about her cramps. "This has to be one of God's cruel little jokes," she said. "Like I need this every month. What a waste!" Sydney had never thought about that aspect of L.C.'s lifestyle before and grew curious. "Did you ever want to have children?"

"Never," the ailing woman said decisively. "I've never exactly had those feminine maternal qualities." She nibbled on an English muffin and sipped hot tea. "It was just me and my dad most of my life, and when I was a kid I played with all the guys in the neighborhood 'cause I was so good at sports. I didn't play with dolls or throw tea parties. And I've never had the desire or felt the need to drop a puppy in order to feel complete, or like a real woman," she said. "How about you? Did you ever want to have kids?"

Sydney shook her head. "No. When we were growing up and all my girlfriends would say, 'When I get married and have children,' I never did. I never wanted that, not even as a little girl. I was a dancer and gymnast my whole life and if I'd gotten pregnant, I couldn't have done the things that defined who I was, the things that made me happy. So I guess that's why I never saw myself in that way."

Sydney's thoughts drifted back to her girlhood days. "Now that I think about it, we were only 6 or 7 when we started talking like that. Lord, we program females at such a young age to want to become mothers." She shook her head in pity.

"And I'm glad I didn't have children during either of my marriages because I ended up divorced twice. It's too hard having all that responsibility dumped on a woman—it's not fair. And child support doesn't take the place of love and affection or life lessons either. I don't know where men get off thinking that a check can relieve them of their parental responsibilities. Anyway, I just think it's better for kids to have two parents, if for no other reason than to keep from overburdening a single parent.

"As far as those two parents being of the opposite sex, I don't know if that's really a plus. Maybe yin and yang energies do make a child better. I know psychologists say a child needs both a male and female role model, but I don't see what great role models men are when they commit adultery and leave their wives for younger girls and aren't around anyway. They skip out on child support, they're overly aggressive—look at our prisons, they're filled with men—and they perpetuate the porno industry. I mean, just what is it about the male sex that you could possibly want a child to emulate? I don't see it."

L.C. agreed with her completely.

Sydney took a long look at the beautiful woman sitting across from her. "Don't you ever feel sad that you won't pass on that amazing voice?"

L.C.'s expression never changed. "Not all children inherit the talent of the parents," she replied.

"And sometimes the children develop even more talent than the parents," Sydney said with some bitterness.

"Well, either way, it ends with me," L.C. said. "What about you? Don't you want to pass on that gorgeous, healthy body of yours—maybe produce an Olympic gymnast in the next generation?"

Sydney's eyes lowered sadly. "I think about that now and then. I suppose that if I were a mother who helped her child instead of hindered…" She faded off, deep in thought. "When I think of how much easier it would be for a child to reach her potential with a loving parent constantly encouraging her and protecting her…what a wonderful life she could have."

"Are you talking about your mother again?" L.C. knew the answer before she asked the question.

The question snapped Sydney out of her daydream of what might have been. "Yeah. My mother was a gymnast too, and when I surpassed what she could do by the time I was only 6, she was so bitterly jealous. And she didn't hide it either. She never lifted a finger to help me. Never drove me to practice, never came to any of my competitions. In fact, she did everything she could to hinder me. After a while she even refused to pay for my private coach. I was lucky my coach had enough faith in me to waive her fees so I could continue with her. And I'm absolutely certain that's why my mother badgered me so hard about going to that conservatory in London. She wanted to put an end to my Olympic dream." Sydney was unaware that her jaws were clenched slightly, but L.C. noticed it. "She was the worst excuse for a mother in the history of parenthood."

L.C. saw Sydney's eyes grow shiny with tears. She knew too well how sensitive relationships with parents were, so she let the conversation go.

Suddenly Sydney came out of it. "You know," she said with a half smile, "it wasn't until just now that I realized something." She looked L.C. directly in the eye as she spoke. "The real reason I never wanted to have children is because of my own mother." L.C. wasn't sure exactly what she meant. "Our parents are our role models for what parents should be like, and I hated that woman so much as child—why in God's name would I ever want to grow up and turn into her? That's why I never wanted to be a mother." She shook her head, looking a bit bewildered. "Why didn't I ever see that before now? It seems so obvious." L.C. didn't have the answer.

"Regardless, I don't regret the decision," Sydney continued. "I've traveled the world many times over, I've gallivanted with the rich and famous, and I've had wonderful adventures that I never could have experienced if I'd been tied to a crib. Oh, I know that's what some women want and need, and that's fine. But it was never for me."

L.C. looked surprised. "You traveled around the world? I thought you didn't fly."

"Ah, but my boycott has only recently been in place, remember. I did a lot of flying when my first husband and I lived in Hawaii. He was a Navy officer and we were stationed there for a three-year tour."

"Wow, that must have been great."

She sighed deeply. "It was heaven on earth. And I don't just mean the weather and the tropical setting. I really learned a lot about the Hawaiian culture when I was there. They're a very spiritual people, and their beliefs made a lot of sense to me. I have it in my will that I want my ashes scattered in the ocean at this beautiful secluded spot I know off Maui. I've always been a water baby, and that just seems like the best way home for me."

L.C. was too busy fidgeting to let the seriousness of the topic sink in. "Well, on any of your trips to exotic locations, did you ever pick up any tips on how to get rid of cramps?"

Sydney smiled sympathetically. "Best thing I've found is either a nice soak in a hot tub or a heating pad." She looked over at the heated pool with sparkling clear water. "Why don't you take a swim? The mild exercise and heat might do the trick."

"I don't know how to swim," L.C. confessed.

Sydney let out a hoot. "You mean you bought an oceanfront house with a heated swimming pool and you can't swim?"

"I enjoy the view and the sound of the ocean," L.C. said with a slight defensiveness to her voice, "and the house came with the pool. Besides, if the urge strikes me, I can float on my back or on one of those inflatable things, so the pool isn't a complete waste."

"You don't ever go into the ocean and play in the surf?"

"I'm afraid it might carry me out to sea and then I'd be screwed."

Sydney felt a little sorry for L.C., missing out on the luxury of a nice swim and the fun of water sports, but since that option was out as far as her cramps went, Sydney fixed her up on the fainting couch in the bedroom with the heating pad on her abdomen. Then she curled up on the bed and read a book to keep her ailing friend company.

"Hey," L.C. said. "In the drawer over there." She pointed to her bedside table. "Get my calculator, would you?" Sydney handed it to her, and L.C. began punching the keys.

"You counting all your money?" Sydney asked.

L.C. was busy concentrating on her calculations. "Good grief! In my lifetime, I have used 6,840 tampons," she announced. "I swear, sometimes I think that if I have to cram another wad of cotton up my crotch I'm going to scream."

"You think that's bad, I had a girlfriend in junior high who had such a heavy flow she had to piggyback two supers."

L.C. grabbed her crotch in sympathy. "And just think, we've got at least another 10 years to put up with this crap." With that thought, her face contorted.

Sydney cracked up laughing at something that popped into her head just then. "Do you remember back when we first started having periods, before the convenience of mini pads, those old bulky Kotex pads we had to use with those elastic belts you had to hook the gauze ends into?"

L.C. cringed at the memory of that hell. "Lord have mercy!" she said closing her eyes, then laughing. "I'd forgotten all about those hideous contraptions."

"And of course the fashion then was stretch pants and shorts. You couldn't hide those bulges in the front and back for anything dressed in those! I used to hate going to school on those days for fear the guys would see those tell-tale bulges and tease me about being on the rag."

"What fond memories," L.C. said jokingly. "Ah, the fun for women just never stops." After adjusting the heating pad a little, L.C. leaned back and closed her eyes. "I can't wait for menopause," she pined. "Why didn't God make us like animals that come into heat once a year? Why does it have to be every friggin' month?"

"Because biologically it increases the species' chances of survival," Sydney responded.

"Yeah, and now we're overpopulated, thanks to the Penis People...horny fucking bastards."

"That's about the only thing they do well, isn't it?" Sydney said, but L.C. didn't respond—she was busy wrestling with the cord on her heating pad. "You know, what you just said about menopause made me think about what my mom went through," Sydney continued. "If she's any indication of what I'm going to go through, you're in for the time of your life."

"Not so good, huh?"

"Uh-uh. I remember one time she'd been out shopping and bought a silver hand mirror for her vanity. One of my girlfriends was over at the time and made a little fuss about how pretty it was, but all I said was, 'That's nice.' Well, Mother got this Norma Desmond look on her face and went off on me. It was so embarrassing, in front of my friend and all. Jesus, she would go completely psycho over the littlest things."

"Gee…I can hardly wait," L.C. said, feigning fear. "You know, since we were little, they've discovered lots of ways to ease the symptoms of menopause. Maybe it won't be so bad for us," she said. "I guess it wouldn't hurt to start eating soybeans now, though—they're supposed to be good for that."

Sydney grinned. "You already have been." L.C. looked puzzled. "I've been spiking your salads and soups with them at least three times a week for months," Sydney confessed.

Normally L.C. would have been angry that someone had been putting things into her food without her knowledge, but in this case she thought it was sweet. She knew Sydney had done it out of caring and affection for her. And there was something comforting about having someone taking care of her and looking out for her well-being. "Thanks," she said softly.

With all the talk of menopause, L.C.'s thoughts lingered in the future. "Gosh, in 10 years we'll have lines in our faces. We'll be looking at teenagers as whippersnappers and complaining about the noise they call music, contributing 50 grand to the Democratic Party to make sure we still have Medicare and Social

Security around when we need it. Oh, God," she said, feeling depressed, "we're turning into our parents!"

Sydney laughed softly. "We all turn into our parents, and it's not from genetics or role playing, it's just the phases everyone goes through in the life cycle. And the funny thing is, men seem to get tamer and women more aggressive as life goes on. How many times do you see an older woman making a stand about shoddy service at a bank or a restaurant? Little old ladies don't take any guff."

Suddenly it hit L.C. that the Big 4-0 was lurking right around the corner. "You just made me realize that in 10 years we'll also qualify for the seniors discount at Denny's." The two pair of eyes met and they both burst out laughing. What else could they do about the inevitable? L.C. sang the chorus from one of her favorite Beatles songs that popped into her head: "When I'm Sixty-Four."

"You know what I can't wait for," Sydney said, "is for my hair to turn gray so I can stop going through the monthly hell of bleaching it. What a relief that will be."

L.C. imagined how beautiful her head of long, thick silver hair would be, glistening in the moonlight every night when they sat out on the balcony side by side in the chaises, holding hands, talking. For the first time in her life she actually was having pleasant thoughts about getting older, as though a peaceful and comforting place were out there waiting for her. And she knew it was because of Sydney. This woman seemed to have such a great perspective on life. And to have her around to grow old with made it seem much more bearable. Let the outside world continue worshiping youth—the two of them would stay right there in their own little world, adoring and desiring each other, celebrating each year that passed, cherishing every gray hair, relishing every wrinkle.

She watched the woman reading on the bed. Sydney was so different from any of her other lovers. She was definitely the prettiest girlfriend L.C. had ever had, but it was more than that. She was smart. And not just book-smart, but smart about life and people. She seemed like someone L.C. could trust, and that was a very comforting thought, especially considering her last relationship. She felt so lucky to have Sydney in her life.

Suddenly the smile dropped from L.C.'s face; her stomach knotted and she couldn't catch her breath for a second. Her heart pounded from deep inside her chest. Whoa—what was she doing thinking that far into the future? She *never* thought about where a relationship was going with a lover, whether she would still be with that one particular person years from now. She always enjoyed a relationship while it lasted, and when it ended, she simply waited for the next one to come along. And another one always did.

It was all that talk about menopause that had started this. She convinced herself this was why she was thinking about the future today and not because of any feelings she had for Sydney. Enough of this. "So what are we having for dinner tonight?" she asked. Not that she cared; she just wanted out of the unknown and back to a time and place she was sure of.

Chapter Ten

While L.C.'s new love affair made her ecstatic, it didn't please many of the people involved in her career. Nearly a year had passed since she started work on the songs for her first album with her new label. Her band and backup singers weren't happy because not working took money out of their pockets. Producers and executives at the record company weren't happy because they didn't have a product to sell, not with only five of the 12 required songs completed by late June.

Finally, during the second week of August, everyone got the call and the first recording session was held. Sydney was L.C.'s faithful companion, practically living at the studio, attending every session, some lasting until dawn the following day.

Three weeks later, they recorded the final song on the album, which was L.C.'s favorite, the one she titled "My Walkin' Talkin' Life-Size Barbie Doll,"—a light-hearted love song obviously inspired by Sydney. By 3 A.M., it was only L.C., Rick, and Sydney remaining in the studio. The two women sat on the piano bench in the recording area, and Rick pulled up a folding chair to listen to the playback with them.

Five times L.C. made Rick play the song through, start to finish, because she felt something wasn't right. "There's a problem," she said, "and I can't figure out if it's the rhythm guitar, or bass, or what."

Rick shook his head. "I think it sounds OK."

"Really?" L.C. said hopefully.

"Yeah, it sounds fine to me."

She listened a while longer then turned to Sydney. "What do you think?"

Sydney didn't say anything right away, then looked at L.C. sort of squeamishly. "There's a problem all right, but it isn't with the guitar." L.C. sat upright, sensing she was about to hear something she wasn't going to like. "It's the music," Sydney said frankly. "It isn't right for this song." L.C. didn't have to speak; her expression said, *Come on—I gotta hear this.*

Rick casually sat back, sensing fireworks about to start, making sure he didn't get singed. Sydney took a deep breath, then let it out. She wanted to be kind, but she also knew L.C. preferred people to just hit the nail on the head when making a point, so she came out with it. "This isn't L.C. Hackett—it's Hal from *2001*. The melody is mechanical, completely emotionless, with no character or personality."

Tension engulfed the room. Rick swore he felt L.C.'s angry heartbeat thumping through the hardwood floors. "You've got peppermint-spice lyrics with vanilla music," Sydney continued. "They clash! This should be a number 1 song on the dance and pop charts, honey. You should have a ball with this—it's sexual and sensual, the lyrics are full of whimsy. But there's none of that in the music. It should have a chorus that's so catchy people can't help singing it over and over because it sticks in their heads after only the first time they hear it.

"But I don't feel like dancing to this—I feel like standing with my hands clasped while I watch the numbers light up waiting to get to my floor." Rick's jaw dropped. Elevator music! My God, could there *be* any worse insult to a songwriter and vocalist? If he hadn't been frozen by the shock, he would have slipped out at this point. L.C.'s mouth cocked to one side; her eyes burned holes in the black and white keys.

"This is the kind of overproduced stuff Streisand has made for years," Sydney continued. "And I see that happen so often in the music industry—they find a fresh, new artist with an original sound, they move her to L.A., and then they start overproducing all the character and personality right out of her music." Rick winced as though he'd just seen someone beaned with a baseball. Then he wondered whether this one had been intended for *him*.

"They did it with Mariah Carey, Whitney Houston. When was the last time either of them had a number 1 song? When was the last time *you* had a number 1 song?"

L.C. recoiled; her eyes narrowed to slits.

"The only thing those women put out now is boring lyrics with that annoying, sing-song beat. It's schlock! And I don't want that to happen to you. I would hate to ever hear people say, 'Yeah, she was good when she first started, but now it's assembly line.' You're better than that. When someone with a God-given talent like yours doesn't use it to its fullest potential, it's a sin."

A full minute passed before L.C. spoke. "Is that all?"

"No, it's not," Sydney said, to the surprise of the other two people in the room. "You're overpowering the lyrics. And not just on this song. Sweetheart, you have a voice that was meant for love songs—both the heartbreaking kind that make you want to cry your eyes out, and the happy ones that make you want to smile and sing along. Both require tender, delicate emotions to come through your voice, but they can't if they're shoved out of the way by a freight train."

She let out a heavy sigh, taking a moment to think. "You have one of the most beautiful, feminine voices ever created. It's like a rainbow—there are so many colors to appreciate, but when you blast us with a full-spectrum, bright-white light, all those wonderful qualities get washed out and disappear.

"And this particular song should start out soft and sensual, then graduate into a raw, teasing sexuality that sort of growls its way up from inside. But there's no climax to this song with either the music or your voice. You know that song, "What You Need" by INXS, how it builds to this tremendous climax? That's what this song should do. It should have a drumbeat and a bass and a rolling rhythm that all get into the base of your spine and crawl their way up your backbone until you just have to throw your head back and shout, 'Oh, yeah!' But it doesn't. It's just flat and repetitious. You've got great control of that voice—I know, I'm lucky enough to hear it every day. Don't deprive the rest of the world of it."

Sydney looked earnestly at L.C. who was still focused on the ivories. "You know why I'm saying these things, don't you?" There was no response. "It's not because I think I know more than you do about the music industry or anything like that, it's because I'm thinking about your future." L.C. didn't know what the hell she meant.

"Everything you do now is creating your legacy, what people will look back on. And if you put something bad out there, it never goes away—you can't just erase it and pretend it never existed. I know you don't sing with the purpose of only winning awards, but the charts and awards are the measure of quality in your business, and there's nothing wrong with either. I just want you to have everything you deserve out of your career, and you deserve better than this. This isn't worthy of you."

She waited for a response, but still none came. L.C. hardly moved except to blink. Sydney lowered her head. "I was hoping you'd appreciate the honesty instead of my acting like a sycophant and saying, 'Oh, it's wonderful!' "

Even though Sydney hadn't directed that bean ball at Rick, he felt the sting all the same and set his jaw, folding his arms in a defensive posture.

"But I can see by that look in your eye and the way you're biting the inside of your mouth that you're pissed, so I'm going to take my cute little buns into the booth like a good girl and wait quietly where I belong." The slender blond got up and tiptoed away.

Good, get the hell out of here, Rick thought, just before L.C. turned to him with a hang-dog expression. "Goddamn it...she's right," the singer groaned. It was difficult to say, but she had to.

"I don't know," he said defensively, "I still think it works."

"No, it doesn't...she's right."

Fine, he thought, *go ahead and take the opinion of someone with absolutely no experience in the business—fine!* He glared at Sydney as she walked away, hoping she'd keep on going and leave the two of them to finish their work alone instead of filling his client's head full of crap.

L.C. buried her face in her hands and shook her head. "Sydney!" she shouted. The blond stopped in her tracks and turned around. "Come back!" L.C. beckoned helplessly.

Sydney walked back and stood at the piano, keeping her distance, not sure why she had been summoned. "I know what you're saying," L.C. said. "You're right, but it still hurts."

"I wasn't trying to hurt your feelings," Sydney said sweetly.

"I know. But no matter how you say it, something like that is going to hurt."

"I understand," she said. "You know, maybe I should take the car and go on home so you guys can work it out."

"No," L.C. said firmly as she stood. "I'm spent. It's late and I'm tired, and it's like you're always saying, people aren't light switches—I can't just turn off this negative feeling with the flip of a switch. I'm going to have to take some time and get all this disappointment and frustration out of my system—get rid of all these negative emotions." She shoved her hands in her pants pockets and turned to Rick. "Let's give it up for a couple of days so I can blow off some steam, all right?"

Rick leaned back, arms still folded, and pleaded his case, reminding her that they were already months behind schedule. But L.C. insisted, and he reluctantly agreed to shut it down for the night.

A mere 18 hours later, L.C. had put the recording session behind her and the two women were ready to go out and tear up the town. L.C. fussed with her hair gel trying to get some lift into her sprigs for a new look, while Sydney broke with tradition and actually had a glass of chardonnay. The svelte blond was feeling a little buzz even before they left.

Their first stop was a new bar on Melrose, but as with any new club in L.A., there was a line winding around the building to get in. L.C. didn't seem concerned. She took Sydney by the arm and escorted her right on up to the entrance where the doorman, who recognized the rock star immediately, let the couple in. Their cover charge also was waived.

A thick cloud of dry-ice smoke hung from the ceiling, and the heavy beat of head-banging music made the walls and floor throb. L.C. took the lead and squeezed through the bodies as they made their way toward the bar. All the stools were taken and all the tables in the club were filled, which didn't please Sydney because she was teetering on the four-inch "fuck me" heels she always wore with her skin-tight, shiny black leather pants. L.C. knew poor Sydney was dying for a place to sit and smiled at her gorgeous girlfriend. "Turn it on."

Sydney stood next to the very hairy guy sitting at the end of the bar who was obviously cruising for chicks. "Oh, I'm so-o-o tired of standing," she said, sounding frail and feminine. "I'd give anything just to sit down for a few minutes." When the gorilla turned around and saw what was talking, he went apoplectic. He hopped up from his stool and offered it to the gorgeous damsel in distress. "Oh, thank you," Sydney said with a dazzling smile. "You're such a gentleman."

The beast was ready to zoom in on her when L.C. walked over and put her arm around Sydney's shoulder. "Thanks, man," she said, then the two women turned around and tried to get the attention of one of the bartenders. But after having no luck, L.C. gave up and walked to the other end of the bar where the two bartenders were mixing drinks for a line of waitresses. She ordered a couple of drinks and leaned on the bar to wait. The guy to her right, a seriously inebriated frat rat in an Aerosmith T-shirt, caught a glimpse of her out of the corner of his eye. He hoped this was a chick to hit on and started checking her out. His eyes scrutinized the face next to him, but because of his altered vision, he wasn't exactly sure what he was looking at. He nudged his friend with the mousse-spiked hair. "Trevor! Dude! Check it out!" he whispered loudly and leaned back for his buddy to see. "Is that a chick?"

"I don't know," Trevor said, able to see only the back of L.C.'s head.

"Chromosome check!" the first one shouted, raising his hand in the air. He laughed at his own joke, then his eyes moved from L.C.'s head down to her shirt. "Whoa! It's got tits—we have our answer."

L.C. heard the remark and turned sideways just enough so that Trevor recognized the distinct profile. He punched his friend in the shoulder. "Ryan, that's L.C. Hackett, you idiot!"

Ryan did the drunkard's squint. "Looks more like Buddy Hackett," he said.

L.C. wondered what it was about drunks that made them think they couldn't be heard by someone standing only inches away unless it was one of their friends. She knew it best not to provoke an idiot, especially a drunk one, so she kept her eyes on the bar and let the jerk ramble.

He tapped a pack of Marlboros on the bar. "Should I offer her a smoke?" he said to no one in particular, then decided to answer his own question. "Nah, chicks like her probably go for cigars...something a little more phallic." His friend shushed him, but to no avail. "You think she's always the one on top, or do they take turns being the guy?"

The bartender set L.C.'s drinks on the bar and she tossed him a 20, not waiting for the change. She picked up the glasses, then looked Ryan Boy square in the eye. "See that blond with the legs at the end of the bar?"

He and his buddy both took a gander at the pair of legs in shiny leather. Trevor gave out a low whistle of approval. "Yeah? So?" Ryan said combatively.

"I get to have sex with *that* every night." She flashed him an eat-your-fuckin'-heart-out grin and swaggered past.

"Oh, bullshit," he said to Trevor, who instantly became wide-eyed; as soon as L.C. handed one of the drinks to Sydney, she planted one on the blond. "Look at this!" he said, his voice turning falsetto with excitement as he grabbed Ryan by the shirt-sleeve.

His friend caught the end of the kiss but wasn't impressed. "Eh, they're probably just friends having a girls' night out." At that point L.C. pried open Sydney's legs with her hips, snuggled up torso-to-torso, and engaged in a passionate kiss that made those long legs wrap around her waist.

"Sweet!" Trevor growled, achieving a semiwoody.

"OK, so I was wrong," Ryan admitted casually as he pulled his stool out from the bar to get a better view. The two fellas sat and enjoyed the hot girl-on-girl action at the end of the bar for a while. "It's like Cinemax in 3-D," Trevor declared.

Later, when the women were leaving, Trevor and Ryan enviously watched the two walk out with their arms around each other, nuzzling and fondling. "I guess it is true," Trevor lamented. "Rock stars do get all the best pussy. Damn!"

Sydney was in the mood to move, so they drove over to a dance club a few miles away. It was more of the same scene—horny college boys and wanna-be actors trying to score a one-night stand. As soon as the couple started dancing, some Gen-Xer in jeans and sunglasses next to them did a double take when he saw Sydney and started going into his routine. "Hey, how's it goin'?" he said, with that "cool dude" head bob. Sydney just smiled back, but L.C. was a little pissed at having her girlfriend hit on right in front of her, and it didn't help when she caught the young one giving Sydney the once-over a second time. "You're a tall one, aren't you?" he said. "What are you—6-foot, 6-foot-1?"

L.C. glared at the interloper. "Does she win a prize if she guesses right?" she snarled, then bopped over and positioned herself between him and Sydney. He gave up and devoted his attention to the girl he'd asked to dance, who was quickly developing an inferiority complex from his rude behavior.

When the song was over, L.C. and Sydney left the dance floor in search of a table. They happened upon a group leaving one just as they approached and managed to slide in before anyone else could claim it. Sydney alternated moving her feet round and round to work out the stiffness. These shoes were good for one dance every half hour because that's how long it took for the discomfort to subside. If they didn't look so great with her pants she never would have bought them, but for some reason comfort never seemed to be a consideration for shoe designers.

As it turned out, the guy from the dance floor happened to be sitting with three of his friends at the table next to theirs. From the way he lit up when he saw the blond in black leather in such close proximity, it was apparent he still didn't get that these two women were a couple. He stood up and turned around, sitting backwards in his chair facing Sydney's back. "Them's some long legs you got, girl," he said, trying to get her attention. L.C. had had enough and scooted her chair out so she could face him. "Can you not see that she's not interested?" she said angrily.

The young man gave L.C. the once-over, just the once. "You got a pair of legs on you too, don't you. Looks like you've got your own little rain forest over there with those tree trunks."

Sydney shot him an angry look. "How dare you!" she scolded. "You know, you might have better luck if you hit on someone who wasn't here with a date." Seconds later she saw sparks flying from the wheels in his brain grinding to a halt as he finally figured things out. "You gotta be kidding me," he said with a laugh.

"No, I'm not," Sydney said.

"No way! Not a babe like you."

"Why is that so hard for you to wrap your little brain around?"

"Because chicks like you don't go for chicks like her. It ain't natural."

"Oh, come on," L.C. said to the boy, deciding to have a little fun, "you can't tell me you never thought about doin' the nasty with one of your buddies there." Her intent to goad worked, and he vehemently denied any sort of sexual thoughts or feelings for his male friends.

Sydney went along with the game. "Me thinks the man doth protest too much," she said haughtily.

"What?" he said.

Sydney rolled her eyes and repeated herself. He stared at her with a blank expression. "It's Shakespeare!" she shouted over the noise. "Crack a book sometime, pretty boy!"

"Hey! This boy is straight as a board," he said. "In fact, that's not the only thing straight as a board." He spread his legs a little wider to make sure she got what he meant. Sydney and L.C. shared a moment of exasperation. "It never fails," L.C. said to Sydney. "Every time I go to a hetero club I end up feeling like Jane Goodall."

Sydney was too appalled by the guy's gesture to laugh. She took a deep breath and glared at him. "In spite of what Freud said, you have *nothing* that I want."

"Who?" the boy said.

"Aw, Jesus," Sydney lamented, fearing for the future of the country. "Come on." She held out her hand to L.C. "Let's dance."

The women burrowed to the center of the dance floor, where Sydney watched her partner dance until their eyes met, and she had to smile. "You cause a commotion wherever you go, don't you?" she teased.

"No more than you, sugar."

The two tore up the dance floor for another hour, avoiding the pest in the sunglasses the rest of the time they were there, then headed out for the next club on their list.

On Monday L.C. went to see Rick at his home and had a long talk with him. She told him she was scrapping the album and starting over. "It's like Sydney's always saying, creative people can't do their best work unless they're downright miserable," she explained. "And I've been anything but miserable since I met her."

Rick was disappointed and angry at the news. Sydney again. Perfect.

"She can't write when she's happy, and apparently I can't make good music when I'm happy, and I've been so wrapped up in this relationship I just want to spend every second with her. So I rushed these songs and I didn't have my heart in most of them, and it shows. And I'd rather kill this album and wait a few more months until I can come up with some songs I can be proud of. I should say until *we* can come up with them. Sydney's going to be working with me this time."

Rick was shocked at this bit of news, knowing L.C. Hackett was strictly a solo artist. "We figured that was the best way to get me motivated to spend some time at the piano. If she's there, that's where I want to be."

Her producer took a moment to get his emotions under control. "L.C.," he began, "I can appreciate your wanting to make the best album you can, but now you're putting me in a position where I have to go upstairs to the suits and tell them that after being several months late with this project already, we're going to have to wait God only knows how much longer to get it done. I was the one who convinced them to sign you, and I promised them a smash hit. My career is riding on this project."

L.C. spoke more firmly. "So is mine. And if I don't have a future, neither do you. It's like they say, better late than never, right?"

Rick continued pressing his point, but nothing he said made the singer change her mind. L.C. told him she'd be in touch as soon as the songs were finished, then got up and left before he could say anything else.

Rick poured himself a drink. He stared into the highball glass, and without even taking a sip threw it against his brick fireplace, shattering pieces all over the carpet. He didn't mind an artist getting a piece of ass on a regular basis, but now this blond bitch was fucking with his career too, and that was unacceptable. He was definitely going to have to do something about this.

Chapter Eleven

The two women spent their days working on songs together, and before long, Sydney was helping compose the music to go with their lyrics, now that her ability to hear symphonies had been reawakened since becoming comfortably enveloped in L.C.'s world. The duo also made great progress in reworking the music to several of the songs salvaged from the attempted album.

Sydney was expecting the two of them to finish reworking the last of the songs from it one night after dinner, but she was unpleasantly surprised when L.C. informed her she was going out to a strip joint with the girls instead and left her sitting at the piano, stunned and alone. Sydney found this annoying on so many levels. First, she couldn't understand why L.C. still wanted to frequent places of that ilk now that she was involved in a serious monogamous relationship, especially considering how happy they'd been the last few months. And second, L.C. hadn't even asked if Sydney minded her going someplace like that. Then, she didn't invite Sydney along. Not that she would have gone. No, it was just cut and dried that L.C. was doing this without her whether Sydney liked it or not—not exactly the way a solid relationship works. And L.C. hadn't even mentioned she was going out until she was literally walking out the door.

Unbeknownst to Sydney, there was something else L.C. had

neglected to tell her. About a conversation that had taken place over lunch that afternoon at a Beverly Hills restaurant between herself and Carol Ann when the idea to go carousing had been broached:

"I'm going to pass—Sydney wouldn't like it."

"Pussy-whipped," Carol Ann taunted.

"Hey! I wear the pants in the family," L.C. boasted.

"Yeah, but *she* tells you which ones to wear."

That was all it had taken to make L.C. change her mind.

There had been a few other changes in L.C. recently that had concerned Sydney. Like the time a couple of months ago the singer had gone out clothes shopping and came home looking like Billy Idol with white spiked hair. The dramatic alteration had been a shock at first to Sydney, but then she thought L.C. looked beautiful no matter what she did to her hair, so she didn't mind. The new look didn't last long, however, because when the black roots started growing out, L.C. hated the two-toned hair and dyed it back to black. When Sydney asked what had prompted the change in the first place, L.C. just said she was tired of looking at the same old face every day in the mirror.

L.C.'s actions tonight caused Sydney to wonder whether she might also be tired of looking at the same face lying next to her in bed every night, which upset her a great deal. She recalled from one of her college psych classes that the initial hormonal high one feels in a relationship usually starts wearing off after about two years and that's when the temptation to stray begins. However, with L.C. and her voracious sexual appetite—and knowing her track record—apparently it had started wearing off a little faster with her. Sydney figured that in order to keep her mate from losing interest, she was going to have to keep their sex life plenty spicy and full of surprises. So she took the restraints off her vivid writer's imagination and let it run wild.

Sydney also decided to use another tip from her psychology studies in spicing up their sex life: positive reinforcement. So whenever L.C. had been a good girl and came home at night instead of partying, she was rewarded with a night to remember. Sydney made sure her hormonal honeybunch never knew what was going to greet her when she walked through the door. One night Sydney had on a cheerleader outfit complete with yellow-and-black pom-poms, and she performed a sexy routine, shaking her pom-poms and bare ass to Toni Basil's "Mickey," only she changed the lyrics to "L.C."

On another occasion when the singer had returned from a short business trip, she opened the front door to find a trail of yellow rose petals that led to Sydney's bedroom. The king-size bed was covered with golden, velvety petals, plus a few scattered strategically on Sydney's nude body, à la *American Beauty*, with Sydney's long hair spread out like a golden corona on the pillow.

And knowing that sex was 90% in the mind, one night Sydney stood her dark-haired beauty in front of a mirror while she undressed her and fondled and pleasured her. L.C. said it was like watching someone else having sex, but she was feeling everything she saw—kind of like Sensurround at a movie theater. She found this voyeuristic experience extremely arousing.

But L.C.'s favorite encounter happened when she came home once after attending a Lakers game with the girls to find two of the high-back upholstered dining room chairs in the middle of the living room floor facing each other with Sydney sitting in one, her legs stretched out on the other. The blond had on a well-tailored pink-and-black suit, black gloves, and black heels. All her blond hair had been tucked under a brunette wig with a '60s flip, which was topped with a pink pillbox hat. The look was conservative yet chic. L.C. asked what the deal was with the chairs.

"I've sent Richie over to Millie and Jerry's for the night, so we have the house *all* to ourselves," came the reply.

L.C. knew right then she was looking at Laura Petrie sitting in her living room. Sydney stood and wiggled an index finger, meaning "Come here." She guided L.C. to the chairs and the singer straddled one in order to sit properly because of their positioning. The woman in pink punched a button on the stereo remote control. "Super Freak" blasted out good and loud, and the lovely Laura began stripping down to the raunchy tune.

First one glove was slipped off and tossed aside, then the other. Next she shimmied out of her skirt, revealing a black lace garter belt and stockings. Her jacket was just long enough to cover her derriere and she looked like a risqué Rockette as she pulled out some of the raunchier dance moves from her younger days that required a supple spine and freely shifting hips.

Off came the jacket, then she put one foot up at a time on the chair across from L.C. and flipped each garter open. Turning her back on L.C., she unhooked the lace garter belt and slingshot it across the room. She strutted over to L.C. and did a roundhouse kick over the woman's head and straddled her, sitting on her lap.

Now that Sydney was this close, L.C. could see the detail in the sheer, black lingerie and the little satin bows over each nipple and on the crotch of the panties that held the fabric together. Sydney delicately took the end of the tiny bow on her right breast and pulled until it came undone and the fabric opened, unveiling an erect nipple. She raised a wicked eyebrow and looked into blue eyes. "You can get to all the good parts without me having to take anything else off," she purred, then pushed out her rounded breasts, inviting L.C. to undo the other bow.

"You know, I always suspected Laura had a little freak in her," L.C. said as she obliged.

Because Sydney was sitting on top of L.C.'s lap, her breasts were eye-level for her lover, and L.C. easily took a nipple into her mouth and sucked hard. Soon Sydney's back arched and her head fell back, causing her hat to tumble to the floor. She screwed up her face as though she were about to cry and whined, "Oh, Ro-o-b!" in an exact Laura Petrie voice, complete with the head bob that made her flip bounce back and forth. This dead-on impersonation was enough to momentarily quell the passionate mood, and L.C. had to laugh. But it passed quickly and she resumed kissing Sydney's firm breasts.

"Is that making you wet?" L.C. asked.

"Why don't you find out?" Sydney whispered, then leaned back until she was lying on the chair behind her. L.C. gently pulled the end of the bow on the panties until it opened. While she massaged the tiny pink rosebud inside, Sydney fondled her breasts herself, which got L.C. good and wet too.

After L.C. had satisfied Sydney, the blond moved the spare chair away and knelt between L.C.'s legs. "What now?" L.C. wondered aloud.

"Oh, honey," Sydney said with a look of pure lust as she wrapped her slender arms sensually around L.C.'s shoulders and neck, "I'm gonna make your eyes roll back and spin like a Las Vegas slot machine." Somehow L.C. knew she was never going to be able to eat dinner in those chairs again without a big smile breaking out on her face.

It was one day in late September when L.C. noticed Sydney sitting with pencil and paper at the piano, and she walked up to see what Sydney was doing. "Making some progress on those lyrics?" she said, taking a seat beside Sydney on the bench.

"No, I'm sketching out an idea for a costume to wear to Amy's Halloween Party." One of L.C.'s friends had come up with an idea for a costume party where the guests dressed as a character from their favorite movie. "It'll take weeks to get an elaborate dress made up, you know. Who are you going as?"

"Scarlett O'Hara," L.C. replied.

Sydney understood her choice, recalling the "M. Mitchell" connection. "And which fancy dress will Miss Scarlett be wearing?" she said in an over-the-top Southern accent.

"That fluffy white meringue of a dress with emerald green flowers and green velvet sash she wears to the barbecue at Twelve Oaks," L.C. replied, touching her hair as if primping her coif.

Sydney imagined L.C. dressed as the Southern belle. "In that dress, with your jet-black hair and a little red lipstick, you should make a great Scarlett O'Hara."

"It's the perfect character for me because frankly I couldn't give a damn if Rhett Butler ever came back." Sydney appreciated her sense of humor. "And I'm always looking for tomorrow, waiting for new adventures to unfold."

Sydney suddenly giggled. "I just realized this'll be the first time I've ever seen you in a dress."

"Yeah, well you'd better take a picture 'cause it'll be the last time too." The thought of being in a dress made L.C. cringe. "So who are you going as?"

"Audrey Hepburn in *How to Steal a Million*."

"Really?"

"Yeah. There's this one scene where she meets Peter O'Toole for a drink, and she has on this gorgeous black lace Givenchy cocktail dress with this ultrachic black lace mask. Can you imagine being in a social echelon where that was in vogue? And through the mask you can see she's wearing this heavy, silver glitter eye shadow. The whole ensemble is really a wild effect."

L.C. sat there, indulging Sydney's sweet enthusiasm.

"Oh—and in another scene she wore the most exquisite diamond earrings—she must have had a dozen half-carat diamonds dangling from each ear. Cartier did all the jewels for the movie, so you know they were grand. I guess I'll have to start shopping the stores for some cubic zirconia look-alikes since I don't feel like spending a quarter million for the real deal." Suddenly she cocked her head like a puppy when she realized something. "Although I suppose I *can* afford it now." She pictured herself at Cartier putting on her brilliant baubles for the first time, basking in the aura of their glittery glamour. "Nah," she said, coming down to reality, "too much of a splurge." Then something else dawned on her. "Oh, Lord! I'll have to find a hairdresser to give me an up-do, otherwise those fabulous earrings won't even show."

"I can't imagine you with your hair up," L.C. said, having seen her only with her long hair flowing down to her waist. Sydney grabbed all her hair and bundled it on top of her head to give L.C. a preview. Not bad, L.C. thought. She certainly had that long Audrey Hepburn neck to carry off a do like that. Suddenly that slender neck beckoned to L.C., and she kissed Sydney sensually up one side and down the other. Sydney dropped her pencil and sketchpad, and fell back into strong arms, just the way she had done that December day almost a year ago, the first time L.C. had touched her. Then L.C. stood up and scooped Sydney into her arms and headed toward the bedroom.

"Hey, wait a minute," Sydney said. "Scarlett was the one carried off, up the staircase that night—shouldn't I be carrying you off to bed?"

L.C. laughed at the thought of the tall, thin woman carrying a load like herself. "Yeah—like *that's* ever going to happen."

In the hours just before dawn, as the two lay bundled up in each other's arms under the covers, bodies relaxed and minds drifting after making love, Sydney caressed the face next to her and said sweetly, "This is the time I love best...when all the lights are out, and everyone's asleep... in the still of the night, when we snuggle under the sheets."

L.C. opened her eyes, smiled, and gave Sydney a snuggle hug. Then they both gazed at the round moon and it's watery reflection billowing on gentle ocean waves. "It's no one's moon but ours," Sydney said confidently. "The night was meant for us... This is the time I love the most, when all the noise, all the commotion, all the voices are silent and we've got the entire world to ourselves."

The lovers' lips met in a long, sweet kiss. L.C. rested her head on Sydney's shoulder and marveled at what beautiful thoughts this woman had, how even her everyday words sounded like songs. She closed her eyes and felt so lucky, not only to have someone to write love songs with, but someone to live them with.

At last Halloween arrived and it was time for the girls to play dress-up. Sydney had spent three hours at the hairdresser's and another hour applying her makeup with a special glitter eye shadow that had to set before she could open her eyes. Adding black false eyelashes gave her big green eyes an even more dramatic look.

She had just finished slipping into her black cocktail dress when she called out for L.C. to come zip her up. L.C. came in with her makeup all done, but she was still in her jeans and undershirt. Somehow the feminine emphasis with the makeup didn't work for L.C. "You are one of those lucky women who actually looks her best without a drop of makeup on," Sydney said jealously.

L.C. zipped up Sydney's dress. "You look pretty without makeup too."

"No, I don't—I look like a duck." Both women laughed.

"You do not," L.C. said.

Sydney turned around and faced her partner. "Are you going to stand there and tell me I don't look a million times better with this makeup on than I do barefaced?" She turned her head side to side, then turned on those wicked eyes.

"OK, you look pretty fantastic with your eyes done," L.C. admitted.

Sydney admired herself in the mirror. "Well, my look is complete. I'll wait until we get there to put on this mask." She picked up the lace mask and carefully slipped it into her purse. "You'd better get dressed, sweetie. It's almost time to go." She took one more look in the mirror to make sure everything was all right. "Oh!" she said, touching her ears, "My earrings! I almost forgot." She dug through the top drawer of her dresser where she kept them, but when she pulled out the box, it wasn't the one she had bought. This box was red with a gold emblem on the lid that she recognized immediately as Cartier.

Inside were a pair of earrings exactly like Audrey Hepburn's in *How to Steal a Million*, and these were real diamonds—Sydney could tell at a glance.

Two dozen fiery stones sparkled as she moved the box around to catch the light. Sydney stood with her mouth hanging open, dazzled by the beauties. Then it hit her how much these custom jewels must have cost. "Why did you do this?" she said, stunned.

"It's sort of an anniversary gift. We met about a year ago, remember?"

The time had gone by so quickly Sydney hadn't even realized. Her smile broadened. "This is so sweet," she said softly, her words full of emotion. "Guys don't do this," she went on. "I've never had anyone mark the anniversary of our first meeting with anything, let alone with something so..."

She gazed at the gems for a moment, searching for the word,

but she was too filled with emotion to think clearly. "Men only give flowers and gifts on birthdays and Valentine's Day when it's basically required, but never on their own, just because they want to say—" Suddenly she looked up at L.C. with teary eyes that also held a glint of hope.

L.C. began fidgeting immediately. "Aw, don't cry," she said, giving Sydney a shot in the arm in a palsy-walsy gesture. "You'll get all that beautiful glitter in your eyes."

Sydney hurried to the bathroom and grabbed a couple of tissues, holding one at the corner of each eye to soak up her tears before they ruined her elaborate makeup. L.C. hooked her thumbs in her front pockets and uncomfortably shifted her weight back and forth, watching Sydney deal with her tears.

When she returned, once again Sydney looked L.C. in the eye and waited for a response to her question. The dark-haired woman strummed her fingers on her thighs absentmindedly. "Well, I have to get dressed," she said, and walked away. But Sydney wasn't about to let things go and followed L.C. into her bedroom.

L.C. had taken off her jeans and was in her undershirt wrestling with the mounds of white-and-green chiffon she had already shimmied up to her waist when the figure in the doorway caught her eye.

"Why do you always run away just when we start talking about our feelings?" Sydney asked, looking hurt. "You do this all the time—you either walk out or you change the subject, which is just another way of running away. When you feel an emotion, don't run and hide from me," she pleaded.

L.C. plopped onto the bed amid a poof of chiffon, the bodice drooping over the full skirt. "I don't know." She looked down at the floor. "I just felt…awkward."

Sydney sat beside her. "But why? I'm not going to laugh at you or hurt you. I *want* you to open up and share your feelings with me. I know you play the aggressive, protective role with us, but you still have to have a feminine side that needs to share her feelings and be reassured in return." She took L.C.'s hand. "I wish you'd open up and let that happen."

The hand retracted and L.C. went back to wrestling with the dress. "Look, we're going to be late—I've got to finish getting dressed. We can talk about this later."

Somehow Sydney doubted that time would ever come.

Chapter Twelve

Christmas Day arrived, and the couple woke up just after sunrise with the enthusiasm of two kids who couldn't wait to open their presents. There wasn't an abundance of gifts around their tree—a dozen or so packages from close friends, but most were from each other. Gifts from business associates didn't go under the tree because those weren't really from the heart. They would be opened later.

L.C.'s special gift from Sydney was a ceramic sculpture about 10 inches high of a sitting dog with a goofy expression on its face. The piece was titled *Jackson Pollock Pup* and was created by a local artist. The two had seen it at an art gallery on one of their jaunts months ago, and every time they passed it, neither could help cracking up laughing. Sydney told L.C. that she had gotten it so she'd keep smiling, that any time she felt blue, all she had to do was look at this precious pup and she'd immediately be happy again.

Animals seemed to be the theme of the day because L.C. got Sydney a stuffed penguin with a knitted scarf around its neck they had seen at FAO Schwarz. Sydney had a collection of stuffed animals she'd been working on since she was a kid that was now in storage with all her furniture and belongings since her divorce, and she had mentioned how she missed having them to brighten up her room. This was L.C.'s small contribution to filling that void.

Soon the floor and furniture were covered with shreds of colorful paper and ribbons, until only one gift remained under the tree. It was a thin cylindrical package with Sydney's name on the tag. L.C. presented it to her with the proud shyness of a child bringing home a drawing done at school. Sydney popped open one end of the container and tapped out the contents: a piece of parchment rolled up and tied with a yellow ribbon. She anxiously unfurled the paper.

In her hands she held a sheet of handwritten music for a song titled "A Bed of Yellow Roses." As soon as Sydney saw the title, she knew what the song was about. It told of the golden flowers that had grown outside Sydney's bedroom window as a girl, but the lyrics had a double meaning that only the two of them would understand—they also described that night the couple had made love on a bed of yellow rose petals after L.C. had come home from being away for several days.

The words were lovely, and they described the scene with such passion and emotion, the love song nearly made Sydney cry. "This is beautiful," she said, taking L.C.'s hand. "Sing it for me, please?" she said as she sat down on the piano bench and scooted over to the edge to give L.C. room to play while she put her voice to those lovely words.

The melody was as simple as the lyrics, but there was something so charming about the composition. It was one of those sweet songs that possesses a timeless appeal. As Sydney listened to the ethereal voice floating on the air, she thought how strange it was that L.C. was able to say all these sweet things in written words but couldn't say them to her face. Perhaps she would bring up the subject again once the song was finished. For now, she was content with the love in L.C.'s voice and eyes...those blue eyes that always sparkled in a strangely familiar way. Where was it she had seen that beautiful, sparkling blue before?

Sydney became lost in L.C.'s eyes and found herself back in the days when she and her closest friends went canoeing on the Illinois River many years ago when its pale blue waters were pristine and so crystal clear one could see down to the pebbles and rocks on the bottom. When a warm breeze rustled the tall elms and oaks on its banks, sunlight filtered through and glistened on the surface of the rolling waters like tiny stars dancing about. That was what these blue eyes reminded her of.

As she drank in the gorgeous face of the woman sitting beside her, Sydney noticed so many familiar, comforting things...her grandmother's mouth and sculptured cheekbones she had touched countless times as a child while sitting on her lap while being read a bedtime story...the infectious smile that made tiny eyes squint up until they almost closed, like on the face of her best friend from school, the one who had lived around the block with whom she spent nearly every waking moment as a teenager at slumber parties and cheering together at football games...the fleshy upper arms of her Aunt Sophie, who used to hug her so hard she couldn't breathe whenever she came to visit, always bearing gifts of frilly party dresses from Neiman-Marcus, and at Christmas, the world's best homemade fruitcake...the strong hands of Mrs. Taylor who had lived next door, that were always callused, their short nails always dirty from tending to her flower garden; the woman who had babysat her nearly every weekend as a girl, driven her to gymnastics practice and dance lessons, the one who had been more of a mother to her than her own. It was then Sydney realized L.C. was all the women she had loved in her life.

Having heard the song played through only once, the words and music were already etched in Sydney's memory. She knew right then this was destined to be one of those songs people would be singing years from now. "This is absolutely the most beautiful song you've ever written," she said, giving L.C. a kiss on the cheek.

"I was hoping you'd like it. I want to make it the title song on the new album." The news took Sydney by surprise. "I can't think of a better one for it," L.C. said.

Sydney forgot about pressing L.C. to say those three little words to her. She wasn't about to spoil this marvelous moment, so she kept it to herself and reveled in the warm, wonderful feelings this very special Christmas gift had given her.

After lunch, they put on warm clothes and prepared to take a walk on the beach since it was a sunny December day. But as they were going out the back door, the phone rang and L.C. went back in to take the call.

Ten minutes later when she stepped out on the deck, she saw Sydney standing at the surf's edge next to giant letters made of footprints in the wet sand that spelled out I LOVE YOU. As she approached, she heard Sydney singing an old Pat Boone song, "Love Letters in the Sand." Sydney's face beamed. "My gift of a song for you," she said, taking L.C. by both hands and dancing her around in circles while serenading her.

Then the two stood, wrapped in each other's arms, watching the tide come in and go out, each time erasing more and more of the beautiful love letter, prompting the two to sing the final verse, about the heartache of watching each wave breaking over the beautiful love letter in the sand.

"This is so sweet," L.C. said, then unashamedly kissed Sydney out in the open.

Many nights found the lovers either sitting out on the balcony or walking on the beach singing old songs with beautiful harmonies, ones where the music didn't get in the way of the vocals, unlike the crap Veronica always had blasting that L.C. couldn't stand. Songs by the Everly Brothers, the Beach Boys, Simon and Garfunkel, Crosby, Stills, Nash and Young filled their nights.

Their joy of singing with each other spilled over into one of L.C.'s recording sessions one day in February when she was putting the finishing touches on the long-awaited album. All the big brass from the record company were in the booth with Rick during the session, celebrating the completion of another project by an A-list artist.

The womenfolk—L.C., Sydney, and the three backup gals—stayed in the studio avoiding the suits, kidding around with one another. Spontaneously, L.C. and Sydney broke into song with "A Bed of Yellow Roses," which L.C. had just finished recording, because it was such an infectious tune.

Rick had left the studio microphones on so he could talk with L.C., and when the stirring voices came through, the conversation in the booth came to a quick halt. They all listened silently for a while, then one of them directed Rick to start the recorder again quickly, which he did.

After the duo finished, Rick rolled back the tape. L.C. had just entered the booth on her way to the restroom, and the suits complimented her profusely on the song and the impromptu duet. She thanked them for their remarks about her work, then excused herself, saying she was on her way to the ladies room and needed to get there quick.

As soon as the door closed behind her, Rick started the playback, and it blew them all away—clear, strong voices beautifully meshed in tight harmony. Suddenly all the suits seemed to have the same brainstorm. "We need to rerecord that song as a duet," said the young one with glasses, as though he'd just gotten a sure tip on the stock market and wasn't about to let it get away. "I agree," said the one in the Polo shirt and jeans whose loafers were kicked up, intruding on Rick's console.

"I know!" said the bespectacled one. "we can release it as a single and have Sydney go out on tour with them and make it the encore number in the concert. People will go nuts, seeing the two lovers performing together, live and in person. Think of all the publicity the tour will get." Again the higher-ups agreed vigorously.

Rick's jaw dropped. The thought of having to kowtow to Sydney as a signed artist and deal with her on a regular basis made him cringe. It was bad enough he had to put up with L.C. and her temperamental ways, but the two of them ganged up on him? His life would be hell. He tried to persuade them that L.C. was strictly a solo act and to suggest adding Sydney to the bill would insult her, possibly enough to make her jump ship again. But they didn't buy it.

The execs rushed into the studio and announced their suggestion with great enthusiasm to Sydney, promoting their genius idea with grand words and gestures. The four women in the room were too shocked to speak. Attentions turned to the tall blond, whose face registered a smile of stunned flattery, and Mr. Polo Shirt walked over and put his arm around her shoulders while he continued his spiel.

Carol Ann and Rick looked at each other through the glass window, knowing exactly what the other was thinking: *Veronica—The Sequel.* Then something hit Rick.

He went into the studio and sidled over to Carol Ann. "Wow, L.C. is really going to be stunned when she hears this," he said.

"Stunned is not the word," Carol Ann replied, shaking her head. "Man! Can you believe this? What a coincidence."

Rick cocked an eyebrow. "Are you sure it's just a coincidence?" Carol Ann wasn't sure what he meant. A diabolical smile crept across Rick's face as he took her aside and began planting the seeds.

As soon as L.C. returned, Carol Ann made a beeline to her, corralled her at the door, and dropped the bomb.

"I can't fuckin' believe this is happening to me again!" L.C. said, falling back against the wall with limp arms, as though she'd had the wind knocked out of her.

"Why not? I mean, what do you really know about Sydney?" Carol Ann said, eyes narrowed with suspicion. "Where does she come from? What did she do before she wrote her book? That only took up the last two years of her life—what did she do before that?"

L.C. tried to remember. "She said something about working at a newspaper in Texas once."

"Well, how do you know she's telling the truth?" she said. "Has anyone ever seen any evidence of her past life?"

L.C. was starting to get the picture being painted for her. "Now that you mention it, she said all her things are in storage in Texas—she got divorced right before she went on that book tour and had to move her things out of their house before she left."

"Have you ever checked up on her story to see if it pans out?"

"Of course not!" L.C. said with great offense.

"Well, you said that she said she knew Sting, but he didn't remember her at all. And she says she has pictures, but they're in storage in another state. How convenient," she said with intense sarcasm. "And you never thought that story suspicious? They just *happened* to be at the same hotel...yeah...coincidence. What if she was some big-time wanna-be singer when she was younger who tried to latch on to some rock star's coattails? Maybe she knew he was going to be on tour and went to Cairo hoping to meet him." She paused, giving L.C. time to soak it all in.

"Maybe she targeted you too," she said, getting closer. "Look at how she's slowly wheedled herself into your career. What was she doing the first time you laid eyes on her? Singing. And she sang that song with you at last year's Christmas show. And today—she knew the microphone was open and the suits would hear her. That's an awful lot of singing for a writer, don't you think? Maybe this is the career she always wanted but never got the chance at. And don't say it's impossible because Veronica did the same damn thing, remember?"

Wheels turned in L.C.'s head, churning out suspicions. Now that she thought about it, there were several things Sydney had claimed that she had no evidence to back up. But they were all harmless...weren't they?

"A few phone calls is all it would take," Carol Ann uttered, tempting her friend.

L.C. shook her head in disbelief. "I gotta get outta here," she said. She looked at the men crowded around Sydney who were still rambling on. "Shit. Sydney's got the car keys in her purse—will you take me home?"

"Sure," Carol Ann said, putting an arm around L.C.

The two left without anyone noticing.

As soon as L.C. got home, she pulled Sydney's book off the shelf and scanned over the biographical information on the back cover for the name of the newspaper she'd worked at. Then she called information and got the number.

"Yes, I'm trying to verify a previous employment of a job applicant—can you tell me if you had a Sydney Sanders working at your paper?"

"What employment dates, please?"

Crap. L.C. didn't know how long she'd worked there, just that she had supposedly quit around two years ago. "I can't read the start date on the application, but it would have ended about two years ago."

"And the last name was Sanders?"

"Yes."

"One moment please."

L.C. bit her fingernails while she waited.

"I'm sorry, we have no one by that name in our records."

Her heart sank. "Are you sure?"

"Yes, ma'am. I searched back over the last 10 years."

L.C. let out a sigh. "All right, thank you."

Slowly she put the receiver back on the phone. That lying little bitch. She buried her face in her hands. Jesus—this couldn't be happening again! She felt the walls close up around her heart and braced herself for the confrontation that she knew would come shortly.

When L.C. heard the key in the door, her heart started pounding and her hands went cold and clammy. Sydney bore a look of puzzlement at seeing her there on the couch. "Why'd you run off without a word?" she said, sounding hurt and a little pissed. Then she saw the copy of her book and the phone on the coffee table. "What's going on?"

L.C. stuck her chin out defiantly. "I called the paper where you said you worked, and they told me a Sydney Sanders never worked there." Her tone was definitely accusatory, and Sydney was stunned.

"You called to check up on me?" she said. "Why?"

"Well, it just seemed a little funny that you go from a Pulitzer Prize–winning writer to a songwriter and recording artist at warp speed. Career changes like that don't happen by accident. It took me *six years* of struggling to get a record deal."

Sydney didn't speak; she only glared at L.C. as she digested all the suspicions Carol Ann had conjured up.

"I'm wondering if I wasn't just the next one on your list to use to get what you really want."

That did it. It took a lot to get Sydney furious, but that did it. "And just what is it you think I really want?" she said, with restrained anger.

"What you just got! A recording deal and a tour, all in the blink of an eye."

The volcano exploded. "I never pursued a record deal or a tour! *They're* the ones who came up with that idea, not me!"

"Yeah, and I'll bet you jumped on it too, huh?"

Sydney grabbed the phone off the table and threw it hard on the couch, just missing L.C., making her flinch. "Since you're so good at checking up on things, why don't you call the studio and ask what I said to their offer?"

L.C.'s tone suddenly softened, feeling like she might have crossed the line. "Well, why don't you just tell me?"

"Because you wouldn't believe me, obviously," Sydney shouted, hands in the air. "I can't believe you think I'm a liar and a schemer." She sat in a chair on the other side of the room, arms folded, looking completely dazed. "That means you must think that everything I've said and done since we met has been nothing but an act." No response. Now her walls were going up too. "You have no idea how deeply that hurts me."

Sydney stormed over and picked up her purse and keys. "While you're doing your telephoning, call the newspaper back and ask them if a Sydney Robertson ever worked there. That was my name when I started working there before I married my second husband. I didn't change my last name until after I quit because everyone in the newspaper community already knew me as Robertson." She flashed a sarcastic smile. "But thank you *so much* for just automatically assuming I'm a conniving liar."

L.C. felt like a fool now. The name change—that was something she and her friends had never dealt with, so it hadn't occurred to her. Before she knew it, Sydney was almost to the front door. "Wait," she shouted, then ran after her. "Where are you going?"

"Oh, *you* can take off without telling me where you're going, but I can't? Bullshit!" She turned and took a few steps, but L.C. grabbed her by the arm and stopped her.

"I'm sorry! Please don't leave," L.C. begged. "I know Carol Ann was wrong now."

Sydney's eyes blazed. "What does Carol Ann have to do with this?"

After L.C. explained things to her, Sydney was furious. She glared at L.C. with hate and anger smoldering in her eyes. "Look, remember how I told you I lost my best friend once by spouting off when I was pissed? Well, I need to *not* be around you right now, otherwise that's going to happen again. I know how to handle my anger, and I need to just go and drive it off and stay away from you until it's gone."

"Well—how long will that take?" L.C. whimpered.

"Well, let's see… I've just been accused of being a scheming liar and a user by the person I love and who I thought loved me, so—" A horrible thought hit her, and her shoulders slumped. "No wonder you never said it—you never felt it, did you? How could you love someone you never trusted?"

L.C. wanted desperately to tell Sydney she was wrong, but she couldn't think, she couldn't move, she had completely lost control of her world.

"I guess you just kept me around for a great piece of ass, huh? How typically male, you fucking bastard." At this point Sydney didn't care whether the comparison hurt L.C. or not. Then she held her hands up like a traffic cop. "OK, see, I'm already starting to lay into you, and I've got to leave *now* for your own good," she said, then stormed out.

"Don't leave," L.C. pleaded, but Sydney slammed the door in her face. Tears came pouring down her cheeks. God, what had she done? She ran to the phone and called her record company to find out what had happened after she left.

"She turned us down," said Steve Barboza, the one in the Polo shirt and jeans. "She was a real class act," he added. "She thanked us for the offer, then said politely but firmly that there was no way she was going to ride on your coattails into a singing career—something about that being your world and she wasn't going to trespass out of respect for you and your relationship."

L.C. wiped her eyes on her shirtsleeve, then put a hand over her mouth so the man at the other end of the line wouldn't hear her crying.

"Then she said too much togetherness for you two wouldn't be good and it might end up being a competition, which she didn't want. Plus she felt she didn't have the voice to make a real career out of singing." A tear fell from L.C.'s eye as her head hung, slowly shaking back and forth.

"And then she said something I thought was so great," Steve added. "She said writing is her gift and singing is yours, and she was perfectly content making beautiful music together with you at home but never on a stage for money, that it was a private and personal thing."

L.C. cleared her throat and thanked Steve for his time. As she hung up, she felt physically ill and gagged, her stomach now tied up in knots. How could she have doubted Sydney and their relationship? Carol Ann—that's how. Damn that bitch! She had despised Sydney from day one and was always causing trouble whenever they were under the same roof.

She phoned Carol Ann to ream her out then fire the bitch, but apparently her so-called friend hadn't gotten home yet and the answering machine picked up. L.C. slammed down the phone.

But she had so much anger and frustration built up that she had to vent it to someone, so she called Mandy. While the phone was ringing, L.C. suddenly grew short of breath and her heart began pounding faster and faster in her chest, quickly doubling its normal rate. Her face was burning up but her hands were ice cold. The phone dropped from her shaking hand because she no longer had the strength to hold on to it, then she doubled over on the couch. What was happening?

She heard Mandy speaking into the phone and reached a shaky hand out and picked it up. "Oh, God," she said, her voice almost a whisper because she was so weakened and out of breath.

"L.C.?" came Mandy's frightened voice.

"I think I'm having a heart attack," the woman gasped. "My heart's pounding 90 miles and hour and it won't stop."

"What? Are you serious?" Mandy said, sounding scared to death. "OK, now stay calm—just sit down and hang up. I'm going to call 911. I'm leaving the house right now."

Mandy made the 45-minute drive in 30, and came screeching up just as the paramedics were packing up to leave. "Is she all right?" she asked frantically.

"She's fine. Panic attack."

Mandy drooped like a rag doll. "Oh, thank God! The way she sounded on the phone I feared the worst."

"Yeah, we know, people mistake it for a heart attack all the time."

"What a relief," she said, then ran toward the house.

"Oh, Miss Gilbert?" said one of the attendants, causing her to stop and turn. "I'm a real fan of yours—could I have an autograph?"

The entertainer gave him a *Not now, you idiot* look, then ran into the house.

She found L.C. lying on the couch wrapped up in a blanket,

shivering. L.C. burst into tears when she saw the familiar face. Mandy sat beside her and took her cold hand, rubbing it fondly. "Hey, you're OK," she said with a smile, giving her friend a hug. "It's a lousy old panic attack—people have those all the time."

"I know, but it still feels like I'm dying. I hate this feeling and it won't go away. Just when I start to calm down, I think about Sydney and I don't know where she is or if she's ever coming home, and I want her here but she's not, and I feel so completely helpless—" She stopped, grasping at her chest.

Mandy watched L.C.'s face go stark white. She checked the pulse on the hand she held. One forty-six. This concerned her. "Honey, you have got to get a grip and calm down. Did they give you a sedative or anything?"

"No, they're not allowed to."

"Do you have anything in the house?"

"Just cold medicine."

Mandy dug through her purse and pulled out an orange prescription bottle. "Here, take one of these." She poured out one of the little pills. "It's a five-milligram Valium. It won't knock you out but it'll sure calm you down, and that's what you need." She held out the pill, but as L.C. reached for it she jerked her hand back. "You haven't been drinking today, have you?"

"No."

"Good," she said, giving her the pill. "These can really be dangerous if you take them with alcohol."

After L.C. took the pill, Mandy sat down next to her. "OK, now tell me what happened."

Mandy spent the next several hours trying to reach Sydney on her cell phone but had no luck. She tried calling the author's agent on the chance she may have checked in and mentioned her whereabouts, but that didn't pan out either.

Around 7 o'clock she made L.C. a sandwich and soup, but halfway through the sandwich it all came up again. When the first Valium started wearing off she gave L.C. another, and that finally put her to sleep. Mandy got a blanket and curled up on the fainting couch in L.C.'s room and slept over that night to keep an eye on her friend.

At 11:15 the following morning, Mandy finally got Sydney on her phone. "Where the hell have you been?" she shouted from the deck.

"Who is this?"

"It's Mandy! Where *are* you?"

"I'm at the Beverly Hills...why?"

"Because I spent last night at your house taking care of L.C. after I had to call the paramedics."

Mandy recounted the events of the previous night. "Her eyes were so puffy this morning from crying nonstop that she could barely open them. She's pale as a ghost, Sydney, and she hasn't eaten all day. She's suffering."

"Mandy, I had no idea she would react this way."

"Look, I don't want to scare you or anything," Mandy said, "but I had a friend who went into a deep blue funk over a breakup just like this, and she ended up in the hospital with an IV stuck in her arm and being force-fed for weeks. I don't want that happening to L.C.," she said angrily, "so get your butt home."

"I'm on my way—I'll be there as soon as possible. Stay with her until I get there, will you?"

"You didn't even have to ask."

Chapter Thirteen

Sydney came in carrying two sacks from Wendy's and saw L.C. lying on the couch in the midst of a graveyard of Kleenex. The ailing woman immediately came to life and sat up when she saw the tall figure standing in the room, smiling. "I hear you've been feeling kinda puny," Sydney said, trying to take the seriousness off the situation.

L.C. burst into tears again, and Mandy looked at Sydney as if to say, "See, this is the way she's been all night long." Sydney sat beside L.C. and hugged her tight. "Stop crying, sugarplum," she told her. "I'm back, and I'm not leaving again. It's over."

But the floodgates had been open too long, and L.C. cried even harder. Mandy got Sydney's attention and waved goodbye, leaving the two lovers to make up.

"Hey," Sydney said softly, kissing L.C. on the neck. "What's this? You cry when I leave, then you cry when I come back?" She laughed a little, hoping it would become contagious, but L.C. only blew her nose again.

"I didn't know if you were ever coming back," she bawled.

"Honey, I thought I made it clear that I was just getting away to blow off some steam. How could you think I was leaving for good? I didn't pack my clothes or anything—hell, I had to buy a souvenir T-shirt and a toothbrush at the gift shop last night. Why on earth did you think I wasn't coming back?"

While the two talked, Sydney casually spread out the hamburgers and chocolate malts on the coffee table as though it were just another lunch. She handed one of the malts to L.C., who shook her head at first. "I'm not hungry," she said, but Sydney held the straw to her mouth and coaxed her into taking a drink. L.C. frowned. "I really don't want this."

"I know, baby, but you have to eat. That's one reason your heart rate won't go down and you can't sleep well. If your body doesn't get enough fuel, it can't make those chemicals that make you sleepy. The human body needs food in order to function normally, and you've missed, like, three meals already." She put the drink into L.C.'s hands then picked up the other malt and drank from it herself. "Come on," she said. "Drink up. Your appetite will come back before you know it."

L.C. followed directions. "Are you still pissed at me?" she said shyly.

"I'm not angry anymore, but I'm still very hurt."

"Then why did you come back?"

Sydney ran her fingers affectionately through L.C.'s hair, neatening her short locks. "Because this is what families do…they take care of each other." L.C.'s eyes filled with tears again. "Sometimes what's best for someone else takes priority over what's best for yourself." Now the tears rolled down L.C.'s face, and Sydney got another tissue and dabbed at L.C.'s red eyes. "I came back because I love you," she said.

L.C.'s mouth opened as if trying to speak, but she burst into tears again and buried her face in Sydney's shoulder. Sydney shook her head. "You just can't say it, can you?" she said pitifully. "Why?"

"I don't know," she cried.

"Yes you do. You have to know. It's your life—you've lived it, you know everything that's happened to you. It's in there somewhere. Tell me what happened to make you bottle up your feelings this way."

"I don't know!" she shouted.

"Yes, you do," Sydney shouted back. "You just don't want to tell me for some reason. Why won't you tell me?"

L.C. struggled to get the words out. "Because I'm afraid," she finally said.

Sydney looked perplexed. "Of what, honey?"

L.C. lost it again, and Sydney was afraid she was about to have another attack, so she let it go, wrapping her arms around L.C. to let her cry it out. She noticed the painfully swollen eyelids from all the crying and decided not to push any further. "Sweet baby," she cooed, "I'm so sorry for putting you through this…I had no idea you were suffering last night." She kissed L.C. on the cheek. "I promise you that if we ever argue again, I won't leave. I'll just go off to my room until Mr. Hyde turns back into Dr. Jekyll…but I won't leave you. Never again."

"I'm so sorry for what I did," L.C. said, her voice cracking.

"Don't say that. That was what I hated about the romantic relationships I've had all my life—guys constantly saying 'I'm sorry' for their bad behavior, yet they never learned to stop doing those things. They never got to the point where they'd think first."

She took L.C.'s hand. "I just want you to realize," she went on, "that every time you say or do something like what happened yesterday, you chip away at the foundation of our relationship. And even though we end up forgiving, it's always there—you can't undo what's been said and done. And over the years, if you get enough chips in that foundation, it becomes damaged beyond repair. Remember that the next time you start to say something hurtful and maybe you'll decide not to say it at all."

Sydney didn't require a response, and she turned on the television as a distraction, then handed L.C. a hamburger hoping she'd unconsciously start eating. Eventually she did.

After L.C. had finished every bite of her food, Sydney got a cold washcloth and put it over the puffy red eyes to soothe them while L.C. lay stretched out on the couch, her head in Sydney's lap. While Sydney stroked L.C.'s soft hair, she reminisced about the different relationships she'd had with females in her life. "You know, I was just thinking about the girls I've known for decades, since grade school...over the years we've argued and said horrible things to each other. We'd get mad for a few days, and then it passed. Somewhere inside us we knew there was this connection that would allow our friendships to survive all that garbage.

"And they have survived. I've had a handful of girlfriends for over 30 years now, and no matter how long we go between calling or visiting, it's always like it was just yesterday when we last saw each other." She gazed down at the pretty face in her lap. "I guess I just expected you to know that we're going to be together forever the way I do."

L.C. moved the cloth and looked up into Sydney's eyes. "I really hope we are together forever," she said. "I don't know what I'd do if I didn't have you in my life. I wouldn't want to go on living without you, that much I do know."

Sydney smiled lovingly, then put the cool cloth back on L.C.'s eyes and stroked her hair gently until she fell asleep.

The next day Carol Ann called, having heard about L.C. from Mandy. Sydney asked if she could take a message, saying L.C. was still too stressed out and needed to rest, and Carol Ann said to relay her apologies. But after they hung up, knowing it was Carol Ann and her meddling that had caused all this turmoil in the first place, Sydney decided not to mention the call at all.

A few days later, however, Carol Ann stopped by to see how L.C. was doing since she hadn't heard back from her. When L.C. said she hadn't known about the call, Carol Ann shot Sydney a vicious look. Sydney just shrugged and said it must have slipped her mind amid all the chaos, which she strongly suggested had been caused by Carol Ann, who immediately blamed the situation on Rick. Carol Ann confessed how he had influenced her suspicions, but Sydney didn't care. She hoped L.C. would chime in and lay into the bitch, but Carol Ann started crying and begged for forgiveness, saying she was just watching out for her cherished compadre. Sydney almost puked when L.C. hugged the woman.

Finally, L.C. walked Carol Ann to the door. After what seemed like a long time, Sydney went to see what was taking her so long and rounded the corner just in time to see Carol Ann kiss L.C.—on the lips—before she went out the door.

"What was that?" she asked angrily. L.C. didn't know what she meant. "That kiss," Sydney stated firmly.

"Just a goodbye kiss between two old friends. Haven't you ever kissed a girlfriend or a relative goodbye?"

"Sure…on the *cheek*! Kisses on the lips are for lovers."

L.C. laughed. "Well, apparently not, because she and I have never been and never will be lovers."

Sydney folded her arms. "Are you sure?" she said, her voice full of suspicion.

L.C. didn't know what the big deal was. "It was just a kiss—she was really upset by all this and she was a bit emotional. Give her a break."

Sydney's mouth fell open. "Give *her* a break? She caused all this! She's been nothing but a troublemaker from the start. She almost broke us up and nearly put you in the hospital, remember? No, I won't give her a break."

L.C. put her arms around Sydney's waist and pulled her close, then kissed her passionately on the neck. "I like you when you're a little jealous. Your nostrils flare out in this really sexy way when you get torqued up." She kissed Sydney again, then started fondling her breasts.

"Are you sure you're up for this so soon?" Sydney asked.

After L.C. assured Sydney she didn't have to worry about her keeling over during sex, the two adjourned to the bedroom and spent the afternoon making love.

While Sydney napped, L.C. went down to see Barboza and demanded that he hook her up with a new producer, which shocked him. She explained how Rick had used Carol Ann as his minion, and said that once someone had betrayed her, that person was out of her life. Barboza didn't want anything stifling her creativity, and if that meant dumping the guy from the project, so be it. Rick was out.

The release of L.C.'s new album in March was accompanied by the usual string of appearances on talk shows and radio stations to get the word out about her upcoming tour. Word of mouth quickly spread that this was one of the best albums released so far that year, and the Grammy buzz had already begun, which delighted the executives at her label and her new producer, Gordon Cavanaugh.

Most of L.C.'s concerts sold out on the first day of ticket sales, both for the U.S. dates and the foreign portion of the tour, which was set to kick off in Rio in mid September, giving everyone a two-month rest after the U.S. tour finished on July 4 in New York. Promoters had wanted her to schedule concerts right up until the end of the year, but L.C. insisted on ending in mid December with a big welcome-home concert in L.A. This way she'd be rested for the holidays with Sydney, who would only accompany her on the U.S. part of the tour in the spring, as she had a year-end deadline with her publisher for the first draft of her next novel and had completed only an outline at this point.

Having done the tour thing a million times, L.C. knew it would be a grueling year and tried to ease Sydney into the rigors once they embarked on the U.S. leg. Sydney started out excited about the adventure because she was getting a first-hand, behind-the-scenes look at a rock star on tour. But by her sixth week on the road, the adventure had deteriorated into a camping trip from hell.

Some people had grown too tired to bathe on a regular basis, and no one got good sleep on the buses, even though the custom vehicles had been outfitted with plush, queen-size beds. The occasional nights at hotels weren't any better. All that plus too much fast food and Carol Ann—ever the thorn in her side—all compounded Sydney's misery.

It was at that point she realized everybody on the tour had a job to do except her. And yet L.C.'s label had shelled out hundreds of thousands of dollars for the tour buses because L.C. told them Sydney didn't like to fly, and they covered her expenses at first-class hotels and restaurants. She finally deduced that her job on this excursion was to provide sex for the star—to keep the talent happy and satisfied. She had begun to feel like the world's most expensive whore.

After eight weeks on the road, Sydney became concerned about the changes she'd noticed in L.C. Almost every night for the last two months, the woman had put herself center stage for 90 minutes, making love to an audience. Night after night she opened her heart and soul, giving her emotions through her words and music. Afterward the audience went home happy and satisfied, but L.C. was left spent, weary, and alone. By the time she crawled into bed with Sydney, it was impossible for her to get worked up to that same emotional and physical high, so they both were left unsatisfied and empty, and feeling neglected. It seemed to Sydney that L.C. had grown unappreciative and unresponsive to her presence and support. She hadn't been prepared for this.

A constant string of technical problems also occurred along the way, which only added to the ever-increasing stress level on the tour: electrical outages, microphones going dead in the middle of a song, screeching feedback, local union problems resulting in equipment not being set up properly. All the aggravation had turned L.C. into an exposed nerve.

During week 10, the concert in Detroit had to be canceled because of a freak storm that dumped 12 inches of snow on the state, which meant everyone had to spend an unscheduled extra night in Philadelphia. L.C. decided that since she finally had a free night, she was going to take a break and let someone else do the entertaining for a change.

The entire entourage ended up at a downtown bar on Market Street but split into factions as soon as they arrived. It seemed everyone wanted a break from each other for the night—including L.C. She had wandered off early into the evening, and Sydney figured the exhausted singer just wanted some space, and decided to let her have it.

About an hour after L.C. had disappeared, Sydney was on her way to the ladies room when she passed by the bar, where she saw her lover sitting, talking with a pretty brunette who had her hand on the singer's thigh. Space was one thing, but this was definitely over the limit. Sydney quietly approached the two, hoping to pick up a tidbit of their conversation, but the drone of the crowd drowned out any hope of that. But the way that hand moved on L.C.'s leg said plenty. Sydney walked up beside L.C. and smiled sarcastically. "Aren't you going to introduce me to your new friend?"

L.C.'s demeanor changed immediately—she knew she'd been busted, and she reluctantly said, "This is Sydney."

"Oh, are you part of the tour too?" the young, smiling face asked.

Sydney turned to L.C. to let her answer that question. "We live together," L.C. said.

The girl's hand moved away from L.C. thigh. "Oh! I'm sorry," she said to Sydney as she got up to leave, "I didn't know."

Sydney watched L.C.'s face the whole time this exchange went on, searching for clues to her feelings, and damned if L.C. didn't check out the girl's ass as she walked away. Right in front of her!

Sydney scooted into the empty seat. "You know, I'm reminded of the parable about the frog that comes across a scorpion at the edge of a river. The scorpion says he needs to get across to the other side, but he can't swim. So the frog tells the scorpion to climb onto his back and he'll swim them both across. But halfway there, the scorpion stings the frog. The frog says, 'Why'd you sting me? You know we're both going to drown now,' and the scorpion says, 'I can't help myself—it's my nature.'" Again she watched her lover's face until she knew the message had registered. "You're just going to take us both down, aren't you?"

L.C. shook her head hopelessly. "What are you so bent out of shape about—just because a fan comes up and talks to me?"

"Oh, please! She was doing more than talking—she was rubbing your thigh the whole time. And you just ate it up. Anyone could see by the look on your face that you were loving it. You just can't resist someone feeding your ego, can you? It feels too damn good to say no, doesn't it?"

"You're making way too big a deal out of this."

Sydney rolled her eyes in disgust. "It's having intimate physical contact with another person, which is inappropriate for you to be doing with anyone but me. And you just let her do it in front of all our friends—people who know that you and I are involved. That's humiliating, and it hurts. It's a slap in my face." She detected no indication of remorse in L.C., who seemed more concerned that her beer was almost empty. "You don't have the slightest idea what I'm feeling, do you?"

"No, I don't," L.C. said casually.

"You, with your songwriting talents and ability to capture emotions, don't have the imagination to put yourself in my place and feel what I'm feeling right now?"

She gave a cavalier shrug. "Guess not."

Sydney was crushed. When she was hurt, her pain either came out as tears or anger, but tonight she didn't feel like crying in public. "Well, let me help you," she growled, then hauled off and slapped L.C. hard across the face.

The singer was in complete shock, as were the people nearby who had witnessed the action. Now Sydney's face registered no sympathy for her lover either. "Don't look so surprised," she said with restrained anger. "If you're going to behave like a cad, you're going to be treated like a cad." Again L.C. said nothing; she simply sat and seethed, having noticed the spectators around them.

"Oh, yeah. Now you know, don't you?" Sydney went on. "It's humiliating, it's embarrassing, and it hurts." L.C. glared at Sydney. "Don't give me that look like *I'm* the problem here," Sydney said. "You created this whole mess, and *don't you dare* try to twist things to make it look like *I'm* the one at fault here."

A couple of on onlookers snickered at the lovers' quarrel. "Could we discuss this later?" L.C. said quietly, hiding her face. "People are starting to stare."

"I thought you wanted people to know how I felt about you, my little rosebud," the blond shot back. L.C. didn't find the retort funny. Sydney stood up and tucked her purse under her arm. "You want to fuck somebody besides me? Fine. Go fuck yourself!" she said, then stormed off to get a cab back to the hotel.

Hours later L.C. dragged herself into their hotel room, drunk and surly. Sydney was ensconced in a chair with a blanket over her, obviously waiting up for L.C. "Well, if it isn't Belle Watling finally come home from a hard night's work."

L.C. scowled. That was low. She knew Sydney well enough to know the reference to the whore from her favorite novel had been deliberate. "Gee, thanks for waiting up, Mom," L.C. spat back.

Sydney waited to speak until L.C. sat down.

"Are you trying to end this relationship?" she asked. L.C. rolled her eyes. "It's not a ridiculous question. You knew I could see you, you knew it was wrong. Why'd you do it?" L.C.'s defiant expression indicated she had no intention of answering. "Fine. If you won't talk, I will. I've spent the last several hours doing some serious thinking about why you're trying to screw things between us."

"And what did you come up with, Siggy?" she retorted.

"You know, you're old enough to know better by this point in your life. You're almost 40 years old, and what's the longest relationship you've had—not quite two years, isn't it? That doesn't even qualify as long-term. That's less than half the time the average marriage lasts in this country. You can't even compete with a sorry statistic like that." Her head shook pitifully. "Let me guess," she continued. You always had your girlfriends move in with you, right?"

L.C. sat up a little, wondering where Sydney was heading with this inquisition. "Yeah," she said suspiciously, "because I had the nicer house."

Sydney smiled knowingly. "Of course. Well, have you ever

been involved with anyone as famous or as wealthy as you, someone who might have a nicer lifestyle than yours?"

"No."

"Of course."

"So what?" she said defensively. "All that means is I had the nicer house. Big fuckin' deal."

"No. It means money and fame are power, and you want all the control, so you make sure you've got more of those things than your partner. Then when commitment starts closing in, you find some way to start an argument or piss her off so she'll leave. But you're really the one ending it—you just do it in a roundabout way that makes you look like the poor suffering one.

"But you don't suffer at all. *She's* the one suddenly without a roof over her head. *She's* the one thrown into turmoil without a home after being spat out like garbage into the streets. But your calm little lake hardly suffers a ripple. As long as you and a lover are living in *your* house, it skews the power structure of the relationship. And that's not fair because it will always be your house and she'll always be the guest...that is, for as long as you permit it. Now I understand why Veronica tweaked you so much. It wasn't because she hurt your feelings, it was because she was the first woman who beat you to the punch."

L.C. was furious. "And just how did you come up with this cock-and-bull theory?"

"Easy. You're textbook. Fear of rejection. I've known so many guys who do the exact same thing with their relationships. Instead of facing their fears and dealing with them and growing into a mature human being, they run from them. You're doing the same thing."

"Well," L.C. said indignantly, putting her feet up on the coffee table, "I hate to brag, but I've never been rejected by *anyone* I wanted to go out with." Then she watched her feet rock back and forth as if that were more interesting than their conversation.

Since L.C. liked people to be blunt, Sydney decided to make things a little more clear. "You're a coward," she said coldly. She now had L.C.'s undivided attention. "And until you're willing to work through those fears and bad relationship habits you've developed over the last 20 years, you're never going to have a successful permanent relationship. You need to grow up."

That blew the lid off. "If you're trying to get me to put your name on the house, I'm not going to do it. I worked hard to pay for that house, and I'm not going to end up losing half of it if we break up."

Sydney laughed. "Have you been listening to Carol Ann again?"

"No, I'm just remembering what you said the first time you saw it—you said it was the house you'd always dreamed of."

"That is such a typical response for you," Sydney said. "Instead of discussing this with me, you try to divert the blame off you and onto me. Well, I'm not falling for it. I don't want half of your house. I don't even want to pay you for half of it and be a joint owner, which I could easily afford—not that that would ever occur to you. I'm not trying to take anything from you, and you know it. And that's not even the real motivation behind your behavior. It's not a material conflict, it's an emotional one. Why are you so afraid to open up and really love someone?" She knew there would be no response to that question. "Or is it that you can't really love someone else unless you love yourself first?"

L.C. jaw dropped. "What the hell does that mean?"

"Do you not like the person you've become?"

"I'm perfectly happy with who I am."

"Uh-huh. Are you going to sit there and tell me it didn't hurt those times when we've been out and guys have made disparaging comments about you? You say it doesn't bother you, but you're a human being—it has to hurt. I know. I've had guys say hideous things about me. In school, guys I'd never even been out with or hung around with said they fucked me. They said horrible things about me because I wouldn't put out. I know exactly what you must feel deep down inside. And it's all right to let people know you have feelings and that those feelings get hurt sometimes. It's all right to cry once in a while, L.C."

L.C. shook her head. "So now you're complaining because I'm a cold-hearted bitch, is that it? Gee, thanks."

Sydney's hands flew up. "There you go again, trying to twist this and put the blame on me. I'm just trying to find out why you won't open up completely to me—why you won't tell me you love me. We don't have a complete emotional connection between us after all this time, and a relationship can't last without one because it's that connection that will keep you from succumbing to the temptation of young brunettes with roving hands."

"What is this all about, really?"

"I'm genuinely concerned about our future, L.C. Early in our relationship you once said your life made you weary because of all the work involved in a music career. But over the months, I haven't seen any evidence of that being the case. You have hardly any responsibilities. Your manager books all the concerts and appearances, your accountant handles your banking and investments, and Trudy, your personal assistant, handles all your calls and correspondence—all you have to do is say 'yes' or 'no' to a few choices they outline for you. They do all the work.

"And if something doesn't go smoothly without some effort from you, you just walk away from it rather than work it out. Or if someone in your entourage doesn't suck up properly, you get rid of them rather than hash things out. Unfortunately that attitude seems to have slipped over into the way you deal with personal relationships. Once a relationship requires some genuine effort from you, you chuck it and move on to the next one. It's like you get to a certain point where a real emotional bond starts to occur and then you bail."

Ice-cold blue eyes glared at Sydney. "I had no idea you thought so little of me. I'm sorry if you don't like me the way I am."

"I *do* like you! I love you. I'm not sitting here saying you're a bad person—I'm saying you're a wonderful person who has a fear she needs to work out, that's all. This relationship has been beautiful up until now, and I think it's worth saving. But that's going to require some effort on your part too, to get past this fear of yours."

"Will you stop talking about this 'fear' of mine!" L.C. jumped her feet. "I don't have any fears—I'm not afraid of anything."

"Really? Then you're the first human being in the history of the world who isn't."

"Well, if I do, I'm sure not aware of them, Miss Know It All." She paced angrily, stomping back and forth across the room with her arms crossed under her chest, hands clenched into fists.

"Yes, you do know, you have to know. Like I said before, it's your life, you've lived it, those experiences are all in your head somewhere—you just don't want to recall them because it's like reliving them all over again, and that can be very painful. But you *have to* in order to get rid of them. It's like being an alcoholic. You can't deal with the problem until you admit you have one. You have to face your life and your fears, L.C. You have to."

Sydney knew she had said something that struck a chord because L.C. stopped pacing and was giving her that cold stare again. "No...I don't," she said resolutely, then walked out the door.

Chapter Fourteen

The final two weeks of the tour were dreadful. The two women hardly spoke to each other, they slept apart, and they never touched each other—not even a good morning kiss. Once they were finally headed home, Sydney hoped things would settle down and they'd go back to being lovers, but even at home it was more of the same, including separate beds.

On the third day back, L.C. spent the entire day locked away in her room. Sydney decided to surprise her with a romantic candlelight dinner to try to put her in a more receptive mood.

That evening, as Sydney was arranging flowers in the centerpiece and putting candles in the candelabra, the doorbell rang. She was surprised to see Mandy, Carol Ann, and Margaret standing at the door. Then L.C. emerged from her cocoon with her black leather jacket slung over her shoulder. "Where are you going?" Sydney asked disappointedly.

"To Lapland," L.C. said flatly.

Sydney was puzzled because she had thought the first stop on the overseas tour was Rio, and that was still two months away. "Are you singing there?

L.C. frowned. "No," she snipped.

Sydney looked around to see if the rest of the entourage was also there. "Well, is everybody going...are the guys in the band going?"

"No, it's just us girls."

"Well...where are your suitcases?"

The three looking in from the outside knew what the miscommunication was and tried not to laugh at the two women. "We're not staying overnight," L.C. said to the idiotic question. Carol Ann opened her mouth, eager to deliver the explanation, but Mandy quickly put a hand over the gaping hole and pulled her aside to make sure she didn't stir things up even more between the couple. Finally L.C. filled in the gaps. "Not the country, you idiot—it's a strip joint in the Valley. I thought you knew."

Sydney became even more furious. "How the hell would I know?" she ranted. "I've never been to one of those places." Her hands went angrily to her hips. "And what are *you* doing going to those places when you're in a relationship anyway?"

"Here we go again. I don't know why you get so upset about things like this. So we're going to look at naked women. It doesn't mean anything."

Sydney's mouth flew open. "I can't believe I'm hearing this. That is such a guy's line. You know, you may as well have a dick between your legs the way you've been acting the last few weeks." The three bystanders decided it was time to come in, sensing the evening's entertainment had begun early, and they took a seat on the sofa.

"That's what a guy says when he's gone and fucked some other woman," Sydney shouted. "And he thinks saying that makes it acceptable somehow, like just because there's no emotional connection it's nothing to get upset about? Bullshit! It's called 'making love' for a reason, and fucking someone you don't love when you're involved with someone else doesn't make it any less abominable. And that goes for letting some stranger rub her hand on your thigh too, and lusting after naked women. Those are a prelude to sex, and even that much is cheating—to a lesser degree, but it's still cheating. And it *does* mean something when you cheat—it means everything." L.C. simply shook her head in disagreement. "You know, you have absolutely no will power." Suddenly an epiphany struck. "Wait...I think I've finally figured out why you've never had a long-term relationship," she said in amazement. The three women on the couch couldn't wait to hear this one. "You're a sex addict," Sydney pronounced.

L.C. was floored. "Jesus Christ! One day you diagnose me with a fear of rejection, and now you peg me as a sex addict? You are so full of shit."

"It makes perfect sense. People can get addicted to that wonderful rush the body puts out when someone's in a new relationship. That natural amphetamine the body produces is why they can't sleep, can't eat, and why they always feel like they're on a high. But with you, as soon as that high starts wearing off, instead of working to make things exciting again or learning to enjoy the love in the relationship and not just the sex, you simply move on to the next conquest. It's the same reason men—mostly men—" she said, giving L.C. the evil eye, "go to strip clubs, and look at girlie magazines, and watch porno movies on TV. They become addicted to that readily available noncommittal sex and the high that comes along with it. And before long that's the only kind of sexual relationship they can tolerate. It appears you might be the same way."

"Now, that's really funny coming from you, Mrs. Petrie."

The three bystanders wondered what she meant by that. Sydney hung her head. "You know, at the time I thought I was helping our relationship by keeping things exciting for you at home, but in this light, I see you're right. I was probably making things worse by feeding your addiction to emotionless sex with fantasy partners. Well, I'm not going to do it anymore. If you want to be with me, it's going to be making love and not just fucking."

"You've got a lot of nerve," L.C. shot back. "Who the hell are you to diagnose me as psychotic? You're just a *writer*, for God's sake."

Sydney held her chin up high to take that verbal slug. "It's a nice defense mechanism you have there, but it's not going to work this time. With or without any clinical diagnosis, the fact is that you've become lazy in your professional life and in your love life. You don't exercise your emotions in either one because it takes effort and it hurts sometimes. But you need to start changing that soon, otherwise you're going to be bed-hopping when you're 50 or 60. That's kind of pathetic, don't you think?"

"No. What I think is pathetic is you trying to change me. I like going out with my friends carousing now and then. I enjoy it, it's part of who I am."

Sydney said calmly, "I'm not the one trying to change you. I like you—for the most part—just the way you are. *You're* the one who's always changing yourself."

"Oh, please! This again?" L.C. was pacing frantically now, hands waving angrily in the air. Mandy and Margaret squirmed on the couch, feeling a little like intruders, but Carol Ann was enjoying the show immensely. "Maybe we should get some popcorn," she whispered, prompting Margaret to smack her on the arm.

"Yes, and again and again until you deal with it," Sydney shouted. "That's why you wake up some mornings and decide on a whim to up and cut all your hair off, to bleach it blond, or to get a tattoo, or buy a motorcycle. It's because you don't like the person you see in the mirror and you want to change her somehow."

L.C.'s hands dropped to her side. "What the hell does a motorcycle have to do with my appearance?"

"Only everything. Feminine little foofie girls don't buy

motorcycles—their boyfriends do because a motorcycle is a psychological symbol of power between the legs. You're always trying to emphasize your masculine side. You never wear a bra, and you refuse to go by either of your very feminine names. It's like you want to hide the fact that you're a female at all."

"Now, why would I do that?"

"Because female means sensitive, and sensitive means vulnerable, and vulnerable means you can get hurt. So instead of passively waiting for other people to sling hurtful insults about your looks, you beat them to the punch by flaunting your appearance and sexuality, in essence saying, 'Yeah, I already know how I look—you don't need to bother saying it.' Because if they don't say it, it can't hurt. But I know it does hurt you because despite what you say, I've seen it in your eyes before you cover it up.

"My point is that you make all these changes on the outside, but I don't think that's where the problem lies. I'm not concerned with *what* you do to your appearance, I'm concerned with *why*." She took a hard look at the woman across from her. "Who hurt you so badly to make you want to run away from who you are?"

L.C. looked away and didn't respond, then suddenly turned around and lashed out. "So now you're down on dykes, huh? You criticize me because I'm not like you? And thanks, by the way, for pointing out my supposed defects in front of my friends."

Mandy and Margaret looked as though they'd rather be anywhere else, but Carol Ann rather enjoyed that last one.

"Well maybe I should make a list of *your* defects," L.C. continued. "You're not so perfect yourself, you know."

Sydney didn't let the words distract her. "There's something you're running from, L.C., and you and I both know that's true. So you can spit out all the insults you want, but they're not going to chase me away. I'm not going to be like all the others and walk away and let you get away with staying emotionally stunted. I'm not going anywhere, L.C., because *I* think this relationship is worth working for. And if you want to stay in it, you're going to have to grow up and face your demons, whatever they may be."

L.C. was running out of patience quickly. "Once again, why should I bother—since I'm so defective?"

"You're not defective," Sydney said, "you're just refusing to evolve. No one's perfect, honey, but I think you're pretty close. You're sensitive, gentle-natured, and thoughtful most of the time. You're just spoiled and lazy when it comes to your emotional side because if you put forth effort, that means you care. And if you show you care, once again, you make yourself vulnerable. And you can't stand that. But you're not like that with material things, you give them freely, so I don't understand why you're that way with your emotions."

"What are you talking about now?" L.C. asked.

"You went through hell to get that motorcycle over here from Germany. And you tracked down your Land Rover for three months until you found one exactly the way you wanted. You go to the ends of the earth for objects that make you happy, but you won't work for a relationship. I guess you just haven't wanted any of them as much as you wanted those toys." L.C. didn't speak, and Sydney's expression became grim. "All I know is, when you want something bad enough, you find a way."

The dark-haired woman was too angry to think straight at this point, which made her even angrier because she couldn't even defend herself in this stupid argument, which meant more opportunities for Sydney to ramble on, hurling insults at her.

"You're a grown woman with intelligence who makes up her own mind," Sydney said calmly. "You're going to do what you want, and I would never try to stop you. So go...do what you want," she said, throwing her hands in the air.

"Fine." L.C. threw her hands up in a mocking gesture as she started toward the front door with her three friends trailing quickly behind her.

"Just remember," Sydney called out, causing L.C. to stop and backtrack with a sigh. "Actions have consequences." L.C. screwed up the corners of her mouth, not appreciating what sounded like a threat, then walked out with her friends.

The four women sat in silence in Margaret's car as they drove along. "Someone say something," L.C. finally said. Mandy, who was sitting next to her in the back seat, turned and said in all seriousness, "You're stupid."

Margaret took a look at them in the rearview mirror, and Carol Ann did a slow turn, wondering what the hell was going on.

"You've got a gorgeous, smart, affectionate woman who loves you and wants to make a home with you, and you risk it all for your stupid pride," Mandy said, causing L.C. to roll her eyes. Now she was getting it from Mandy too?

"You better open those blue eyes of yours and see what you've got," she warned, "because let me tell you, there are about a million chicks out there who would kill to be in a solid relationship with that woman." L.C. knew Mandy herself was included in that number.

"She's right," Mandy added. "You do this in every relationship when the sex starts wearing off a little and things start to get serious and require some emotional work." L.C.'s jaw clenched, thinking that if she heard the words "Little Miss Hit 'n' Run" come out of Mandy's mouth, she'd punch her dead in the face.

"I've got to admit," she continued, "I've wondered about you myself at times...if there wasn't something you needed to see a therapist about. It just doesn't make sense why you've never in your life had a successful relationship. I'd kind of like to know why you're this way, now that Sydney brought up all those points. And I agree with her—you can't possibly be happy with your life this way."

Silence prevailed again. The two women in the front made eye contact for a second, wondering what the hell was going on here, then turned their attention back to the road.

The candles had burned halfway down and overflowed at each base, sprinkling Sydney's white linen tablecloth with droplets of hot wax. She finished the last bite of the cold lasagna and looked across the table at the clean, empty plate. She was pouring herself another glass of wine when she heard the front door open. Moments later, in the shadows cast by the candlelight, she saw L.C.'s silhouette in the dining room doorway, barely able to distinguish the features of her face in the dim, flickering light. "You know how you said I needed to grow up," L.C. said softly, then took in a deep breath and let it out. "I think I just did."

"What do you mean?"

L.C. didn't respond, which Sydney thought was typical, but then she noticed the woman's shoulders slightly shaking. Then she realized L.C. was crying.

The two sat on the living room couch wrapped in each other's arms until L.C. stopped crying and was able to speak. She dabbed her eyes with a tissue. "You were right when you said I've been hiding something," L.C. confessed, unable to look Sydney in the eye, "and I didn't want to think about it because it hurts too much. But now you've made me dredge up something I've spent years trying to forget, and maybe I can finally get over it if I let it out."

Sydney gave her lover a reassuring hug. "I'm listening, baby. Tell me what happened."

L.C. fiddled nervously with the fringe on one of the couch

pillows. "I want to, but I don't know if I can. I've never told anyone before, not Carol Ann, not Mandy, no one."

"I understand it's difficult," Sydney said, "but until you deal with it, it's going to fester inside and have a hold on you. And I hate seeing you suffer. Don't allow this thing to get the better of you any longer. Face it and free yourself."

It took several more minutes for L.C. to muster up the courage to speak. "Well, I grew up in this little town in Colorado—Pagosa Springs. It's a dirt-water town of a few thousand people and there's absolutely nothing to do there. My dad drank a lot, and my parents fought constantly when I was little. So when I was only 5, my mother finally got fed up and left us. Why she left me with that bastard I'll never understand." She sobbed a moment, and Sydney thought she might lose it again, but L.C. wiped her eyes and got it under control.

"I couldn't understand then, and I still don't. I was only 5, for God's sake, and all I knew was that my parents had had another fight and the next day the person I loved the most had packed her things and left me...she just left. I woke up the next morning and she was gone—no explanation, no goodbye."

Sydney hugged her and stroked her hair sympathetically and said, "Believe me, I know that a child's only source of love is its parents, and when that love is taken away, it leaves an emptiness that's always there. You're not alone in that one," she whispered.

"Well, I was a wreck," L.C. continued. "I cried myself to sleep every night for the longest time. I couldn't eat, I got sick because my dad wasn't taking care of me, you know, making sure I ate and got enough rest. I had all this rage and anger and pain inside me and no one to talk it out with. And my father—he was a pathetic excuse for a parent. He didn't know how to deal with it himself let alone help me.

"And this was back long before all the schools had grief counselors to deal with school shootings and that sort of thing. In those days the only option was a psychiatrist, and that was just for clinically insane people—average people with family problems just didn't do that. Hell, the town we lived in was so small I don't even think it had a psychiatrist anyway.

"So I kept all that garbage inside, eating away at me. God, I wanted out of that life so bad. At first I stayed in my room all the time, then that wasn't far enough away from reality, so I took a quilt and made a bed inside my closet and I started living in my closet when I wasn't at school. But even that wasn't enough after a while. I had to get that grief out of my system somehow. And that's when I started writing poetry.

"I must have been about 7, I guess. I started out writing all this dark, depressing stuff the first few years, then one day I found my grandfather's guitar in the top of a closet and started playing. I taught myself to play before long and started putting my poetry to music.

"So my dad and I went on this way for years and years, and just when I'd gotten a handle on my emotions and my life was in a nice routine, my body started changing. Only it didn't change like all the other girls' bodies. He used to make fun of me because I had hardly any boobs and no waistline, and when he was drunk he'd say stuff like he'd gotten the boy he wanted after all—things like that. Just the sort of encouragement you need from a parent, huh?" Sydney held her tight, knowing how that must have hurt, coming from her own father.

"Like that wasn't bad enough, when I got older, during my senior year in high school, he came home one day and caught me with a girl I'd been secretly seeing. We weren't doing anything, but I guess he could sense the guilt in us, and he figured out I wasn't your average daughter," she said, raising an eyebrow. "He teased me every chance he got about that too, calling me horrible names and stuff.

"Then, I guess it was about a week after graduation, he came home roaring drunk one night and got me out of bed and started in yelling at me for not having the house cleaned up. He slapped me around, saying what a worthless daughter I was and what a pervert I was. Then he started looking me over and said what I needed to straighten me out was a good man, the way it was meant to be for a woman." She hesitated a moment and closed her eyes. "And then he started touching me."

Sydney felt ill, and now she too was fighting back tears. She didn't want to hear any more but knew she had to—she couldn't abandon L.C. at this critical moment. So she tightened her grip on the strong hand she held.

"He tore off my nightshirt and knocked me on the floor," L.C. said coldly. "He got on top of me, but he was so drunk he couldn't get it up, thank God." She paused again, looking like she might become sick. "So he used his liquor bottle instead."

Tears rolled down both their faces. Sydney softly kissed L.C.'s hand. "What did you do?" she whispered.

"Oh, I was scared to death. I was bleeding—I didn't know if the bottle had cut me or if something inside had ruptured. I thought I was going to have to go to the hospital and have an operation. I didn't know that's what happened to all girls the first time—I didn't have a mother around to tell me about those things.

"Anyway, I hurt so bad the next day I could hardly walk. But I did," she said resolutely. "I packed my things and hitchhiked to Denver and I never looked back on that son of a bitch." L.C. broke down and sobbed. "That was the last time I ever saw any of my family." She blew her nose, then snorted a pathetic laugh. "Some family! They all knew what a bastard he was all those years, and none of them ever offered to rescue me from that hell—none of them."

After a few minutes L.C. stopped crying and stared off into space, her face void of any expression as the shock and anger of reliving that awful experience set in.

"Did you call the police?" Sydney asked.

"I was too humiliated. If I'd called the cops it would have been plastered all over the newspaper. And even if the newspaper didn't use our names, you couldn't keep something like that a secret for long in a small town. I couldn't bear that. I already had to live with people looking at me like I was a freak just for being alive in that little Peyton Place. I could just imagine what it would have been like facing the kids at school and our neighbors if they knew about what my own father had done to me."

Sydney cuddled L.C. up in her arms and hugged her tight. The poor baby was shivering and having trouble catching her breath since she couldn't breathe through her nose anymore. "So what did you do when you got to Denver?" Sydney asked.

"I got a day job at a McDonald's and after a couple of months got a singing gig at a bar at night."

"Where did you live? Did you know someone there you could stay with?"

"One of the girls at McDonald's let me crash on her couch until I could afford my own place. That was Carol Ann."

Sydney cringed, knowing how dangerous it was to move in with a total stranger. She tried not to think about all the other horrible things that could have happened to L.C. in that situation, then she thought of the awful thing that had prompted her to leave home and understood how nothing could seem worse by comparison.

Then she laughed at herself. So she had been wrong about L.C. in a sense. The woman had wanted control in her relationships, all right, but not because she was a power freak and a user; she just didn't want her partner to have the power to walk away and abandon her as her mother had done. Well, so much for playing amateur psychologist.

After a while L.C. stopped shivering and her breathing evened out. Their lips met in a sweet kiss, full of intense emotion. Sydney stroked the woman's soft face. "I want you to know that I'll never tell anyone what you've shared with me. This is your life and it's not my place to open it up to anyone. This is just between you and me, I promise."

L.C. played nervously with Sydney's hand, as though working up the courage to say more. "There's something else I've never told anyone," she said shyly.

"What's that?" Sydney said, bracing herself, almost afraid of what she might hear next.

L.C. breathed in deeply. "I love you," she whispered.

Sydney was stunned at first, then overjoyed. At last she was hearing those three words from the woman she loved. Her tears flowed, and L.C. held her tight, with a sense of desperation and relief. "I'm sorry it took so long to say it, but I just couldn't—I hope you understand now. But you knew, didn't you?" L.C. said, her voice full of hope.

Sydney touched the pretty face she gazed into. "I suspected that was what I was sensing at times," she whispered. "The way you smiled when you looked at me, the way you touched me so gently, the way you talked with me and laughed with me. I hoped...but it's so nice to hear you actually say it."

They kissed again, then L.C. began crying hard. "I guess I've been betrayed so many times in my screwed up life, I've just never trusted anyone enough with my feelings to open up this way." She blew her nose again.

"And I was so sure I had figured you out," Sydney said with a pitiful laugh. "Sometimes I think I'm so smart."

"You knew there was something," L.C. said with admiration.

"But you were definitely right about one thing—I'm almost 40 years old and I'm tired of feeling alone in the world, of not having a home—a real home with my own family, someone to love and to love me back.

"I've missed out on the comfort and security of real love and family for so long. I said I didn't want them, but I did. And it hurt because I felt I'd been cheated out of all those wonderful things my whole life. I guess I eventually got to the point where I accepted the fact that I'd never find it again and just gave up." L.C. laughed sweetly and smiled, combing her fingers through Sydney's long soft hair. "And then one night, this beautiful blond came singing her way into my life, exuding this innocence and honesty. I think I fell in love with you the first time you touched me, when you took my hand in yours and you spoke that strange greeting that was so full of emotion. Then you worked your way into my heart the first night we spent talking here at home. Oh, I tried to block you out, believe me—it scared the hell out of me what I was feeling at times. But it felt so good, I was just drawn to it—to you—to the way you made me feel."

"And how did you feel?"

L.C. smiled shyly. "Happy...and beautiful...and loved for the first time in ages, because somehow I trusted you enough to let myself feel those things now and then. But even though I never said it, I want you to know that I felt it for you—it was there the whole time. I just denied it because I was afraid."

They embraced again. *What a wonderful feeling,* L.C. thought. The security of Sydney's arms wrapped around her, being held so tight she could feel the comfort of another heartbeat through her chest...both breathing in and out in the same rhythm...it was almost like sharing the same body, and she was certain there simply could be no more sublime feeling in the human experience.

At that moment L.C. knew she was home, that no matter how

badly she misbehaved or screwed up Sydney would always be there, accepting her with all her faults and shortcomings, yet loving her and helping her to grow out of them and become a better person. She had finally rediscovered the comfort of that unconditional love she had lost as a child—the love of a family.

The following night Sydney came home to find L.C. standing in the living room dressed in her Armani tux looking absolutely stunning. She had an Elvis Presley charm about her, with her black hair combed back, dark eyebrows and lashes accenting sparkling blue eyes, sculptured cheekbones, and that dazzling, disarming smile. Her hands were in her pants pockets, and she rocked back and forth, looking a little shy and insecure. "I figured that with all the special evenings you've arranged for me to come home to that it was your turn to be surprised." Sydney smiled with delight. "Go put on an evening gown," L.C. instructed.

Minutes later, Sydney reappeared in the black strapless gown she had worn when they performed at the Christmas benefit on the first night L.C. had kissed her. The big woman hooked her arm inside Sydney's, preparing to escort her, but to Sydney's surprise L.C. led her toward the glass door at the back of the house and out onto the deck.

There in the middle of the sandy stretch of beach was a large canvas tent that glowed from the inside with candlelight like a giant luminaria. A warm breeze tickled the flames, creating silhouettes that danced across the fabric, beckoning the lovers to enter. A long red carpet stretched from the bottom step to the tent, which Sydney knew was for her so she wouldn't stumble from trying to walk in the sand wearing high heels.

Inside the tent, Sydney saw two waiters setting the table and a dinner cart from Granita, Wolfgang Puck's restaurant in Malibu. "I wanted it to be nice, so I didn't cook," L.C. laughed.

Then Sydney noticed it was L.C.'s large mahogany dining table and chairs that were now in the middle of this tent out on the beach. "How'd you get all this out here?" she asked, looking stunned.

"It wasn't easy," L.C. said, lifting up a hand to show bruised knuckles and a scratch.

Sydney affectionately squeezed the injured hand. "Now I know why you sent me out on all those errands today." She looked around the tent once more and smiled. "I can't believe you went to all this effort for me."

"Well, you know me…when I want something badly enough, I find a way." The lovers shared a sweet kiss.

After dinner, they kicked off their shoes and took a romantic stroll on the beach in the moonlight. Sydney was singing, so L.C. knew she was happy. L.C. started making figures with footprints, then made their initials in the sand. She positioned herself at the bottom of the set of letters and told Sydney to come join her. "We'll make a heart around our initials," she said enthusiastically. "Hurry, before the tide gets them!"

While they both reprised "Love Letters in the Sand," the two walked off in different directions, then around and back until they met at the top of the heart. "Perfect!" L.C. said, admiring their artistry. "Ah! One last thing," she said, then ran around to the left side of the heart and began patterning an arrow piercing the heart. She leapt into the middle, took a few steps, then leapt across to the right side and made the point on the arrow. She turned, striking a pose as if she were a gymnast who'd stuck the landing. "Ta—da-a-a!"

"A thing of beauty!" Sydney declared.

"This time I'll say it in front of God and everyone… I love you," L.C. declared just before wrapping up her blond beauty in a lingering kiss. Afterward the two admired their creation while the tide slowly erased it.

While walking along the water's edge, L.C. was quiet, and Sydney asked what she was thinking about. "Well, it occurred to me today that for the entire time we've known each other, you've basically been living in my world, helping me with my album and writing songs, being dragged all over the country on tour, and that's not fair. So I was thinking that this spring, after the Grammys and when I'm finally through with all my promotional commitments for the album, that we'd take off six months or so and take a trip around the world." Sydney's face lit up. "No planes—just ships and trains," L.C. said reassuringly. "I'd like to see the world you've seen...have you teach me about art and history and all the things I missed out on because I didn't go to college and because I've spent so much time on my career. I haven't had any time for *me*, and now I want a personal life."

"Oh, L.C., that sounds heavenly," Sydney cooed.

They walked a little farther, arm in arm. "I've been thinking about something else too," L.C. said.

"What's that?"

"How would you feel about leaving L.A.?

Sydney was shocked. "You mean permanently?"

L.C. nodded.

"It wouldn't bother me a bit."

"I was thinking maybe we could build a home of our own, maybe in Aspen, and just keep the Malibu house for vacations. Aspen is so pretty all year, and we both love the snow and skiing in the winter. At least we'd get a change of seasons—Christmas is always sneaking up on me because the weather never changes here." Sydney laughed, knowing exactly what she meant. "Besides, there are too many temptations in L.A. It's too easy to be decadent. Too many people willing to stab you in the back to get ahead. And we both have careers that go wherever we do—I can write songs wherever I am, and you can write books or screenplays any place you can take your computer. I don't see why either of us has to live in L.A. to be in the entertainment business."

"You know, a change of scenery might be good for us," Sydney said. "That sounds wonderful." She looked at L.C.'s blue eyes twinkling in the moonlight. "*You're* wonderful," she said, then kissed her softly.

Chapter Fifteen

The months during the hiatus before the world tour began found the couple busy with architects designing their new house to be built on the side of a mountain in Aspen. Their 10-acre lot had a small lake on it, which the back of the house would overlook. Sydney made sure the master bedroom had two walk-in closets—with hers the size of one of the smaller bedrooms to accommodate all her designer clothes and shoes. Sydney was also excited about finally getting to send for her furniture and belongings, now that she was going to have a real home. She couldn't wait to show L.C. all the pictures from her life before they'd met, sharing her childhood experiences with the one she loved. The home would be ready to move into by the time they returned from their trip around the world a year from now, and the couple delighted in the anticipation of their life together.

However, the three weeks preceding the overseas tour were so hectic for L.C., she had barely any time to devote to Sydney. Her days were busy with working out last-minute details and changes, and she walked around with her cell phone glued to her head.

Their last night together, as the two lay in bed talking after making love, Sydney noticed L.C. wasn't her usual smiling self. It didn't take her long to figure out that L.C. was starting to get homesick already.

"Are you sure you won't go with me?" the singer pleaded, even though she knew what Sydney's reply would be. "You won't have to worry about unused airline tickets or any problems with delayed flights and lost luggage because we have a charter jet."

"Sweetie," Sydney said, stroking the soft face resting on her breast, "I need to stay here and finish this book. The first draft is due by the end of the year, and it's going to be a struggle getting it finished even without you around as a delightful distraction. Besides, you know I can only write when I'm miserable—that's why it took me over a year to even start it. Hell, I should be able to crank this baby out in two weeks because I'll be good and miserable without you."

That's when the tears started flowing from those blue eyes. Sydney was so touched at seeing this strong woman show her emotions, but she also sympathized with the love of her life because she knew L.C.'s heart was breaking. "It won't be so bad," she said reassuringly.

"I suppose we can call each other every day," L.C. said with a sniffle. "Hell, we can afford it, right?"

"You know what I'd like instead, sugarplum?" L.C. looked up at her. "Write to me," Sydney said. "I can't remember the last time I got a real letter in the mail. No one writes letters anymore, what with e-mail and phones and faxes. But there's something so special about a letter, about you putting your hand to paper, and me having that same paper in my hands. And it's something I can touch and keep forever to read years later. You can't do that with a phone call." L.C. sobbed quietly. "Besides, you won't have time for me while you're away—look at how little time we've spent together the past few weeks, and you're not even gone yet."

L.C. wiped away her tears. "I'm sorry about that," she whined sorrowfully, as though begging for forgiveness.

"It's not your fault, honey, I know it couldn't be helped. I remember well," Sydney said, referring to the U.S. tour. "But there's always going to be something that can't be helped. It goes with the territory." She ran her fingers through L.C.'s soft black hair. "Look at it this way, this is your time to shine and to renew your individuality. When two people spend too much time together, they start losing themselves. Too much of even a good thing isn't good after a while."

"But I don't want to be an individual," L.C. sobbed loudly. "I want to be a couple."

Sydney's efforts were hopeless, and the two stayed up for hours until L.C. eventually cried herself to sleep.

The charter flight was scheduled to leave at 2 o'clock the following afternoon, and L.C. woke up early to run some last-minute errands, taking Sydney along, saying she wanted to spend every moment possible with her love. After a trip to the drug store for a few personal items, L.C. made Sydney promise that she'd FedEx one of her favorite California pizzas from Granita or a dry ice-packed Wendy's hamburger to her during the six weeks she would be in Europe, partly because L.C. hated the strange cuisines, and partly because of mad cow disease affecting Europe.

The last stop was to her attorney's office, where the singer said she had to sign some papers. But to Sydney's surprise, she was handed the documents and a pen after L.C. finished signing them. She scanned the papers and saw that L.C. had added her name to the deed to her Malibu home and all her bank accounts. Sydney's mouth fell open after she mentally tallied up the dollar amounts. "This is close to $25 million here," she said, in total shock.

L.C. took her hand and softly said, "Just in case anything

happens to me, I want to make sure you're taken care of...that you have a roof over your head. I don't want it going to any of my relatives. And I don't want anyone else ever living in either of our homes. I want them always to be ours, always filled with our spirit."

Suddenly Sydney felt sick and started crying. "What an awful thing to say—stop it."

L.C. hugged her tightly. "I know it's a small possibility, but it could happen. Maybe not on this trip, but maybe 20 years from now. And just because the state of California says two people who happen to be the same sex can't make the same commitment as a man and woman doesn't mean they can stop me from doing it in my own way." She tenderly fondled Sydney's delicate hand, lowering her eyes. "I guess this is my way of saying I want to take care of you forever...and that I love you."

Their eyes met, then they kissed each other sweetly. L.C. thought everything was fine, but then Sydney's face screwed up and she burst into tears. "What's the matter?" L.C. asked.

Sydney wiped the tears away. "It just hit me...you're leaving," she whined, then burst into tears again. The two male attorneys in the room couldn't handle any more of the intimate scene and left the couple alone for a private moment.

"You're going to be gone for *three whole months*," Sydney lamented. "God, I'm going to be so miserable."

A secretary brought in a box of tissues, then efficiently exited. Sydney dried her tears and looked deeply into L.C.'s eyes and into the soul she had grown to love. "You'd better come back to me," she said, full of anguish. "I don't know what I'd do without you."

L.C. cupped Sydney's face gently in both hands. "My love...for the rest of my life, no matter what separates us, I will always come back to you. I promise."

The lovers kissed passionately, then Sydney dried her eyes and L.C. called the attorneys back in.

The tour followed the same routine as it had in the states, starting out like summer camp, but then problems soon turned it into a hassle. On top of everything else L.C. was heartbroken, pining away for Sydney, and her bad case of homesickness got worse every day, which was hardly inspiring for a singer to give her best performance.

Back at home Sydney had gotten into the routine of sequestering herself in her room sitting at the computer 14 hours a day. And she had deteriorated into a mess. Her daily attire had become a T-shirt and undies that she frequently slept in. Her hair was in a constant scraggly ponytail, and she never put on any makeup. Why bother? She had absolutely no incentive to spiff up. She was good and miserable, which, of course, made the words flow.

The only thing that allowed either of the women to keep her sanity was the FedEx packages delivered almost every other day from each other containing precious love letters. Sydney had been able to keep track of L.C.'s concerts too through the newspaper clippings sometimes included in the packages.

When Thanksgiving arrived, Sydney was miserable and lonely. She had invited Mandy and her new girlfriend over for dinner, but they were going to visit Mandy's parents in Chicago. Because Sydney ended up spending the holiday alone, she didn't have any incentive to make a whole dinner, so she dined on a Swanson's frozen turkey dinner with a cranberry sauce dessert. And she cried with every mouthful. At nine weeks into the tour, she wished she hadn't vetoed the idea of phone calls, desperately wanting to hear L.C.'s voice. Around 7 o'clock that night, she did.

"Where are you?" she squealed with delight when she recognized the beautiful voice at the other end.

"We're in Stockholm," L.C. said, "and I'm freezing my ass off. You wouldn't believe the snow they get here—Jesus!"

"Well, you're staying bundled up and warm, aren't you?"

"Yeah, but I'm so worn out—I hope I don't catch a cold or get a sore throat. I'm not used to this kind of weather."

The two talked for almost half an hour; Sydney tried to make it sound like everything was fine with her, but the only good news she had was that she was mere days away from finishing her first draft. She tried to sound as though that made her happy, but as soon as they hung up she started crying again.

Days later, Sydney finished the first draft of her book, and she was so happy to be through with the chore that she broke open a bottle of champagne to celebrate. She cranked up the stereo and sang and danced around the house, drinking her bubbly. But that evening as she ate dinner alone again she realized she now had nothing to occupy herself with to keep her mind off L.C. And she still had almost three more weeks of torture until her baby got back home. She decided the best way to get her mind off her misery was to start getting the house ready for Christmas. Tomorrow would be December 1, and she determined that wasn't too early. After all, the stores had put up Christmas decorations the day after Thanksgiving.

So the next day she bought a live pine tree that they could plant once the holidays were over, and she put it up in front of the glass wall in the living room. Before long the whole house smelled like a pine forest. Sydney spent the entire afternoon decorating the tree with lights and ornaments and silver icicles. Later on she stopped by the florist to put in an order for flowers for L.C.'s homecoming and to pick up a wreath for the outside of the door and holly garlands, which were strewn over the fireplace mantle and along the Steinway. Candles of bayberry and vanilla were placed here and there, and L.C.'s favorite ceramic Santa figurine that she'd had for ages went atop the piano. Sydney wanted the house looking pretty and festive for L.C. when she came home on the 19th.

It was after midnight when she finished transforming the house, and she did feel better as she basked in the aura of the holiday spirit and a cozy fire. She turned on the TV to see what the late-night fare was, and to her surprise she discovered one of her favorite Christmas movies that she hadn't seen since she was a girl was coming on in half an hour. This would give her just enough time to brew up some hot chocolate and get nice and snuggly in a soft blanket on the couch.

The movie was *We're No Angels*, starring Humphrey Bogart, Peter Ustinov, and Aldo Ray as three convicts who escape from the prison on Devil's Island on Christmas Eve in 1895. They hide out at a local store, masquerading as handymen, intending to do harm to their hosts in order to escape. But the Christmas spirit comes over them after spending an evening with the family, and they end up helping them instead. After only a few minutes, Sydney began to wonder what it was about this movie that had touched her so when she had first seen it. Then, during the Christmas dinner scene, she remembered. Suddenly an idea came to her, and she smiled with girlish glee.

Three days later at the Hotel de Paris in Monte Carlo, a FedEx package awaited L.C. when she checked in. Inside was only a cassette tape—no letter this time, which she thought strange. She scrounged up a Walkman from one of the crew and played the tape:

> Hi, sweetheart—this is your living Christmas card from the one who loves you back home. Everything is turning

Christmas around here, the decorations are up on Rodeo Drive and around the city, people have colored lights on their houses, and I've been decorating our house.

Last night I was watching TV after I finished with the house, and they played an old movie I hadn't seen in years, this Humphrey Bogart film called *We're No Angels.* After the family finishes their turkey dinner, they go into the parlor and the mother sits down at the piano and plays this lovely, sweet song while she sings. It's called "Sentimental Moments." And it brought back so many memories of Christmases past—in fact, it was one of the first songs I learned to play on the piano, and it made me think of you. If you listen to the words, you'll understand why.

L.C. listened to the sweet, simple melody Sydney played on the piano and her beautiful voice, full of touching emotion as she sang.

Sentimental moments
Moments that you shared with me
They will last forever, and ever, and ever
In my memory.
Sentimental moments
How I treasure every one
And I live them over, and over, and over
When my day is done.
Those happy endless walks, the quiet talks, the music.
The crazy things that lovers do when love is new.
Sentimental moments
Share them once again with me
And they'll bring us closer, and closer, and closer
Like we used to be.

"I love you, sweetheart," Sydney said in closing. "It won't be long now."

L.C.'s tears had started at the second verse, and once the message was over, she took out the cassette, held it to her heart and cried softly. How awful to feel happy and sad at the same moment. Right now she wished she could say "screw it" to the rest of the tour because she just wanted to go home.

Two days later, Sydney received her package, which also contained a cassette. She couldn't wait to hear L.C.'s sweet voice again and played it immediately. After a brief audio letter, L.C. sang two of her favorite Christmas songs from her old Carpenters albums, "Merry Christmas Darling" and "I'll Be Home for Christmas." The lyrics told the couple's own story so perfectly and with such bittersweet melodies that Sydney couldn't help crying. The holidays were a time for families to be together, and here they were, half a world apart. It wasn't right. She didn't know how she would be able to bear another two weeks of this separation.

It had been eight days without a letter from L.C., which had begun to concern Sydney. The couple had exchanged at least two letters a week since L.C. had left, until now. She knew the old saying, "Absence makes the heart grow fonder," but her heart was about to burst. She didn't understand this at all.

Sydney got out the copy of L.C.'s itinerary and checked today's date on the schedule. Copenhagen. With the time difference from L.A. to Copenhagen, it would be about 2 A.M. there. If she called, she might wake L.C. up, but at least she'd catch her in her room. She debated for almost half an hour then gave in to her feelings and called the hotel listed on the sheet. To her surprise, Carol Ann answered.

"L.C.? No, she's not here...oh, she's having another powwow with Inge, I think."

"Inge? Who's Inge?" Sydney asked.

"This gorgeous blond promoter here in town."

The shot hit its mark. Sydney's smile disappeared when her jaw fell open. "What time did she leave?" she asked, trying to hide her concern.

"Gee...they took off after the concert about 11:30."

"And she's not back yet?!"

"Well, she didn't get back until 3 A.M. last night when they were discussing things, so..."

A harsh silence ensued, which Carol Ann broke by saying, "Look, she just hit the Big 4-0 a few weeks ago, and she's not handling it too well, OK? Besides, you know how L.C. is," she added, as if it were no big deal.

Sydney bit her lip. "Just tell her I called," she said flatly, then hung up.

As soon as Carol Ann hung up the phone, L.C. came out of the bathroom with a towel wrapped around her, fluffing her wet hair with another towel. "Who was that?"

Carol Ann was slightly startled and quickly said, "Uh, I was putting in another call to Sydney. I left a message again."

"Still no answer?" L.C. said with great disappointment as her arms dropped to her side. "Damn. You know, I haven't had a letter from her in almost two weeks. That's not like her—she loves to write," she said, toweling her damp hair again. Then she stopped. "You don't think anything's wrong at home, do you?"

"Probably not. Maybe she got the hotel addresses wrong, maybe the FedEx guys delivered something after we checked out." L.C. sat on the bed, her thoughts thousands of miles away. "Yeah, I suppose that could happen. And you haven't been able to get through to her at all?"

"Nope," she said, shrugging her shoulders. "I left a message twice. Maybe with the holidays she's getting a lot of messages and they just got bumped. Or maybe since she finished her book she's been out blowing off some steam and partying. Who knows? It doesn't mean she's up to anything wrong."

L.C. frowned at the suggestion. "I didn't think she was." And she hadn't...until now.

After a moment L.C. said, "Hey, would you mind calling the hotel in Stockholm and finding out if anything came for me after we left?"

"Sure," Carol Ann said, delighted that L.C. had kept the ball in her court. "Be glad to, first thing tomorrow."

L.C. smiled sweetly. "Thanks. You're a real friend, taking care of all these things for me since Trudy had to go home. I tell you, it's hell being on tour without a personal assistant."

"I told her not to drink the milk in Stockholm," Carol Ann said with a laugh.

"Oh, speaking of letters, would you mind shipping off another one to Sydney tomorrow?" She went over to the desk and fished out the FedEx envelope from the pile of papers. "I guess I may as well keep trying—who knows if she's even getting them," she pined.

"Don't worry," Carol Ann said reassuringly, stroking L.C.'s wet hair, "I'll take care of everything."

L.C. gave her a hug and handed her the FedEx envelope, which Carol Ann took back to her room. And with great satisfaction, she stuffed it inside a pizza box in the trash can next to her bed. *Let's just see how Sydney likes it when messages don't get delivered,* she thought with a smug grin across her face.

Sydney couldn't sleep that night, fighting the image of a hand on L.C.'s thigh attached to a pretty brunette in a Philadelphia bar. Then the hair turned to blond, and the creature suddenly had a name: Inge. She pictured L.C. in bed with Inge, doing the things only she and L.C. should be doing with each other. She tossed and turned for hours trying to shake loose from the clutches of this nightmare, but it was impossible knowing L.C.'s past. Apparently this old dog was up to the same old tricks.

This left Sydney with an awful feeling—missing someone she loved yet hating the object of her affection at the same time. But she knew she couldn't just act like one of those wimpy wives who tolerated their partner's indiscretions by letting them get away with bad behavior again and again, always forgiving and forgetting. Plus, she knew there was always the chance she was misinterpreting the situation. Still, she wouldn't be able to rest until she found out for sure.

Sydney got out of bed and got on the Internet to check airline rates and schedules, then remembered her passport had expired because it had been so long since she'd flown, which meant she wouldn't be able to get into another country. And by the time her applications for a new passport and a visa got processed, L.C. would be back home anyway. But then it occurred to her that L.C.'s last stop before coming home to L.A. for the big welcome home concert was Honolulu.

She went and got the itinerary and saw that L.C. would be in Honolulu a total of four days, two before and one day after the concert to rest and recoup in paradise. Perfect. Sydney booked a first-class ticket for December 16, the day L.C. was scheduled to arrive in Hawaii.

Chapter Sixteen

L.C. entered the Sheraton Moana Surfrider, greeted at the entrance of the Victorian hotel with a choice of leis made of tiny yellow-and-white or purple-and-white orchids. The yellow flowers had a pungent fragrance like gardenias, so L.C. chose one of those. As she walked into the lobby, the stunning view of Waikiki Beach through the back doors and a giant banyan tree in an open courtyard beckoned to her, and she sat in the midst of this tropical paradise sipping on a Blue Hawaiian as she unwound.

After finishing her drink, she went up to her ocean-view suite and stopped just inside when she saw not only her three trunks beside the couch, but a suitcase she recognized as Sydney's. She ran to the bedroom doorway.

"I can't believe what I'm seeing," L.C. said upon seeing Sydney sitting on the bed in her travel clothes, arms folded. She didn't even notice her lover wasn't smiling. "What are you doing here?" She ran over and hugged Sydney tight. It wasn't until she kissed Sydney that she realized something wasn't right. "What is it?" L.C. asked.

Sydney asked why she hadn't heard from L.C. in weeks, but before L.C. could say anything, Sydney asked about Inge. The singer denied any involvement other than a business relationship with the woman and said she hadn't even been out with Inge the night Sydney supposedly called. Each said they had sent several letters during the past two weeks that the other never received, but neither had an explanation as to what had happened to them.

Sydney said she'd called FedEx, and they said they hadn't had any pickups from L.C. Hackett since December 3. But the singer vigorously defended herself, saying she had sent them, that she'd given them to Carol Ann to send after Trudy got sick and went home. That was all Sydney needed to hear, but L.C. had a hard time believing Carol Ann would stoop that low. Yet there seemed to be no other viable explanation. The only way to find out for sure was to confront the woman.

L.C. decided it would be best if she went alone, afraid Sydney would go ballistic straight away, but as soon as Carol Ann opened her door, L.C. started ranting, asking what the hell she'd done with all those letters she'd trusted her with. She half expected her friend to deny any involvement, but Carol Ann admitted right off the bat that she had intercepted their love letters and seemed almost proud of it, which only angered L.C. even more.

"What the hell do you mean, messing with my personal life that way?" she shouted.

Carol Ann stood her ground. "I was just doing it to protect you. She's all wrong for you—she's just out to use you."

"Whoa, whoa—you're not my mother—you don't decide who's right for me," she said, getting up into the woman's face. "You don't mess with my life, you got that? Just because you don't like her doesn't mean she's not right for me. You haven't liked her from the day you met her. Why?" L.C. demanded. "Why do you hate her so much that you would betray me this way?"

A bewildered expression came over Carol Ann's face. She stood, unmoving, for a long time. "Are you that blind?" she finally said, gazing into the lovely blue eyes across the room.

L.C. threw up her hands. "What are you talking about?" she shouted, her hands landing on her hips.

Carol Ann laughed pathetically, her eyes now moist with tears. "It never even occurred to you, did it...in all these years, you never once noticed I was in love with you."

This revelation hit L.C. like a ton of bricks. A strange feeling crept through her. She stepped back.

Watching the woman she loved recoil unleashed Carol Ann's pain and anger and tears. "Who always took care of you when you'd drink yourself sick, making sure you didn't pull a Jimi Hendrix?" she shouted, brushing the tears from her face. "Who ran your errands when you had a cold and couldn't get out and do things for yourself? Who always had a shoulder for you to cry on at 4 in the morning when you'd had another spat with your girlfriend du jour. Who was always there for you? *Me*!"

She hated that look of shock still on L.C.'s face, wishing her words would have erased it. But now she realized it was hopeless. L.C. had never felt these things for her and never would. "You never had a clue, did you?" she said dejectedly, putting a hand over her mouth to hide her quivering chin. "Why? Because I wasn't pretty enough for you—or sexy enough, like your frilly little doily? What is it about me that makes it so ridiculous to think of me as a lover?" She waited, but L.C. didn't make an effort to respond, which brought out Carol Ann's anger even more.

"Why not me?" she shouted, even louder than before. "I was the one with the most time invested in you—why do you think I packed up and hauled my ass across the country, leaving all my family and friends when you wanted to move to L.A. and look for a record deal? I did it because I couldn't bear the thought of never seeing you again," she cried hysterically. "That's why I threw away your letters," she snarled. "Because I couldn't bear seeing you with someone who's not me." Carol

Ann buried her face in her hands, and her shoulders shook.

None of this confession of the soul touched L.C. the way it had been intended, and she remained unmoved. "Well, you'd better get used to the idea of not seeing me anymore, because you're fired," she said firmly. Carol Ann looked at her in disbelief. "I can never forgive you for this. You should have been honest with me long before now, but you've been deceiving me all these years. And after that business with Rick, how can I ever trust you again?"

Their eyes met in a cold stare—15 years of friendship and affection had been destroyed in the blink of an eye. "I don't want you in the band, and I don't want you in my life," L.C. said calmly. "Have Allan book you a ticket home tomorrow—I don't want to see your face ever again." She turned away from her long-time friend and walked out without looking back.

The next morning, L.C. and Sydney slept in, then decided to enjoy the free day before the concert by renting a pair of mopeds for an afternoon tour of Honolulu. They stopped at the aquarium just down the street from the hotel, then the zoo, the Blow Hole and the Pearl Harbor Memorial. At dusk, Sydney went for a relaxing swim in the ocean while L.C. played in the pool under the banyan tree, afraid to go into the foamy surf, which Sydney teased her about.

The day after the concert, the 19th, Sydney woke L.C. at 6 A.M. "What? Is something wrong?" L.C. asked.

"It's time to get up," Sydney said enthusiastically. "I have a surprise planned."

L.C. looked at the clock on the bedside table. "It's 6 o'clock in the fuckin' morning," she whined, falling back onto the nice, warm bed. "I wanted to sleep in this last day." She bundled herself up in the warm sheets again.

Sydney tugged on her arm. "Come on—we have a plane waiting."

"A plane? Where are we going?"

Sydney beamed. "Heaven," was all she said.

After a short plane ride to Maui, the couple rented a car, and Sydney drove directly to a hotel where a picnic basket and a bottle of champagne were waiting for them. Then they headed down the Hana Highway until Sydney spotted a pair of twin palms growing from the same base. Twin palms could be seen all over the islands, but this pair had grown into a heart shape, their tops curving in toward each other. She pulled over and parked the car. "This is it," Sydney announced, smiling.

L.C. looked around. "We're out in the middle of nowhere," she groused. "Are you sure this is the right place?"

"This marks the trail to a place only the locals know about," Sydney said, pointing to the palms. "Trust me." L.C. grabbed the picnic basket and followed Sydney.

They first walked through an open meadow until they came to a small pool beneath a waterfall. The trail began to rise, and the two walked up and up until they arrived at a bridge over a stream where two waterfalls joined in a pool. After carefully crossing the stream, they came to a giant mango tree. Sydney smiled when she recognized it. "My dear," she said with a grand smile, "you are about to enter paradise."

Beyond the mango tree lay a forest so lush and fruitful, everywhere they looked they were surrounded by brightly colored tropical fruits and flowers growing thick and wild: bright red raspberries, tiny strawberry guavas, wild bananas, papayas, and passion fruit.

They walked through a carpet of purple, yellow, fuchsia, and white orchids, dotted with the occasional bright orange bird of paradise. Above was a canopy of fuchsia flowers growing in the trees. L.C. felt as though she really had stepped into heaven. They strolled through, picking handfuls of fruit and flowers, putting them in their picnic basket to enjoy once they reached their destination.

Eventually they entered a bamboo forest, where 25-foot-tall leafy stalks blocked the sun and cooled the air. The breeze swirled up and caught in the leafy tops, causing the shafts to clack together in an almost musical way. As the couple left the forest, they came upon another waterfall cascading down a cliff. "Put your on hiking shoes," Sydney warned. "It's long way down."

Later, when they arrived at the pool, the tired hikers spread out two rattan mats and the contents of the picnic basket and ate a lunch of Hawaiian delicacies. The pungent smell of damp moss and ferns mingled with the aroma of fresh water splashing on rocks that had been heated by the sun. L.C. took one of the fuchsia orchids out of the basket and put it in Sydney's hair just above her right ear. "Uh-uh," Sydney corrected. "A flower over the right ear means you're available." She switched the orchid to the other side.

"You really know this culture, don't you?" L.C. said, impressed.

"Yep. They have such wonderful beliefs. Do you know how the natives greet each other?" she asked.

L.C. shrugged. "They say 'aloha' and put a lei around the other person's neck?"

"Close. But when they say 'aloha,' they put their foreheads together and say it at the same time. They believe an exchange of breath is an exchange of the soul. Isn't that beautiful?" The two put their heads together and "exchanged souls" according to the custom.

Sydney laid down on the mats, took a deep breath, and

looked up at the heavens. "For some reason, part of a song from *The Sound of Music* keeps going through my head." Then she looked at L.C. "I must have done something good at some point to deserve you in my life."

L.C. curled up beside Sydney, full of contentment and joy. "You say things that make me feel like I'm the most wonderful person in the world sometimes." Sydney smiled and kissed her. "I'm so glad you came to Mandy's that night," L.C. said.

"So am I."

L.C. fondled the petals of the orchid resting above Sydney's ear. "So you don't have any regrets about the changes you've made in your life because of me?"

"Nope," Sydney said. "I learned a long time ago to live my life with no regrets." L.C. asked what she meant. "Oh, it has to do with my mother." L.C. could tell by the tone of her voice that this wasn't something Sydney was keen on discussing, but she gave her a pleading look, having avoided the topic for so long. Sydney sighed in acquiescence. "Right before she died, she talked about how she hated leaving this world because of all the regrets she was taking with her for things she always said she was going to do someday but never got around to. All the unrighted wrongs, the unfinished business, unfulfilled dreams. That was when I decided I wasn't going to end up that way—I wasn't going to leave this world with regrets nagging me if I could help it. So I started taking care of the ones I could do something about."

"What did you do?" L.C. asked.

"Remember that girlfriend I told you I'd lost because of my big mouth?" L.C. nodded. "I tracked her down and finally apologized...20 years after the fact. But 'better late than never' was never so true."

"Did she forgive you?"

"Oh, yeah, but I still was the one who suffered. I missed out on 20 years of a great friendship. That's pretty sad. Anyway, it was shortly after that I realized I wasn't happy as a newspaper journalist, that all my life I'd wanted to write books—I just didn't know if I had the talent and was too afraid to find out. But I finally decided to stop being afraid and to pursue my dream. And my life took a new track that eventually led me to you." Finally she smiled again. "That's how I know I did the right thing. Because only good things have happened to me since."

L.C. basked in the glorious feeling that flowed through her. "I wish we'd met a long time ago so we could have had 10 beautiful years together instead of just two."

Sydney shook her head. "No, you don't." She could tell L.C. was puzzled by her response. "Things wouldn't have turned out the same way," Sydney explained, which only seemed to upset L.C. Sydney put a comforting arm around the strong shoulders before going on.

"Remember that night we first met? I said I'd never bought any of your albums. Well, it was because every time I saw a picture of you—in a magazine or on an album cover—I got this weird feeling, and I'd look away immediately." Sydney read L.C.'s expression. "No, you've got it all wrong—as did I, until recently. It wasn't you...it was me." Her words did nothing to ease L.C.'s confusion.

"I didn't look away because I was repulsed by you...it was because I was attracted to you. But when you're raised in the Bible Belt, you grow up learning that it's wrong to feel those things for another woman. And you stood for things that I had learned were wrong, and I didn't like feeling as though there was something wrong with me. So I ran from it."

L.C. began to understand and stroked Sydney's soft hand. "You don't feel it's wrong any more?" she asked.

Sydney hugged her lover sweetly. "I don't see how loving another person can possibly be wrong. How can the way I feel about you hurt anyone else? Yes, I know our social mores and laws are based mostly on the Bible, but to those who say our relationship is an abomination against any religion, I'd simply remind them that the Bible also says, 'Let he who is without sin cast the first stone.' So even if they think our relationship is a sin, it's still not for them to judge. And I'd never deny my feelings about you to anyone, not even to God...if he—or she—even exists."

L.C. looked deeply into Sydney's eyes. "Even though there are several hundred million people who believe you're going to burn in hell for living with me?"

"I suppose if I believed in hell I might be worried, but I don't. Oh, I'm not an atheist or anything," she said. "It's just that when I grew up, religion meant some man pounding on a pulpit screaming that we're all going to hell if we don't do this or that. It was all such a negative experience to me. I never learned anything positive in church, about how to live a good life or how to be a good person. That stuff I picked up along the way, mostly from my parents. The people at church seemed more interested in us memorizing the correct order of the books of the Bible. What does that do to make you a better human being?" Sydney sighed. "No, to me, God is the big bang, physics, the almighty forces of nature that created everything that exists in the universe today. I prefer to think of Mother Nature as God, as the force that creates and nurtures rather than smites and lays waste. I don't think a male spirit could have created a rose with a scent that's so wonderful you just have to smile. Or a sunset with all the beautiful colors. I think that's why I migrate to the Hawaiian culture, because Mother Nature is based in its religion—you've got Pele, the goddess of fire, and so on. It just makes more sense to me."

She looked over at L.C., then stroked her fine black hair. "What do you think?"

"Well, you know my parents tried to raise me Catholic, but I never followed any particular religion because I couldn't find one that had everything I believed in. So I basically just followed the Golden Rule and believe that people should live a good life and be nice to others."

"That's a pretty good philosophy," Sydney said. "So sweet, so simple—it doesn't have to be any more complicated than that, does it?"

L.C. shrugged. "It may seem simple to you, but then, you've studied philosophy and psychology and you've traveled the world seeing other cultures. But believe me, it wasn't that easy to learn by experience."

"Oh, honey, I didn't mean to say that is was," Sydney said, concerned that L.C. had misinterpreted her tone.

"I know, it's just that sometimes I wish I'd gone to college so we could talk about more of the things you're interested in."

"So what's stopping you?" Sydney said encouragingly. "Take the time and just do it. You obviously don't need a degree to survive, so school should be fun this time around. And think how inspiring it would be to young girls to see a big success going back to school and earning a college degree. You'd be a great role model."

L.C. thought about it for a moment. "Maybe I will once we get settled into our new home."

That made Sydney smile again. "Our new home," she said with anticipation. "Only eight more months and we're there."

The two shared a peaceful moment off in the future, then L.C.'s mind traveled back to their earlier conversation. "So anyway, did you and your mother get things patched up before she died?"

Sydney laughed coldly. "She didn't apologize and neither did I. We both said we wished things had happened differently, but that was it. No apologies."

L.C. squinted. "I'm guessing there was something more between you two than just the London conservatory thing...am I right?"

Sydney pursed her lips, working up the courage to speak. "I spent my 11th birthday at my father's funeral," she said with a coldness in her voice that masked any emotion.

L.C. sat up and took Sydney's hand. "I'm so sorry."

"The real shock," Sydney said, "had come three days before when my mother came home earlier than usual from her afternoon bridge club. Aunt Sophie was with her, which was unusual, and Mother was crying. Before I could even ask what was wrong, she blurted out, 'Your father's dead.' Just dropped it on me like a ton of bricks, no warning, no preparation for an emotional shock—nothing. Well, I knew he'd been sick because he'd had nurses at the house for several months and then he went into the hospital, but what my dear mother neglected to tell me during all those months was that he was dying of cancer. Sometimes, when I look back, I think I should have figured it out, but then what does a 10-year-old know of death?

"Well, Mother Dear finally told me that afternoon," she said with a snort. "I couldn't believe my ears. I didn't cry—I was too shocked. I was enraged, furious. I could have killed her right then and there, I hated her so much. Oh, she said she didn't tell me because she wanted to spare my feelings and not upset me, but I know her—she was just making it easy on herself. She always was such a coward when it came to life. She just didn't want to have to deal with it, so she let me take the shock. Great parenting skills, huh?"

L.C. knew no response was required.

"I hated her from that day forward for depriving me of those last precious days with my father. I never got to tell him how much I loved him. I never got to say goodbye. And that's the one regret I can never do anything about, through no fault of my own." She smiled and patted L.C.'s hand. "But I sure learned something from that...I learned that you'd better appreciate the loved ones in your life every day because you never know when they're going to be taken away."

"I'm so sorry," L.C. said. "I had no idea."

"I know. It's just not the most pleasant thing to talk about. It wasn't that I didn't want you to know."

"I understand," she replied, then kissed Sydney on the cheek and cuddled up next to her once more.

"That's why I appreciate our time together so much," Sydney said, hugging L.C. tight. "I want to drink up every drop of happiness you give me."

"So, no regrets about me...about us?" She had to ask one more time for reassurance. The look she saw in Sydney's eyes would have been enough to satisfy her.

"None," Sydney said confidently. "This is the most honest relationship I've ever had. We talk about everything, we share our thoughts and feelings. I love you mind, body, and soul." Sydney leaned over and kissed the woman next to her, and the two lay in the fragrant breeze cooled by the waterfall's mist, soaking up nature's beauty surrounding them.

"Thank you for this beautiful day," L.C. said.

Sydney's face beamed. "Believe me when I say it's my pleasure."

L.C. fastened her last trunk and flung it off the bed onto the floor. "I can't believe we're leaving already."

Sydney's bag was already packed and positioned by the

front door. "I know," she said, bouncing on the bed in front of L.C. "I'd like to stay another four days."

"If we didn't have the L.A. concert booked, I would." L.C. helped Sydney to her feet, putting her arms around the tiny waist and holding her close. "Sure you don't want to wait and fly back with me? It's only another couple of hours."

"No way! When would I ever get back the other half of my airfare?" Sydney said with a laugh. "No, it's all right if I go now. I'll get there in time enough to unwind and prepare a little surprise for you when you come through the door."

That got L.C.'s interest. "A surprise, huh? What kind of surprise?"

Sydney shook her head. "All I'll say is it has something to do with the grass skirt tucked away in my suitcase. Let your imagination run wild for the next eight hours." She stroked L.C. under the chin in a teasing gesture.

"I'll be climbing the walls."

"Like I always say, anticipation can be the best kind of foreplay," Sydney said with a look of pure mischief. "Oh, I got you something for your trip." She broke their embrace, dashed into the other room, and produced a lei of golden orchids.

L.C.'s mouth fell open. "I got you one exactly like that," she said, then went to the closet and brought out the hidden gift. They both laughed at having had the same impulse. The two exchanged rings of flowers, placing them around the other's neck, then put their arms around each other. "So what do Hawaiians say when they say goodbye?" L.C. asked playfully.

"They don't," Sydney explained. "They believe that once souls have joined after they say *aloha* they stay together forever. So they simply say, *A hui hou kaua.* That means, 'Until you and I meet again.' There is no goodbye—only the time that passes until two people are together again."

L.C. sighed. "That's beautiful." The two women gently put their heads together, repeated the Hawaiian phrase, then shared one last kiss before they parted.

Chapter Seventeen

"How much longer are we going to be delayed?" Sydney demanded of the uniformed woman behind the counter at Gate 12.

"They say about half an hour, ma'am," came the discourteous reply from a stout woman in her 30s with what Sydney considered was way too much makeup for this time of day.

Sydney looked at the clock; it was a quarter after 6—more than an hour past her scheduled departure time. "You said that an hour ago. And now they say another 30 minutes?"

"Ma'am, they're having to switch out an engine. It's not exactly Tinker Toys. All I can tell you is what they tell me."

"This is the last time I fly—I swear to God," Sydney said, storming off to find a seat, where she stewed with the people on either side of her.

"Why don't they just put us on another plane?" one of them said.

"Oh, that would be too convenient for the passengers," the other replied.

Thirty-five minutes later Sydney stormed back up to the counter. "OK, I have a friend who's going to L.A. on a charter flight—I'm just going to hitch a ride with her. How do I get my suitcase off that damn plane?"

The woman cocked her head in a combative posture. "You

can't. You'll have to wait for the plane to arrive in L.A. and pick it up at baggage claim."

To Sydney, the face she was looking at seemed to be taunting her, as though this creature were glad Sydney would be further inconvenienced by this attempted escape from the living hell the airline had deliberately created for her. She wanted to slap that expression right off this ugly face. "There's no way to get *one* suitcase off that plane? Why not? It's just sitting there. Let me on and I'll go pick it out myself."

Just then the phone rang at the counter, and Sydney blew her stack when the woman answered it, completely ignoring the conversation she was in the middle of. "Bitch," Sydney mumbled to herself.

As soon as the clerk hung up, Sydney opened her mouth to continue her tirade, but the woman held up a finger to stifle the angry blond, flipped the switch on the microphone in front of her, and announced they would begin boarding immediately. After she finished the announcement, she folded her hands on the counter and gave Sydney a disingenuous smile, as though she had fixed the plane herself and was saying, *See how wonderful I am?* Sydney rolled her eyes and got in line with the rest of the first-class passengers.

Because her flight was so far behind schedule, it had to be squeezed in with all the other flights, which were no doubt behind schedule too, judging from the way the runways were packed with waiting aircraft. Sydney sat another 45 minutes lined up on the runway.

Finally she couldn't stand it anymore—she had to vent. She got out her cell phone and called L.C. "Hey, baby—change of plans. You're going to have to fix up some kind of grass-skirt show for me 'cause you're going to beat me home.... No, I'm not kidding—we're still sitting on the goddamn runway."

After Sydney explained the situation, L.C. said she'd wait for her at the gate and they could ride home together.

L.C. was surprised to see Gordon waiting for her when she got off the plane at 1:45 A.M. He walked over and without saying a word held out a copy of *Billboard.* "Aw, you shouldn't have," L.C. said mockingly, as if she were being presented with a bouquet of flowers. He opened the magazine so she could read the headline at the top of page 2: "L.C. Hackett Grammy-bound." That got the desired reaction out of the singer.

"The nominations come out the first week of January, and if you don't get multiple nods for this baby, I'll give back every cent I made last year," Gordon said. L.C. couldn't wait to read the story and took the paper from him. "Come on," he said, tugging on her arm. "You can read it in the car."

"Oh, no, Sydney's plane was delayed, so I've got about an hour until she arrives. Let's just go grab something to eat and I can read it while we wait."

Gordon said he was surprised to hear Sydney had been in Hawaii with her, and L.C. said she'd explain while they ate.

Sydney was awakened by the pressure building in her ears, so she yawned a few times until they popped. This must mean they were starting their descent into L.A. Thank God this nightmare flight was almost over. She snuggled her head against the pillow again and closed her eyes, hoping to fall back asleep for a little longer, then a monstrous boom shattered the quiet. Suddenly the plane tilted hard left and people began screaming. Plastic cups, books, purses—anything loose went flying. Seconds later the plane leveled out, and the captain's voice came over the speakers.

He informed the passengers that they had lost power in one

of the engines and would have to make an emergency landing, which would require them to make a quick descent and start dumping the remainder of the fuel while they were still over the water. He instructed the flight attendants to prepare the passengers and the cabin.

The flight attendants went into their routine and told everyone to fasten their seat belts and stow all loose items under their seats, then they started gathering up the objects that had been scattered about the plane, handing them to the nearest person, not caring to whom they belonged.

The elderly man next to Sydney was still gripping her hand, which had gotten to the armrest between them a split second before his. She extracted her limb and shook it a few times to get the circulation back. "Sorry," he said with a forced smile. "I've never had anything like this happen before."

"Yeah, it can be pretty scary, but I've flown around the world several times, and I've been through everything from losing an engine completely off the plane to blowing a tire on landing, and we always managed to get down safely. The engineers who make these things take into consideration every possible situation, and when you consider how many thousands of flights there are every day around the world, the odds are so tremendously in our favor. I'm sure everything will be all right—it just won't be pleasant."

Sydney sat back and double-checked her seat belt, then looked at her watch. L.C.'s plane was probably landing right about now. She closed her eyes and was imagining herself safely on the ground, wrapped in L.C.'s strong arms, when suddenly the plane banked hard left again. She let out a shriek, then looked out the window and saw the moon disappear from view. Then she saw flames coming from one of the engines. In an instant several of the overhead luggage bins popped open and suitcases began hitting people as screams filled the plane.

Shortly before 3 A.M., L.C. and Gordon arrived at Sydney's gate only to find the area buzzing with people. "Oh, damn—it looks like her plane already landed," L.C. said, jogging down the concourse. "I swear, if I've missed her, I'm going to be so pissed." But as she got closer, something didn't seem right. Instead of happy faces and people hugging each other, she saw grief-stricken faces and people crying. Suddenly she and Gordon were in a crowd following behind several people in airline uniforms, and the two were pushed out of the way up against the wall. "I don't think these folks are arriving from a flight," he said, "unless it was a really bad one."

The two eventually made their way to gate 26, which was almost empty. Then L.C. saw an airline employee who had obviously been crying taking down the white plastic letters and numbers on the flight arrival and departure board behind the counter, and a sense of doom crashed down upon her. "Oh, my God," she said, her eyes flooding with tears. All the strength ran out of her body, but Gordon grabbed her before she hit the floor and carried her to one of the seats inside the gate.

"Now, don't go to pieces yet—you don't know what's happened. It could be any number of things," he said. But it was too late—L.C. was crying hysterically. "I'll go find out, so get a hold of yourself until we know for sure." He gave her an affectionate pat on the arm before rushing over to the woman who had taken down the flight information.

Just then a cameraman and a reporter from one of the local TV stations charged up the concourse. "Damn!" said Teresa Villanova, a veteran field reporter. "Looks like we missed all the action. They've probably corralled the relatives into a conference room with the airline's attorneys shoving releases in their faces to sign before they get their senses back."

"So now what?" asked Larry, her cameraman.

The reporter shrugged. "We wait. I'll find out where exactly they took them and see if I can get any more on what happened to the plane—be right back." She headed over to the check-in counter at gate 26.

She walked up just after Gordon and leaned on the counter, waiting her turn to talk to the employee. But her reporter's ear caught the conversation between Gordon and the clerk, and she ran back over to Larry.

"You are not going to believe our luck," she said to him as she flipped open her cell phone and dialed. She waved him closer so he could hear her conversation. "Martin! It's Teresa—I've got a scoop on that missing plane. Yeah, we just got here, but get this," she said, looking very pleased with herself. "Sydney Sanders, Pulitzer Prize winner and lover of L.C. Hackett, was *on that plane*! No, I'm not shittin' you. L.C. is about 20 feet away from me sprawled out on a chair totally losing it… I know… I will—*I will*!" she snapped, then clapped the phone together and shoved it in her pocket. "Follow me," she said with a devilish grin.

"No! I don't want to hear this," L.C. screamed when Gordon broke the news. She doubled over and cried hard against Gordon's chest, gripping his shirt, resisting his gestures of comfort.

"Jesus," Teresa said out of the corner of her mouth as she watched the scene from a few feet away. "Someone should tell her they only give Oscars to actors." Then she glanced over at Larry. "You gettin' all this?" she asked with eagerness.

"Oh, yeah," he said, keeping his camera focused on the lead story for the day.

Gordon finally got L.C. to her feet, which Teresa took as her cue. "Let's move," she commanded, then she and Larry made a beeline toward the pair. The two jumped in front of Gordon and L.C., blocking their way. When the camera lights hit her, L.C.

jolted to a stop and put her hand in front of her face to block the blinding glare. "L.C.—is it true that your lover, Sydney Sanders, was on that plane?" Teresa shouted, then shoved her microphone in the woman's face.

Gordon reached out and pushed the camera away, which didn't please Larry. "Hey, buddy—hands off the equipment," he warned. Then he and Gordon got into a shouting match that only unnerved L.C. even more, and every time she tried to escape, either Teresa or Larry moved too, blocking her in again. She grew more and more hysterical, screaming at both of them. "Jesus! Leave me alone," she cried. "Get away from me." The commotion caused the employee at the check-in counter to come over and try to quell the disturbance, which had the attention of everyone on the concourse.

Gordon put one arm around L.C.'s shoulders and held up the other like a battering ram and charged his way through, hustling L.C. down the hall with the news hounds on their heels and Teresa shouting, "L.C.! L.C.! Can you tell us what you're feeling right now?"

After the third time she was asked that question, L.C. stopped and turned on Teresa. "*What is wrong with you?*" she screamed with so much rage that both the reporter and cameraman jumped slightly as they came to a halt. Gordon tried to coax the singer on, but she wanted to unload and wouldn't be moved. "This is my life," she screamed. "This is not entertainment! What kind of soulless creatures are you?"

Just then, camera crews and reporters from the other L.A. news outlets arrived. They quickly surrounded L.C. and her producer, and the feeding frenzy began. L.C. felt suddenly weak again; the heat was suffocating and she felt closed in. Her heart was pounding, her arms and legs went weak, and she panicked, screaming again for them to leave her alone. Gordon grabbed her by the arm and practically pulled her through the crowd, the hoard still leeching on, impeding their escape. Finally L.C. snapped. "Get away from me! Get away from me, you vultures," she shouted as she began pushing and shoving at anything in her path until two security guards arrived and escorted the pair away.

It was almost 4 A.M. when the airline spokesperson entered the conference room and informed those gathered that the Coast Guard had been deployed and was searching the coastline for any signs of wreckage, and that emergency crews were making an air and ground search over a 100-mile radius of where the plane had last been spotted on radar. But so far nothing had been found. She explained it could be hours, or days if the plane went down in a remote wooded area or in the water. Therefore it was suggested everyone go home and wait where they'd be more comfortable. Transportation had been arranged for anyone who needed it, and those few who insisted on staying at the airport to wait were told they would be provided a cot and food. Grief counseling was offered to all to help alleviate the stress, and two local clergy were present.

Mandy arrived at the airport a short time later, having been awakened from a sound sleep by a phone call from Gordon. He felt that since he had only known L.C. for such a short time that she would probably feel better having a close friend nearby instead. Mandy suggested L.C. go home with her to wait, saying it would be too traumatic to go into that empty house right now, but L.C. insisted she be taken to her own home.

As soon as she walked in and saw all the Christmas decorations Sydney had worked on and the presents under the tree, L.C. broke down. She walked directly to Sydney's room and stood in the doorway, wiping away the tears, looking around, as though she were afraid to go in. All Sydney's clothes were still hanging in the open closet just the way she'd left them. L.C. went over and gently touched the garments, remembering the times Sydney had worn each of them: the pink-and-black suit she'd worn the night she played Laura Petrie, the black evening gown from the Christmas show when she had sung so seductively to L.C. from atop the piano on the night of their first kiss.

Some of Sydney's makeup and her electric curlers sat on her vanity. The stuffed penguin L.C. had given her last Christmas rested on her bed between the two pillows. The book on her beside table had a marker sticking out halfway through it to remind her where she'd left off. The room looked as though Sydney might walk though the door at any minute, but L.C knew there was a chance that might never happen and her strong shell cracked. "What if she never comes back?" she sobbed. "Oh, God, I'll just die."

This kind of talk concerned Mandy, recalling how L.C. had reacted when Sydney had walked out during their fight—the uncontrollable crying, not eating, pulse rate going sky high—and she immediately ushered her friend out of the room, saying she wouldn't allow L.C. to stay there, that L.C. was coming home with her. But in spite of L.C.'s state of turmoil, her will was stronger, and she insisted on staying in her own home and sleeping in her own bed. Mandy gave in, supposing it might do the woman some good to be in familiar surroundings after months of traveling, that maybe she could find some comfort here. But Mandy declared that she was staying over, just in case she was needed.

The only comfort L.C. found was in a bottle of bourbon, which she nursed until 6 A.M., when she dozed off on her fainting couch. The rain woke her around 7:30, and she went into the living room where she found Mandy asleep on the couch with the TV still on. L.C. didn't wake her friend; she curled up in a chair and flipped through the channels.

After watching TV for a while, L.C. still felt frazzled and went to the refrigerator, where she found a bottle of Dom Perignon. No doubt part of Sydney's welcome-home plans. Some homecoming. L.C. popped the cork and chugged almost half the bottle while standing at the open fridge.

She stood in the doorway to the living room and guzzled a couple of times from the bottle. The curio shelf in the corner caught her eye, and she walked over and stood for a long time looking at the objects it held. She picked up the *Jackson Pollock Pup* Sydney had given her last Christmas, but its magic charm didn't work this time—it didn't make her laugh, or smile, or feel the least bit better, and the tears returned.

She had almost finished off the bottle of champagne, which she clung to like a pacifier, when she grew queasy and fuzzy-headed and went out onto the deck for some fresh air. She bundled the pup under her arm and took him outside with her and stood in the rain, hugging the ceramic puppy, thinking about how she and Sydney had shared so many conversations out there, how they had shared their lives. Soon her tears poured, and it was impossible to tell whether it was raindrops or teardrops falling to the sand below.

The pup was carefully placed on a chair out of the rain, and L.C. took a walk on the beach. The sand was wet and cold beneath her bare feet, but she didn't care.

Some time later, while her mind was drifting, L.C. was startled back to reality when she heard Mandy's voice calling out to her. "It's someone from the airport!"

L.C. ran back to the house, holding out anxious hands for the phone. "What did they say?" she asked Mandy as she ran up the steps to the deck.

Mandy shook her head. "They wouldn't tell me anything. They said they had to speak to you."

A sinking feeling hit L.C. as she put the phone to her ear. "Yes...oh, my God, I don't believe it—they found it?... Is everyone—do they know who survived?... Well, which hospitals?... All right, yeah—thanks." Mandy noticed L.C.'s expression wasn't any more hopeful than before she had taken the call. L.C. paced frantically, gripped by frustration.

"The plane went down about 20 miles inland in the mountains just north of here. One of the police helicopters spotted the wreckage because someone had built a signal fire, so they know there are survivors...but they don't know how many. There aren't any roads where it landed, so they have to trek in to the site on foot, and they said it's going to take time.

"There were over 200 people on board, so they're being taken to a bunch of different hospitals. I guess I'm going to have to call every hospital on the West Coast myself to find out anything," she said, growing angry. "Why didn't they wait and call when they had an answer for me instead of telling me this? I don't know if Sydney's alive or not, and if she is, I don't know where she is—I can't do anything."

Her big shoulders heaved, and she buried her face in her hands. Mandy gave her a hug, but L.C. didn't want to be comforted—she wanted to get this agony out of her system, so she went back down to the beach to be alone.

For 45 minutes she walked up and down the water's edge, angrily throwing pebbles and old bottle caps at the taunting surf. She tried hard not to let her thoughts wander, and she fought back images of bodies floating on the sea amid splintered wreckage.

When she heard Mandy calling to her again, she ignored it at first. What was the point—more updates on what they still didn't know? She didn't need that garbage. But Mandy's persistence finally got her attention and L.C. looked over at the tiny woman holding out the cell phone, jumping up and down on the deck. "It's Sydney!"

L.C. brought Sydney home from the hospital a few days later, on Christmas Eve, even though Sydney was still in some pain from the cuts and burns she had suffered. But she had insisted on being discharged because she didn't want to spend Christmas in a cold, sterile hospital—she wanted the warmth and comfort of her own home and the one she loved.

When she walked in the door, she commented on how pretty the house looked with all the Christmas decorations, sounding as though she were complimenting L.C. on a good job. When it hit her that she had been the one who decorated it weeks ago, she cried because of how the events had affected her mind.

The two spent a quiet day together, snuggling and talking, and they went to bed early. But Sydney awoke from a restless sleep around 3 A.M., and after tossing and turning for a while she got up and laid down on the fainting couch so as not to wake L.C.

The drapes were open, and the light of the full moon, which was perched in a clear sky just above the horizon, streamed in and filled their bedroom. The deep yellow of the two orchid leis hung over the corner of the vanity mirror stood out in this silver light and drew her eye. One string of flowers was still perfect; the other was a little shorter from where a few flowers had been lost and the broken string reattached. It was the only thing Sydney had come away with, besides what she had been wearing.

She glanced over at L.C., who was sleeping so peacefully, and noticed how the silvery moonlight bathed her beautiful face with dramatic yet blended shadows that made Sydney feel as though she were gazing at one of those stunning George Hurrell silver-gelatin photos of the great movie stars like Greta Garbo and Marlene Dietrich, where every pore, every eyelash was perfect.

She'd never seen L.C. in quite this light before, and the urge to capture her ethereal beauty prompted Sydney to retrieve her sketch pad and charcoal pencil from her room.

She followed the lines of the face resting on the pillow with an ease, as though her hand had drawn this face a million times and was familiar with every curve, every line, every angle, every hair, every lash. But when she had finished the sketch, something seemed to be missing. Something wasn't quite right. Sydney studied the drawing—the whites and grays and blacks that for some reason seemed so cold and soulless. She had captured all of L.C.'s exterior beauty, but her inner warmth—her soul was missing. Then it dawned on Sydney.

She tiptoed back into her room and sought out her box of pastels, taking them to the living room, where she sat on the couch with her things and turned on the table lamp beside her. She took a blue pastel from the box, which she used to color the eyes of the portrait.

That was it. That's what had been missing—those beautiful, endless sky-blue eyes of L.C.'s; the windows to her soul. Sydney sat for a moment, admiring the likeness she had captured and thought it might make a nice Christmas gift for L.C.—something from the heart.

"Is this what you see when you look at me?"

The voice from behind Sydney caused her to jump and let out a tiny shriek. "Good Lord, you scared me," she said, trying to push her pounding heart back into her chest. After she caught her breath, she said, "I'm sorry, sugarplum, did I wake you up?"

But L.C. didn't hear a word—she was awestruck by the drawing in Sydney's hands. "Is this what you see when you look at me?" she repeated as she took the sketch in both hands and sat beside Sydney.

The blond put an arm around L.C.'s broad back and sighed.

"That's the face that saved me," she said softly, then she swallowed hard, on the verge of tears, which made it difficult for her to speak in anything above a whisper. "After we hit the ground and the plane was breaking up, and there was fire and smoke all around me, people pushing and shoving, I panicked, and things started going black. But I knew that if I passed out I'd never make it out. It was so hard to get myself together," she said, resting her head against L.C.'s shoulder.

"I was in so much pain from being knocked around... It was difficult to walk. And then I saw your face," she said, looking at the drawing, "and I thought about how I had waited so long to find you...and it just seemed wrong for it to end so soon. From somewhere inside I found the strength to save myself because I *had* to see that face one more time. I wasn't ready to say goodbye."

Sydney put her other arm around her love and hugged L.C., who was now wiping away her own tears. "I remember the first time I looked into those blue eyes," Sydney said with fond remembrance that made a smile blossom. "It was the most incredible feeling. I took one glimpse and..." She paused to find just the right way to describe that moment. "I knew exactly how Howard Carter felt when he first glimpsed the treasures inside King Tut's tomb."

The comparison took L.C. by surprise, and she lowered the portrait and focused on Sydney, waiting to hear the rest of this story.

"Carter and his patron, Lord Carnarvon, had searched for years, looking for this treasure, and one day they discovered the sealed entryway to a tomb. At first they were afraid that, like most royal tombs, this one had been looted and resealed with nothing of value left inside. But when Carter drilled a tiny hole into the entry wall and held up a candle flame and peered inside,

Carnarvon asked anxiously, 'What do you see?' and Carter said with great awe, 'I see wonderful things!'

"And even though the fabulous things he was able to see at first glance were only a small portion of the treasures that lay sealed inside the other chambers, he still knew, with just one glimpse, that he had been lucky enough to come across something magnificent—a once-in-a-lifetime find." She took L.C.'s hand, gazing at the portrait resting on her lap. "That's what I see every time I look into your eyes," she said, her face beaming. "I see *wonderful* things."

L.C. cried harder, and Sydney instinctively held her tight and stroked her hair in a soothing manner. "I don't know, I suspect all that glittering I see are gold records and Grammys you still have locked away inside you because making beautiful music seems to be your purpose in life. I don't know whether you simply lost your way and forgot how to find those treasures, or whether you purposely sealed that part of yourself away, but I want to be the one to help you find your way back to them and bring those unique treasures out for the whole world to enjoy and appreciate and marvel at for generations to come."

It took L.C. a moment to regain her composure before she could speak. "You know," she said, nuzzling Sydney's neck, "I always loved the way you're able to look at things so differently from anyone else…and for the last few days, I've been looking at the world through different eyes myself.

"When I thought I'd lost you, I really started thinking about things—what we've made of our lives, what will happen after we're gone, and…I don't know, for some reason it didn't scare me anymore. I think it's because I used to feel kind of guilty about being the end of the Hackett line, what with all the breeding my ancestors had done for generations," she said with a pitiful little laugh, "and I felt like everything sort of came to a dead end with me. But now I realize that, when we're gone, it doesn't really end with us. We still have our songs to carry on our names...that's sort of our legacy that we leave the world."

L.C. lowered her head again and fought the tears, but without much luck. "I know this probably sounds silly coming from me, but...it's like the songs we create are our children. They're part of you and part of me. Our souls mingle to conceive the idea, then we labor over the words and music until one day we bring something so beautiful into the world—something that will live on long after we're gone."

Sydney kissed L.C.'s round cheek. "That doesn't sound silly to me," she said sweetly. "It sounds beautiful."

The two sat in stillness, holding each other, then L.C. took hold of Sydney's soft hand, fondling it affectionately, yet somewhat nervously. "You know, sometimes, when we sit just like this, side by side at the piano writing and playing songs, or when we're out on the balcony on our chaises holding hands talking, I get this wonderful, strange feeling," she whispered dreamily. "I feel like I'm in there with you," she said in amazement. "It's like I can feel everything you're feeling, and I know what you're thinking, and I'm looking through your eyes, seeing things from inside your world. I feel so much a part of you, it's impossible to tell where you begin and I end. I never made that kind of connection before," she continued, "not with anyone. And it's totally effortless...it just happens.

"In all my other relationships, whether they lasted two months or two years, it always felt like it was just the next relationship, like something I was only passing through. But not with you. Right from the start it felt different. And I could never figure out what it was I was feeling...until just now."

Sydney wiped a tear from L.C.'s cheek. "What is it?" she asked.

L.C. looked deeply into the most beautiful eyes she'd ever known and smiled. "This is what forever feels like," she said softly.

The two women embraced, and cried, and kissed. When Sydney felt her own teardrops falling on her leg, she moved the sketch pad onto the coffee table, saying she was afraid they were going to get tear stains on it. "I was going to make it a Christmas gift for you," she confessed somewhat sadly, "but now I can't because it won't be a surprise."

But L.C. was overjoyed. "It can still be my Christmas gift," she said, glancing at the clock as she dried her eyes. "It's 4:30—so it's officially Christmas," she announced, before scurrying over and turning on the tree lights. "Come on," she beckoned with a sweet smile as she sat cross-legged in front of the tree, "let's open up our presents!" She held out a hand, inviting her love to come join her on the floor.

Sydney and L.C. huddled together in front of the glowing Christmas tree, handing presents back and forth. Smiles soon replaced tears, and the couple began opening their special gifts to each other.

Afterward, the two went out to the deck, where they gazed at the full moon now resting on the horizon, casting a reflection on the surface of the still waters like a long, white, celestial carpet rolled out, leading off into infinity. The night seemed to be calling, so the two went down to the beach for a walk.

They strolled along the sand, hand in hand, as they talked in the quiet moonlight, while everyone else was still asleep, and they had the whole world to themselves.